Beasts

Beginning of the End

Volume I

ANA LEVLEY

This is dedicated to Sadie Levley.

Her sweet personality and intelligence are what had me understand animals like I never did before. This is for you my furbaby. I will love you forever. This is also for all your friends, the cows, the pigs, the chickens, and more who are lost every year due to humans. Lastly, it is for the Earth. I hope we can be more proactive in helping her heal so that my imagined future never becomes a reality.

CONTENTS

ACKNOWLEDGMENTS

I would like to thank C.L. Hogan for the constructive edits and comments she provided. I would not have been as inspired or driven to complete this book had it not been for her constant support. I would also like to thank Jonathan Levley, my husband, who tirelessly edited this book for me. I know how hard it was for you to let go of some grammatical rules - but also thank you for your keen eye.

Sadie, thank you for being so patient with Mommy. I know you wanted to play, cuddle, and eat treats all day, which I tried to fulfill while I was busy writing this novel. Thank you for just snuggling beside me when I needed it most. You are my best friend and I love you so much.

Thank you, Josh, for additional edits and Maggie for being extremely supportive during this whole process. Thanks to their littlings (Pulgo, Thomas, and Olive) for inspiring some of the animals in this book. Thank you to my sister-in-law for editing what she could - I really appreciated her insights.

Thank you to one of my best friends A.R. Hellbender for helping me figure out what to do with this book and how to reach the world with it. I was truly inspired by her books. I think our high school selves would be proud of us.

Thank you to the Vegan Business Exchange. You all have been so supportive, and I could not have done this without your support.

Thank you to every little dreamer who reads with integrity, hoping to gain knowledge through storytelling. I was a little dreamer like you, and without stories I am not sure I would have ever made it here.

1

UTOPIA

I wish I could remember the light. You might not care right now about the light, but when it is taken from you, when you start to forget how it looks, that's when you realize how important it is. If you listen, you may be able to keep this luxury. If not, you may find yourself without it forever.

Light is a gift. The light that sways before your eyes as you rise, or even the sunrise dotting the Earth as it wakes - reflections I believe they were called. You really don't know what light is, how much of a blessing it is until it is taken from you. Imagine. Everything dark. A desolate gaping hole of nothingness. The lack of light fills you with a feeling of emptiness. The darkness consumes you as you try as hard as you can to hold onto anything, even if they are just memories of light. Even if you close your eyes, your mind tries to trick you that it's still there. With small bursts of blue, yellow, so faint, and the illusion of light it satisfies you just a little. If I could show you everything, it would blind you.

So, I will start with the small pieces, the shiny pieces, shimmering with hope until you finish my story. This is the story of Atlia, the blackened, the deserter, the murderer, the martyr, the whatever you would like to call me. To me, I am just a person who has a choice to make, a decision that could change my life forever, and yours.

If I sound different, it is because I am thousands of years beyond your time. I know to your naïve species, this sounds

1

insane, I read your books of saviors from the future that you chose not to believe in. Most of what I will tell you will sound like it is not real. This will happen if it has not already. All of this is real, and it is a warning. If you feel your chest going in and out as you breathe reading each word, and if you like that feeling, then I suggest you heed this warning. If you are reading this around the world, then good. Someone has listened. But is it enough?

Our language is created by feeling, so I will try to translate the best I can, in an old language that seems full of feeling, but rife with misunderstanding. My life started thousands of years after you destroyed the Earth with your people. After all the blood you spilled with your conceited leaders who could not see past war. After saying violence was the only way of life, pretending it was the last resort - when it was your first move. After saying "it is what it is" without trying to actually listen to each other, without trying to even see the humanity in "the other". When you decided your life was worth more than another's, or you witnessed others who felt this way and did nothing. When all animals, including your own species, were murdered for the pleasure of a few. I have read about you. How you made something called money, a non-existent item. That you were so untrustworthy of other people, you put their merit into pieces of paper or "digital currency". You are known to my people as the brokenhearted, for your hearts must surely have been broken to stoop so low as to treat lives as things. However grave your crimes are, it can change, while I cannot change mine. I might as well be brokenhearted too.

I lived in Kalea, a domed state surrounded by a force field. We polished toxic rain and nourished an ecosystem for our city. Since the air was toxic outside, due to the Greatest War, we created the force field to let in all the good elements: sunlight, clean air, and water. Our city was the epitome of peace, just like the rest of the World Collective. I loved my city and all the northern provinces. My people were beautiful, and we were all one family. No one human belonged to another person - we all belonged to each other. Our community was our family, and everyone lead with feeling, as was our way. We felt each other's pain when a community member passed, we felt each other's love when people loved one another. There was no such thing as creating a system to value each other - we just did value each other. We chose different projects we would like to do, from intentioneering (the duty of maintaining and watching the telegraphic, the device that connects all of us telepathically), to creationing (those who invent), and so on. We were never at a loss since all of us were different. It puzzles me how your world existed. I could not imagine trying to have a person only fit into one project, one that they may not even care about. For us, we were one. Each had a different culture and tradition, but we all came together to bring peace to the northern provinces. Unified against the Southern Founders who tried to take away our ways of life. The Southern Founders and the volatile state of the Earth after the Greatest War kept us strictly inside the dome. If only I had known the truth, it might have changed everything.

I remember how the day that diverged my life began. How the sun had shone through the reflected dome and how the real flowers looked when I brushed past them to read in the garden. I loved the feeling of real flowers, how they felt light and soft, my pink fingers disappearing into the petals. My Prime Avo (my direct mother) insisted on keeping an old English garden, a garden from ancient times. I looked more like my Prime Avo than Avia Carlo (my father). Her curly, fiery red hair, her tight pink lips and pink skin. Her orange freckles that covered her, all over her body. Her blue eyes that were beautiful, they were slit and sideways tilting. I got the color of my eyes from Avia Carlo, his dark brown eyes that matched the beautiful darkness of his body in contrast to his bright blond hair. He loved the garden as well, I remember his beautiful dark fingers brushing over the flowers when I was little, telling me *touch it leafling, it feels like an old cloth from ancient times called velvet.*

My Kamma (grandmother) had created the garden and though my Kamma was not to be spoken of, it seemed like my

Prime Avo still loved her and kept it to remember the good in her. We had the last of the roses in the entire world here in our garden. My Avo was a child of one of the foundlings of the World Collective. I was very proud of my Avo and her accomplishments. She was one of the leaders of the World Collective, and the Grand Avo of Kalea. The World Collective is made up of four hundred leaders and they had the most important job - sustaining our World Collective rights. Yet all of us were held equally.

We were so fond of our rights that most other nations from the International Unity were not allowed in the World Collective as to not taint our rights. We were taught that the other countries were of no interest to us, and that our nation had real peace because of our rights. Other nations were thought to be fraught with inequalities to this day. But we joined the International Unity as a truce. We don't impose on them, they don't interfere with us. Our world rights were sacred, we all believed in the rights and upheld them as a family. We were taught family unity and keeping the utopia we built was more important than connecting with others who would not understand our way of life.

I, too, was extremely fond of our World Collective rights. I believed them so much that I was planning on being a leader myself - until that day. That day, the day that changed my life, I was in the garden reading via Eden in my telegraphic. I intentioned my telegraphic to activate a projection, and it shot out from my opened eyes to form a real imprint that only I could see, regardless of my curly red hair that fell into my face. My hair was always impossible to tame, a gift from my Avo's genetics. By having a telegraphic, you never had to worry about anything, including pesky hair getting in the way of seeing since it was in your mind as well. I could have changed my appearance with my telegraphic, but I never felt it was really that important. We were taught what is important is who you are, not what you looked like.

We connected through our different appearances on a deeper level through our telegraphics, really feeling the unique person behind the outside. Ever since we have had telegraphic technology, it has made us closer. We can see memories and can do anything our ancestors did on the network machines in the telegraphic. We can do more than they ever imagined.

Telegraphics are biotechnical creations and are now a part of our human species. They were created with the tissues of a human and other elements that could grow within us. My Dalta (sister), Beleeka, could tell you more about how telegraphics are made. Personally, Creationist intentioneering bores me. Though I do love the feeling of my telegraphic.

All humans now have telegraphics and there is no removing them, only blocking. It is as much a part of us as our hands, arms, or legs, but it is most likened to the heart. For there is no living if you remove your heart, yet one can walk around heart-blocked. There is no such thing as shame, as we all know each other's thoughts and feelings. We can turn on and off different channels if it becomes overwhelming. *Relations* I intentioned my telegraphic and a map of my family showed before me and where they were. An intention is a thought that we speak to each other and to our telegraphics with. It can also just be a feeling, it does not always have to be a thought, our telegraphic can read us like you used to read books.

I was really torn that day whether I was going to go see my Dalta in the eve room or if I was going to spend time with my Avia Carlo in the concealer. Looking back, I cannot believe that was even thought of as a "hard decision". The concealer would be cooler, and I would have to change my mask, an image displayed over all my skin to other people's telegraphics. That is how we typically decorated our skin, to express ourselves. It was also common for us to choose little metal mirrors that we wore as jewelry on our bodies, they stuck like magnets to our skin. Most people wore them between their hair down to their third eye, acknowledging our growth into empathy and mindfulness as a human species. I typically wore mine on the side of my head tucking away my curls on my right side that would travel in a triangle to my third eye. I also wore an arm band of purple mirrored squares that wrapped around a few times. Our telegraphics we could use with the mirrors to display a different color or illusion as well.

Our telegraphics could change the color and was limitless to create whatever illusion you desired. Our telegraphics also could change the warmth and cold measures of our bodies, so I would have to heighten mine, so I could withstand the sheer chill of a concealer. My Avia loved to ski, an ancient practice still around due to my Avia who romanticized the ancient Creationists. The concealer was made from inspirational Creationists for the benefit of us to enjoy the nature that was once a part of this Earth. Those who hated the warmth could enjoy the concealer and all that the white has to offer. I did not like the cold that much, though my Avia was the reason I could be found there. I loved watching him as he was doing showings.

My Avia Carlo was my favorite father and my direct father. It was not typical to be close to direct fathers, since we had so many, but Avia Carlo was everyone's favorite father. He was fun, bright, imaginative and supportive. He always had a sarcastic humor that put the other Avos and Avias on edge, but he would make us laugh. He made us feel like he understood us and our generation. We cared about the World Collective, everyone did, but our generation wanted to do more. We wanted to explore outside the domes, a risky idea that no one had explored in thousands of years.

Avia Carlo instilled that sense of adventure in us, taught the few of us who loved the old language how to write and speak it, and was always there when anything went wrong. He was the one person you knew you could trust because he loved all of us no matter what we did. When we got into trouble, he would negotiate with the leaders to let us be forgiven, giving us love through our telegraphics. Our leaders blamed him for making our generation rasher and more impulsive, but he argued with them that our species was meant to use this adventurous side for good, and that due to the World Collective and its teachings, that we were more than capable to explore anywhere in the universe.

Avia Carlo did not care what the leaders thought and continued to nurture us in the art of adventure, the history of our species from the early Creationists to the Intentioneers who created the telegraphic, to ways to communicate before telegraphics. My siblings, Beleeka, Nurium, Telepa, and I were always there, wanting to learn everything from him. He would speak in this melodic voice through our telegraphics that had us engaged from the minute he started. He would read us stories of the old world and teach us about their adventures.

He was the kind of Avia that when you were sick he did not care. He would still hug you while comforting you, feeling what you were at its height to lessen the feeling of being sick. We usually were not sick for that long, our telegraphic being able to heal us. He would still hold us close when others were concerned about catching whatever you had, even if their sickness blocker was turned on. He let us snot all over him as we cried all sick and he would even hold us closer, shushing our sad feelings and lolling us to sleep. I had not seen him for a while and wanted to visit him in the concealer, but at that moment I was more determined to beat Beleeka at our next game.

I decided instead to go to my Dalta's and maybe play a game with her in the Eve room.

When we played games in the Eve room, it was as if time stood still. Both Beleeka and I were intense when it came to games. It was the only place we could really have a fun competition, since it was banned in most areas of our life. Competition was thought to be a warning sign of becoming a lesser, that is what the people in the past who destroyed the Earth were called.

One time, when in the Eve room, Beleeka and I were playing a movement game, Fidget. Our telegraphics displayed different color boxes on the floor and each of us would start at one end or the other. The color of the boxes would change, and we would have to jump on that box before it changed back. The goal was to get to the middle of all the squares. I remember feeling Beleeka as she felt me, gauging what each other's next move was.

What if we turn off all channels on our telegraphics? Make it more interesting Beleeka proposed, her eyes glimmering slyly. *Okay* I responded and when you turn off your channels on your telegraphic you feel such a loss of sensation, it is scary. What you had been feeling for years, everyone else, that feeling of connection - just gone. It feels as if you are standing at the edge of a cliff, teetering on it, half fun, half frightening. Even though I turned it off, I still felt... something. *Odd* I thought for a moment and then I had to pay attention to the game.

All of the sudden the color of the box I was on changed, and quickly I jumped to the next one. Beleeka and I were both closing in on the middle. The one to my right then changed and flashed for a second. As I was about to jump, I saw out of the corner of my eye the one to the left and front stayed solid. I jumped across three boxes to it and waved my hands to balance. I saw Beleeka was close to the middle, except she was now in front of me. I had no idea how she got there, it was a great move. Sometimes the game gives you two different paths, so you can box out your opponent. I saw her box that she was on change to my color and I smiled at her and jumped. She jumped quickly off before I could push her off, to the right, so elegantly. We looked at each other, now the same distance from the box in the middle, both ready to jump.

It flashed both of our colors. Usually I could feel Beleeka before she jumped, but with my telegraphic off, I had no idea how fast she was. Beleeka and I both jumped, her a little before me and landed on the square holding each other up. Now it was a matter of who jumped there first. We felt the announcement in our telegraphics that Beleeka was the winner with shining sparkling powder bursting from the area around us in our telegraphics. We turned our channels back on both laughing and Beleeka gloating, feeling so excited she won against me. She felt my acceptance, annoyance, and amusement. I felt her excitement and happiness.

The day my fate came calling, after practicing without my channels on in the game by myself, I decided it was time for round two. I had been studying her movements for weeks without my telegraphic on. I got up and stretched my hands floating to the top towards the dome sky, getting ready to port to the Eve room.

As I rose I heard a rustle in the bushes. I looked, stunned, wondering maybe if someone had lost a pet. I looked closely, and something rushed out of it. I screamed and jumped up on the sitting plank. I was then extremely curious and told my telegraphic to go back to see what I saw. When I saw in my telegraphic that there had been an odd mysterious creature *that can't be...* I thought and I intentioned my telegraph to pull up what that was. It came up in my ear as Mus musculus BALB/c. I started - *that must be mistaken* I intentioned. The only living things other than Homo sapiens were gone. The ancients wiped out every living animal and plant except for humans and rare species of plants like the roses. Even the roses were the last of the plants alive - other than the plastic plants. It was impossible. Now I had to go to my Dalta (my sister) and tell her what I saw. As I was about to leave I felt a huge pain in my head and cried out as I landed on the rock pathway.

2

LOSS

I woke up cold and was still outside. I moved my arms around myself and intentioned my telegraphic to warm me and I started to feel warmth. It must have been afternoon, but by then it was pitch black and the cold had come in through the dome. I got up a bit unsteady and tried to walk. I then intentioned myself to my living space and as I looked around I saw my Dalta, staring at me. She then laughed, shaking her golden head. Her dark eyes sprinkling with laughter. My Dalta was a beauty to behold. With her obsidian skin and her large forehead, her huge eyes, and tiny mouth. She had her typical flower print on her skin as her mask, with brown stems, dark green leaves, and purple flowers that elegantly wrapped around her body. Her mirrors on her forehead went through her parted straight blonde hair and down to her third eye. She wore it like our Grand Avo wore her hair, she always wanted to be like her.

Fell asleep reading? she intentioned to me - my telegraphic filling me with her amusement. She felt my sarcasm and laughed harder.

Beleeka I intentioned, finally feeling her laughter to the point where I ended up laughing as well. *No, I was reading and then I saw something....* Actually, I thought I did not know what I saw and had no idea... I shut off my intentions and only felt hers.

She made a frowned face. *Do you think you will hurt me with what you saw?* I felt in my head. In our culture we only shut off our intentions if we felt we would hurt the person we were connecting with. My Kamma believed that concealing the truth could save other lives, especially if the information was fatal. I paused and used the technique my Kamma taught me to put my unintended intentions deep in my mind, hiding them in a private channel. This was technically illegal, but Kamma always thought our thoughts and feelings should be our own and that they were not supposed to be classified as intentions. I followed the laws precisely, usually, but at that moment I did not feel as if this was something I could share. I was still shaking, scared, curious, and nervous.

No Beleeka I shared my love with her and could feel her filling up with the love I had with her. I had created a side thought channel by then, just like Kamma taught me - one that not even the best of Intentioneers could reach.

I could then feel my telegraphic signaling that nourishment was ready. Both Beleeka and I intentioned ourselves there. Standing at the plastic nourishment cube - my whole family. My whole family consisted of cousins, brothers, sisters, and more. There were one hundred and twelve of us and, like our community, not all the Avo and Avia were directly related to us. Though we were not all blood, we were treated the same. Since we could not all fit in the same place for nourishment (there are about six thousand two hundred of us in our northern dome state of Kalea) we had different buildings for each main family and most families were as big as ours. Though there were main families, all of us in the World Collective treated each other as family. My family were Clippers, and we were part of the line of the Foundlings, those who founded the World Collective. All the main families took on names of ancient artifacts that were found after the Greatest War. I am not even sure our last name has a meaning, though I heard it had something to do with an archaic device to cut things. The cube was magnificent, with three levels spiraling up to the top where the Avos and Avias sat together. We could join them at our levels, but Beleeka and I liked spending time together during nourishing. My Prime Avo, who is the Grand Avo (which is my direct mother from where I came) started waving. I felt Beleeka's embarrassment first. *She makes me feel so embarrassed with that old custom* she intentioned to me and she felt I agreed with her. Beleeka was closest to the Grand Avo, though not her direct mother, she looked up to her and thought she was one of the best leaders in the World Collective. The Grand Avo reached for us with her intention and felt our embarrassment and filled us with her laughter, letting us know that she felt our embarrassment as cute. She then continued to wave at all her littlings. She started this custom every night, finding the old custom charming.

With the sound of a bell, the nourishment had arrived.

I was so excited to smell that burning, juicy meat it sent tingles down my spine. We sat on hammock chairs and there was the nourishment cube in front of us. Nourishment was ported to the cube where it could stay warm until we consumed it. The nourishment came through the cube in a bubble floating to our laps and I could see the most delicious flower meat in front of me. You had to intention the bubble towards you as it floated and rest where you intentioned the bubble to stay.

The blue and purple colors around the bubble swirled and you could see the steam rise from the nourishment. It was my favorite - the yellow meat with milk sauce! It floated in the air inside the bubble. I intentioned my excitement to Beleeka and felt hers as well. She preferred the brown meat and had a couple of nubs - her favorite thickness. This meat was beautifully adorned, broiled all around, making a flower. The milk sauce was creamy and flowing onto the meat. I intentioned to cut the meat with my telegraphic. Some blood and sauce oozed from the flesh and I intentioned a bubble around it to bring it to my mouth. With the bubble hovering over my open mouth, I popped the bubble with my finger and the nourishment and flavor teased my taste buds and olfaction in my nose. I intentioned to cut another piece, piercing into the flesh; sometimes you really had to cut into it. I then intentioned it into a nourishment bubble. That bubble popped and released the nourishment into my mouth. I tasted the sweet, savory, juicy meat.

The yellow meat was supposed to be the most well-bred, free range, and most delicious. In my society it was well known that our farms respected the nourishment; we gave everything to our nourishment, so they had the best lives. We say it tasted like the best type of cow, a mystical creature from the ancient times. With my intentions, I carefully sliced to avoid the bone, though I would plan on sucking on the bone later - the Creationist nourishers did amazing things with bone marrow - especially from the youngest of the herd.

Nourishment was a time during the day when we could connect with our loved ones, as we all did different things the rest of the day. Our society was all about sustainability, and none of us ate more than we should. We respected the nourishment as well as one another. During nourishment time, we discussed anything ranging from what we did on our projects to our free time. Beleeka was telling me about her day in the beach dome, where there is water and sand - the sand was made from plastic and the water was from the dome turning rain into drinking water, the dome made the water warm and it was supposed to be like how it was in the ancient days. Beleeka sat on a hammock and internalized about the World Collective's original Intentioneers who created our telegraphics and how they evolved with our species. I personally was not so fascinated by what she learned, though she intentioned everything to me so I would have knowing as well. I could feel her happiness, so that made me happy. I loved how she got so excited about the intricate details of creationism.

As I was nourishing and feeling Beleeka, I felt the tremble of a terrible, horrifying sadness. I dropped my intention of holding my nourishment and grabbed my elbows feeling the intense pain. Someone died. Someone close to me. It was then visually intentioned *my Avia had passed*. This pain was felt by everyone. We mourned as a community, feeling the pain and then seeing what happened. My Avia's telegraphic recorded memories came into my telegraphic. And then I saw the unimaginable. It was me - me arguing with my Avia, my father, looking crazed. I then saw myself fill him with hate, so much hate. I cried out trying to stop the memory, but the hate filled my Avia. He terminated himself from all the hate and sadness he felt and fell to the floor. In the next second, the Peacers had my arms, holding them to my sides. *No!* I intentioned. *I don't know what happened! I am so sorry, but I didn't do it!*

I felt my Prime Avo, my Dalta as well as all my other siblings, and the collective horror of every mother, father, and sibling in the community. My direct Avo's face was watering - her whole face was covered in tears. She intentioned to me lovingly and gently *Intentions do not lie, my spring.* I immediately felt hands of the Peacers switch from my arms to my back and I did not resist. I was still sobbing, feeling the pain of my Avia passing. The Peacers took me away. I was so ridden with sadness that I did not notice that they installed a blocker in my telegraphic, so I would not do what my Avia. I did not fight back. I did not know what to do except to let my heavy head hang and feel the grief I needed to feel over my Avia. If only I had been able to focus, then maybe, just maybe, I would have been able to escape what happened next.

In my community when someone commits a crime, ever since the intention was created, once the memory was seen from the telegraphic, it is final. It is known as the intentioned truth. What the person sees and hears is what happened. You can verify it, and usually they do, however, I had no memory to verify. Regardless of my memory, this was not something that happened. My community did not know what to do as it was a very mysterious case. My people, we did not know how to deal with something like this - murder. This was an ancient horrific act that people used to do. You would probably compare it to the ancients who made human sacrifices. In our lifetime it was unheard of because you could feel everything. You could feel the person's fear, pain - you felt their bones crack, or the intense pain in their hearts or brain or however you hurt them. You felt it as if it was hurting you too. In a sense, it was thought of as murdering a part of yourself. When you felt the person's emotions, as well as how you hurt them physically, how could you go through with it? It was almost impossible. Maybe if someone numbed their telegraphic it would be more probable.

This was not the case for me though. I felt everything, and this was someone I loved. Usually, feeling the other person's emotional and physical pain is what stops you. Once you feel their fear or sadness. Once you feel as if your heart is being ripped from the middle of your chest. Or as if your brain is exploding with sharp knives cutting deeper and deeper. It just made no sense why anyone could be capable of such a thing. That was why the sentence was so high, because you must be a lesser, there must be something inhuman in you that made you want to kill a part of yourself. Our whole community was thought to make up one person. All of us working together to love and share happiness with each other. That was the goal of our whole nation.

To me it even made less sense how I could do something like that. I was so confused feeling his body as his soul left. Feeling as if a part of myself left with him. It was not my freedom I felt leave, but my being. Who I was, who I thought I was, that left with him. I don't think I ever truly recovered from that day. When you murder someone, especially someone you love, it is called blackening. We believe that your soul is blackened, which makes you the worst kind of lesser. The one that is barely human, for it is human to feel each other, to share the good feelings and to help and love one another. To try to live happily with everyone. Lessers were those who thought of themselves - they were lesser than human.

The holding building where they put potential lessers was small and plastic, the walls see-through. That way others could see us as they walked past us in the Smooth Square, reminders of what we were, and warnings to what others could become. I was in a holding cell overnight, the first time I spent the night on hard ground, no hammock, nothing. The people usually thrown into this cell were the very few lesser beings who were convicted. They want you to know how it feels to be a lesser, when you lay on that cold hard stone ground. They hope that in those moments you would realize your wrongs if you did a lesser act, which is anything but murder.

I felt the hard, stone ground, cold in my hands. I just ran my hands over it back and forth, slowly feeling the smooth surface, connecting somehow with this part of the real earth, of what was left, of what was saved. I felt as if I was pleading with it, to save me from what just happened. Reality set in. It didn't matter to me at the time where I was or what would happen to me, because the pain of my Avia being gone consumed me. I was in shock. I tried so hard to remember. I force played my telegraphic repeatedly in my mind until I was screaming in agony, trying to force something different to happen that just did not exist. I started scratching the stone, it filed down my nails and they started to slowly rip one by one. I did not care, I wanted to feel something real, something that was not my Avia passing. After hours and what seemed like days, I lay there, waiting for my fate to be decided. Not caring about fate, not caring about myself. Just in and out of consciousness, wishing it was over. At times I held my legs to my chest in ball, holding them so tight my knuckles turned white just to try to keep myself from screaming the whole time I was in the cell, trying to hold in all the pain I felt. I ignored the pain in my fingers from scratching the stone so much, I made a few dents, my nails almost all bloodied and gone by then. I was confused and just did not understand how I could see myself killing the one person in my life I was closest to, my Avia Carlo. How could I do such a horrible thing? How could I live with myself? These thoughts occupied my days and nights.

When the Peacers finally opened the door, the light shined in from the outside, and my telegraphic being muted, I felt how it was like to not control how much light I was exposed to. I cried out, my eyes feeling the burn of the light. I knew in that instant that my fate was decided as they grabbed a hold of me. Since there was no evidence of my memory during that time (which was shocking to the Intentioneers since there has never been a case like this), a small trial was conducted.

I was brought into the Equality Hall, which was a plastic pink bubble, flanked with hammock seats for the leaders. I was at the bottom, below all the leaders as they looked down at me. I looked up and I could see the bigger dome and the clouds and sky above it. The sun that showed very orange peered at me. For a moment I let myself feel how nice that was, one moment of enjoyment. I then looked around and felt eyes watching me since I teleported in and walked to the center. My telegraphic feelings were turned on, so I could feel everyone. The shock, disgust, concern, disappointment. All these people knew I was originally following in my Grand Avo's footsteps. For months I had stood beside where she was now, learning how the leaders worked in Kalea. I was an appointed pre-leader and was learning from everyone how to make decisions to help Kalea.

One time, rebel forces from the south were trying to sneak into our dome by faking that their telegraphics were connected to those in Kalea. Each one of our telegraphics can be appointed to a certain place or allied region. These people faked theirs. I was one of the people who found that we could point them out due to their way of thinking, how their thoughts of the south and certain other intentions that the Intentioneers watched could show who had successfully infiltrated. I read everything I could on the people from the south, studied them and their intentions until I was well versed in them. Not many could get past the dome, so it was usually their best spies. I was told that my way of thinking differently would be good for Kalea, my Grand Avo trying to be humble. However, I could not help but feel her bit of pride that I was one of hers, following in her footsteps.

I was trusted amongst all these people, and now I could feel their fear of me. Of what I did, of how I was capable of such an inhuman act. How I was one of the blackened now, the people who I had fought against. I looked up to see all the leaders, feeling as if one of them had the answers that I was lost to have. They felt this, and I felt their pity. They now knew I had no idea what happened, but I felt their sadness - and their commitment to our laws.

My Prime Avo was crying. She felt my sadness and could tell I did not know what happened. She had to make the trial decision because in the World Collective it is the law that if we had clear evidence of the memory of the individual who died from an attack and another does not, that we would automatically go with the intact memory. She was the Grand Avo first, my Prime Avo second. The memory was released to everyone's telegraphics. We saw again through my Avia Carlo's eyes looking at me committing telecide. He was looking at me with love, and then I filled him with my hate, *hate* - I could not believe I ever had hate in my heart for my Avia.

It was then that I felt him, my Avia Carlo, as if he was next to me. His hand on my shoulder intentioning love. I could see him, in my memories. His dark eyes with excitement, he looked at me. *Atlia, I am coming to get you.* I giggled and Beleeka was next to me giggling too. We were in something called a "fort", an old structure the ancients used to make. We made it with the recycled plastic cloth and ancient wood chairs my Avia had in his sitting room. I could see amusement in his cunning eyes, his mischief dancing across them. As his big hands swooped into our tiny fort, we giggled more and intentioned *No* as he tickled us. I found a hole through the back of the fort and ran away just to be caught by his big gallant hands. He picked me up, the sun shone through the window onto us, blinding me with beautiful light. I felt the warmth from it and my Avia as I could not stop laughing as he kissed me all over in it. *Avia* I giggled out and he then caught Beleeka too, she could not stop giggling either. He held us together, and I looked up at his face, tracing my hands over his smile, hoping I could hold his smile in me forever, that I could absorb it.

His face, that smile, is what I could feel looking at me. I felt hate, uncontrolled hate, fill him. It had no origin, it just existed. I felt his mind, his sadness, and his fate. I felt the pain in his heart, and mind, like fire eating his insides. I felt him suffering, though it was only for a moment as he tried to breathe, as the hate created a tightness around his chest that stopped his heart. I felt him look at me, my face cold with determination. He looked at his hand holding his heart. *Atlia* was his last intention filled with love, for me. We felt his pain and sadness, we felt his body in pain and then give out.

As his body gave out, I released a breath. It was as if my own body had died. My face was wet from the tears that were uncontrollable. I felt betrayed by myself and searched my memory for anything. There was nothing. No memory of murdering him, no memory at all except for reading in the garden.

After viewing the memory again, very painfully, we saw the murder. It was clear - it was me. My Prime Avo intentioned *My little one, there is nothing I can do. The law is clear, you have been found as a lesser.* My heart dropped knowing that that was the worst sentence possible. Murder was not tolerated in the community and we had no belief in rehabilitation when it came to murder. I was considered a lesser, be sent to the farm, and I was never coming back. My shoulders slumped as the tears continued to drop down my face. My Prime Avo, as well as the other leaders, could feel my sadness, and I could feel theirs. They felt my pain over losing my father more so than the pain of knowing where I was going.

3

FALLING

Since the Peacers blocked my transportation access in my telegraphic, we teleported via their telegraphics to the farm. Everything was happening so fast, I felt all the pain, the pain of my Avia, the pain of my Prime Avo losing me, the pain of my family and community losing me. Soon they would not feel my pain. It would be as if I did not exist to them, I would be blocked on their telegraphics by the Intentioneers.

We arrived at the farm.

I was instantly hit by the smell. That smell is what scared me out of my grief. I think it is instinctual to feel pain when you are hit with that stench. Like the creatures of the past, that thing that connects us is the fear of dying. I lashed out, trying to get out of the hold of the Peacers. Something inside me screaming to run far away from the place that they had brought me. I fought against the Peacers even though I knew it was useless. They could not feel my pain, though I saw their faces were pained. They were sad and petrified themselves that this was my fate. I was just one of them. Now I was to be viewed differently. I was no longer one of them, I was something different, I was a monster since I murdered someone. Therefore, I was now considered a lesser being.

I could tell that because this happened to me in what seemed to be an instant, it terrified the leaders and the Peacers, because this could happen to them. We were taught how to find lesser beings so that we could avoid the violence that comes with them. Even as littlings we questioned and watched each other closely, to see if we would share nourishment, or just eat it ourselves. To notice what our first instincts would be. Here I was, the next leader of our community, and now I'm a lesser-being - and no one knew. I knew what this would do to my community - create fear, as the leaders would tell everyone how I was an anomaly. They would try to calm the community, help them realize that I was the worst kind of lesser - a psychopath. One that learns the ways of the community and waits for the moment in glee to strike the community, to shake it. Even if I did not feel this way, this is what they would say to console everyone.

I heard screaming of the lessers and I knew that this would soon be my fate. I was quickly teleported to my cage, one of the Peacers hugged me as she was crying and locked the cage. The Peacer was Nurium, another Dalta with whom I was close. I hugged her back and tried to intention that I loved her. But I was blocked so she felt nothing from me. She quickly turned and teleported away. It was so painful not to feel any intentions. Only sadness, fright, and grief from the murder were the only intentions I was permitted to have, every day, for the rest of my life.

It was then I realized I was sitting on the floor and I stood up. It was pitch black and I hit my head forcefully on the cage above. I tried breathing, but it was difficult because the foulness of debris, flesh, and other objects that were floating in the air. Even breathing through my mouth provided no relief. A violent shock flowed through me and I fell unconscious, as I was already weak from the holding cell. Thankfully I remained unconscious and did not feel them moving me to a multicage.

I woke up to sounds that I was not familiar with, and they frightened me. It felt as if clouds formed and crusted on my eyes, which fell from my face as I scrubbed the matter off, I could see only faintly, still not used to the darkness. I tried to look around as much as I could, not having my telegraphic to fix the light I saw. It sounded as if many creatures were in pain, that they were being tortured. It was moaning and sobbing I realized - I only heard once when my Avo cried over one of my siblings who passed too soon from an accident. It was not so much how loud it was, it was the tone of sheer pain and such deep sadness. I peeled the rest of the crust off of my eyes, my eyelids tugging with the crust, feeling like they cracked to open. I thought I was in a nightmare.

Our telegraphics usually keep nightmares at a distance, so I have never experienced one before. But when I was passed out, I had dreamt that I was in a facility that reeked of a disgusting stench, the smell of melted rusting metal and terror. I soon realized I was smelling blood, I was in a pool of it, and I could feel the intention of every lesser in pain. I was in the darkness and I could feel the lessers, I could feel the pain of their bodies. How they could not move or speak. I opened my eyes to barely make out a lesser in the dark who was in my face, dark circles under its eyes. Its mouth was agape with foam, and spit was falling out, the mouth halfcocked. Its eyes bloodshot and so much fear and sadness in them. I felt the lessers asking me for something, but I could only see their eyes wide in fear. I told them I could not speak their language, which was groaning and moaning. I told them I can't feel how I could help them. I tried to get away, slipping in the pool of blood, and I screamed. I woke up to the nightmare and I am still not sure if it was a dream because it was the same except for no telegraphic feelings. I was with five other lessers in a crowded cage, so small at least two body parts were touching another lesser. The pool of blood still beneath me and other noxious leavings I did not want to identify.

I immediately felt the grief and dreadful intentions from the death of my Avia Carlo and was consumed by it again. Playing in my mind repeatedly, even drowning out the sounds of the place I was in. Though I woke up in my nightmare, I could not tell if I was more saddened by my situation or the grief of losing my Avia. I could feel him dying over and over again. His sadness, his love, his life slipping. *How could this happen?!* I thought, thankful for once that I learned old language, so I could think more colorfully and did not feel totally lost with my telegraphic being blocked. I continued played the scene in my telegraphic. I realized I could still access all my memories, it must have been my Prime Avo giving me this exception since usually your telegraphic is made useless when you are sentenced to the farm.

I played the memories of me and my Avia. He was an amazing Avia, I could not help the tears from proliferating across my face. I remembered a time when I was young and running with Beleeka, I accidently broke a vase from the ancient times. My Avia collected many ancient artifacts and he was very proud of the history of our species, though others saw that as a possible lesser trait. My Avia came over as he saw I felt his sad intentions that came naturally from the loss of this artifact, and I started to feel the sadness myself. As my eyes teared up, I felt caring and dearness from my Avia. *Little leaf, don't feel bad* my Avia intentioned his eyes with smiles in them. *I care more for you than I do that ancient vase, though I am sad it is gone, I love you.* That made me feel worse as I felt sorrier and then Beleeka started to cry too. *Awe my little ones* he hugged us until we stopped, kissed our foreheads and smiled mischievously. *Now go break something else!* He intentioned love and silliness, and we ran away smiling and giggling.

Those hugs, if I could intention you the hugs he gave, I would do that right now. It was his hugs that could stop the world, make you feel safe in an instant. My Avia. The grief struck again in my stomach, my emotions making the sad and terrifying intentions stronger, seeing my Avia's last memory. I didn't care - I needed to feel this pain. I could feel my Avia as he is dying, I could feel his sadness and love for me, but also, for some reason, his understanding. That made it harder, even when I was evil, even when I could not remember slumping down to that of a lesser, he still loved me so much that as I killed him he chose to understand and love me all the same.

I then heard the sounds get louder and saw some Peacers come in. This time farmers had come with them. They looked at all the lessers on the other side, pointing, and it seemed they were intentioning to one another. The lessers huddled in the back crying out trying to get away. I watched with curiosity and fear. This was not the picture the World Collective painted to us of how lessers were treated. We were taught they were in an open area where they could roam and have families. Here they were with me in these cages that smelled of the dead. The Peacers went in and pulled out two lessers, hitting them with painful intentions, forcing the lessers to move with them.

One lesser male had a small lesser, which the farmer pointed to. The male cried out and all of the other lessers in my cage moved forward making noise, screaming so loudly and shrilly, pushing me forward with them. The Peacer tore the small lesser from the male, and it cried out trying to grab the male lesser, tears running down her face until it contorted with pain. She cried in pain as they took her. All of them teleported out of the farm and the whole place resounded with banging and screaming, the male still screaming for his lesser that was just taken. He lay in the cage and something remarkable happened. The other lessers went over and started to pet his shoulders and were crying too, as if they felt something for the lesser. It seemed as if in some archaic way they were trying to comfort him.

I did not know what to feel. My feelings of my Avia. Me being put with these lessers. I could not help but feel there must still be a good reason that I and the other lessers were put into this particular farm. Maybe the other farms were better and this one was for those who were blackened.

But still, a small lesser could be blackened? I wondered as I watched the male, as he acted as if he was still holding her and stroked the air where she was as if to comfort her. My heart tore apart again and I let the sadness, fear, hurt, and grief consume me. I lay beside my lesser cage mates and cried until I slept - a sleep with many nightmares.

The first nightmare was of my Avia Carlo. I saw him, and he was fine. I ran to hug him, but I never reached him. His face started to melt, along with his body. *Stop* I cried out as he started to scream, feeling his face and looking at me with his eyes, piercing through me. *Why Atlia?* was the only intention he managed before exploding. I shielded my face, crying, looking for any of him, but there was nothing I could hold - he was everywhere. Nothing I could say goodbye to.

I thought this can't be real, but something in me told me it was all too real. The nightmare continued, and I was in another room. It was ancient style with Avia Carlo's books, his study he used to call it. He was reading in what the ancients called a chair. He looked up at me *What's wrong?*

Then he started to choke. Blood came out of his mouth and dribbled down. *Wait* I intentioned and ran over to him, reaching out and his blood fell onto my fingers. *Stop, stop, stop* I cried, as I attempted to hold up his head, I futilely intentioned healing. I felt my telegraphic numb.

I was pushed into a place filled with stale air, the smell of hundreds of people, wedged together. The nightmares stopped, but this terror I could not escape. I saw I was in the farm *NOOOO!* I screamed in my head *Stop it please* I cried as I was put into a dark cage with another crouched and defeated lesser. It smelled, and flies were all around it. I was shoved closer and I saw that the lesser was decaying. *Let me out please* I sobbed, and the flies anxiously investigated my skin, focusing more so on the parts of my eyelids that tore from the crusts. *Ahhh* I intentioned with a cry and somehow woke up to the same decaying stench I was dreaming about in my nightmare. Tears felt raw on my face as if I had been crying for hours.

That was my first introduction to what being a lesser was, and I had no idea until I was there myself.

4

HISTORY

As I said, I have always been supportive of the law. Like everyone, I was a believer, but there is something about thinking differently that isolates you from a community regardless. When your whole community and family thinks a certain way and they love you, it can be very hard to think differently. It is hard not to think of yourself and you never want to offend people you love, even if morally you are right. All of us, our whole community being one, united us in a way that it would be like losing a limb or to create a tear in perception. We could think differently, but it had to be in the confines of our moral laws that our ancestors and their ancestors had created. This is what kept the peace for thousands of years, or so we were told.

So yes, I believed that lessers were just that - lesser than humans. I realized that I should probably explain what a lesser is and why I thought lessers were really that, lesser beings, not able to think or have feelings. I was taught that lessers were happy, were on farms where they could be with their families and roam around. That the mother lessers who provided the milk were with their babies until two years of age. That the younger lessers who would be used for nourishment were already failing somehow in their bodies. That we turn on telegraphics in their brains for when we are about to turn the lesser beings into nourishment so that they are able to block the pain, so that the kill is "humane".

Yes, if you are realizing what I am talking about now terrifies you, then I apologize because all I can do is explain how I was taught. It was not a choice - I did not know. Lesser beings are nourishment and since humans are the only beings left a thousand years ago after the Greatest War, humans were split up into human and lesser beings. The world was in a terrible place. The ancestors before us were told to be unintelligent, cruel, unkind, and greedy. Therefore, they were later classified as not human. At first it was nuclear war that spoiled everything, but then climate change took over and killed most of the remaining humans, animals, and plants. Since the world was ruled by lesser beings, it was then decided after Earth was mostly destroyed that the lessers would pay for what they did. Since they could not be human beings, they were sent to farms to become nourishment. We created the World Collective with humans and some very amazing Creationists, who created the domes to keep us alive so that we would not starve, and the planet could rehabilitate itself. They said it would take a million years for that to happen.

I never had met a lesser being, I had only ever eaten them. I did not know that lesser beings were even human, that they could even be people. I knew pets were lessers, but I never thought of them as the same as the lessers we ate. I had no idea that these lesser beings could feel pain and I had no idea what we were doing to them.

Even if I did think that they were humans, it was illegal to talk about. I remember when I was younger, we had a sibling who refused to eat the lessers.

She began telling others about her theory that we were only told lies by the World Collective. She said she visited the farms, and that she saw what happened to the lessers. What she said sounded impossible, that lessers could be like us, that they were held in horrible conditions. At the time, I was too small to even have greater thoughts than what I was going to play with that day. She was sweet and one of my older siblings. She was very intelligent and always kind to me.

She was sent to the rehabilitations center every time she did not eat a lesser.

I remember seeing her hauled out of nourishment as she came in with other siblings and sat at the table, covering their mouths with both hands. We felt the intention that she was doing something illegal and even as I sat on my Avia Carlo's lap, as we nourished, I felt him intention in a side channel to me his disgust at the Peacers for taking her away. She grew her own leaf concoction. I am not sure how she even had it, but when she was arrested they found ten plants that were never seen before. We thought almost every plant, except for a handful of radiated decorative ones, had died. Hiding any type of living thing was treason since our community was founded with sharing everything with the community. She was then found guilty and sentenced to be a pet at the pet rehabilitation facility, where she was found to be a lesser. We were always told that compassion for humans was always to be held above compassion for lessers since lessers were inferior beings.

I was not close to this sibling, but I remember seeing her as a pet after the rehabilitation. She looked blank, like nothing was there. But I remember she looked at me and I felt she was looking through me. She could not intention to me anymore, but I remember thinking I could feel the intention, her gaze was so powerful, fearful, it sent shivers through my body, even to the bottoms of my feet.

That was the sole time in my life that I can remember anyone close to me having been sentenced as a lesser. After her sentencing, my other siblings had dropped their protestations and went back to eating the nourishment. They completed rehabilitation and were determined to be humans, not lessers.

The nourishment, I hate to say, tasted amazing. For some people it was like an addiction. We honored our nourishment with milk sauces, and color. We would filet the nourishment into beautiful flowers, bushes and other plants and animals that were ancient. Our community does not support eating more than what makes you full, with sustainability in mind of course. So those that ate more usually were given a full intention beforehand, so they did not eat more.

Now that was me, that is what I thought. Most people would think I was sad that I was about to die and nourish my family. At the time I did not think that way, though I was scared. My mind was clouded with grief. We are taught that if we are found as a lesser, it is the highest honor to become nourishment and to be able to nourish our family. To become nourishment as a non-human was normal, necessary, a tradition, and an honor. If you were found not to be human any longer, then the next best thing you could do is to feed the family. We were taught that lessers were dangerous if not eaten and they would tarnish the community. We felt it was our purpose to make sure that lessers were found and farmed to protect our family. And that, as nourishment, they would be lifted to the highest level of being a lesser could be.

I did not know that this would be my greatest sadness and my greatest blessed awakening that would change my mind forever.

5

HEART

It was days that I was in the multicage, maybe months. I didn't know; I felt hot all the time, and my back hurt from laying down. I had sores that would pop sometimes when I moved too fast. Though I could roll over, I could not stand. I did not try to interact with other lessers, at the time it seemed useless to me since I still did not believe I was a lesser. They did not even have the feeling of intentions. How was I to communicate with them after all? I ignored their cries and the many times the farmers came in. I held hands over my ears, replaying the memory of my Avia, just to see his face right before he was killed, his last smile. I held onto that moment. After a while, my grief started to pass, and I became obsessed with an idea.

Someone did this to me. There was no other way around it. Maybe it was one of the Intentioneers or Southern Founders that infiltrated the World Collective. I am not sure, but someone had killed my Avia Carlo and made it look like it was me. Someone other than me murdered my Avia, so I must not be a lesser. I kept going over and over it in my mind, keeping my strength only for thinking of who could have done it. We were a peaceful society and not one person has been murdered for over a thousand years.

I felt something wet and I squealed. One of the lessers was licking me.

"Ahhh," I exclaimed and tried to push them away. I saw it was licking my shoulder. *Ewwww* I thought and tried to intention to the lesser. I saw looking back at me a woman, a little older than myself. She had bright green brown eyes and her hair was a deep red and smooth, unlike my very curly, very orange hair - hers was beautiful. Her skin was a chocolate brown and her face petite and oval shaped. She nudged my nose with her small nose. There was something about her that seemed familiar, but I could not find out what that was. Something, inside me said I, I *knew* her. I squealed again and tried to get away, hitting the other lesser on my other side. The lesser I bumped into groaned. He was a very skinny old looking man with frail white skin, who looked at me with brow furrowed and grunted, trying to shoo me away from practically being on top of him. The woman then proceeded to lick my arm after I fell on it and I held it, crying out in pain.

"No!" I shouted at her and she stopped, startled. The woman looked at me sadly and I felt like those eyes reminded me of someone, but I shook my head letting it go.

The woman then said, "Wow, well I kept my promise." She said out loud in a smooth, silky voice in the ancient language. Begrudgingly, she sighed and looked at me.

Stunned, I said nothing. *She speaks the ancient language - how is that? And without a telegraphic!* She laughed at my stunned face.

"I mean just - wow. Okay, so what do we do now? It has been almost a month and I have done nothing, we need to act," she said plainly.

"I have no idea!" I said, not having spoken in a long time the old words stumbling out, rusty. Most people never used their voices, so it was very awkward for me, though I sometimes practiced with my Avia.

"Well, what we do is entirely up to you." She lay down and looked up at the top of the cage.

I looked around then and saw the faces of every lesser looking at me. Their gaunt faces, women, children, men all different ages - just staring. Some had lost eyes, others had lost limbs. It was horrifying, it was the first time I really saw the lessers as individuals. I got extremely nervous and was shocked *why are they all staring at me and how do they know old language?*

The woman then somehow knew how I felt without a

telegraphic and said, "Obviously she does not remember anything, she seems a bit overwhelmed, but," she smiled and said, "the plan worked."

The moaning and crying had stopped by then, and the next thing I knew, everyone had raised their voices in happiness, hooting.

"What is happening," I croaked out terrified. I had no idea what was going on.

"I am Dina, and we did this to you." She saw me looking around, hoping that no Peacers could hear the roar of happiness. "They can't hear us, they installed a device to make sure no one can hear us - our screams of pain and sadness." She stretched out lazily, like how my sister Beleeka took forever to wake up in the morning.

We did this to you ran through my head. "You did what?!" I screamed at her glaring. My anger suddenly ignited. The grief in my heart taking over. There was no emotional control anymore from the telegraphic, my anger seared.

Surprisingly she looked angry back at me, "We killed the Avia Carlo, gladly. Do you know how many of your people have killed of us? How many fathers, brothers, sisters. Of course, you don't," she sighed and changed to a kinder tone. "... you don't know. You don't know what has happened here, do you?"

I shook my head, overwhelmed, and could not stop the tears, "I have no idea what is going on. I... my Avia died and I saw myself kill him. Why would you make it seem as if I killed my Avia Carlo? I am like everyone else. I did not know..." I trailed off as I saw everyone staring at me again.

Their blank sad stares were haunting. That is when I took even more notice in their appearance and I could see their eyes. Those eyes, so human like! Even though some were yellowed. They were like skeletons. I still was unsure at how smart these lessers were. The one I was talking to, though, I am not sure if I would be able to tell her apart if she did not speak and had a telegraphic.

"Are you from the World Collective?" I asked her.

She stared at me, "No, I was a pet at one point. Let's just say, I was not a very good pet." She smiled slyly at me and it sent a chill down my spine.

That disturbed me, but also intrigued me. There was talk of a pet that blinded her owner. Could she be that pet? Could she be... dangerous? *But why* I thought.

As if she could read my mind she responded, "You are the eldest of the Grand Avo's children - her direct line and her successor. We needed to make a stand and this plan has been in motion for a long time, so it is nothing personal," she said.

"Nothing... personal?" My anger flared, "How is murdering my Avia nothing personal - I am going to tell a Peacer the truth and get myself out of here! I am sorry you are stuck here, but maybe you deserve to be here."

Before I called the Peacer, she grabbed my arm and looked at me pointedly, "Maybe *you* do deserve to be here. They can't hear you and I suggest you get comfortable, we are going to be here for the rest of our lives. Call it revenge, call it what you want, but that is the reality."

Terror ran through me. *There is nothing I can do. There is no way out.* I screamed and turned to my side and cried. Dina let me cry and she didn't say anything, no one did. It was silent, and I was the only one crying.

I could hear my own sobs and felt pitiful, processing everything. *They did all of this to me - for what reason? Are lessers so unintelligent emotionally that they don't get the impact they have?* I stopped crying and paused. It was then I decided I would stop crying or feeling sad. I was done with that. I had to get out and I was going to find a way. These lessers might not be smart enough to get out, but I would, and I would gladly leave them behind.

6

ESCAPE

I planned my escape over the next few days. I studied those cages, thinking of how I could get a Peacer in here. I noticed the trough tray they filled with the nourishment. It was not the same nourishment we received in the World Collective. At the farm, the nourishment was totally different, a wet grain-like mush. *How did they make a plant like mush?* I wondered. *That won't help you get out of here* I told myself to stop getting distracted. I realized maybe if I did not eat, then they would come in. After all, they say in the World Collective that they take care of the lessers until the day they died. How would it help them if I just died through starvation? I would be one less piece of nourishment to feed the World Collective.

Dina took notice and laughed, "You think you can get the Peacers' attention by not eating? That is unlikely since there are so many of us. They don't care if one starves to death. Look to your left at the end there." I did and saw a small lesser, looked like a small littling - it was not moving. "You see that lesser? That lesser is dead from starvation." That is when I noticed the flies around her as well.

I gasped revolted, "But that - that is a littling!" I noticed how tiny the body was, and tears welled up in my eyes. It was lifeless, and rotting. I tried to ignore the smell for a long time in order not to vomit. Every day I focused on my Avia Carlo and getting out, but right then I could not control myself. Seeing that defenseless lesser, one that was so small and the fact that the Peacers just left it there was horrifying and disgusting. I felt vomit come up and there was nowhere to vomit. I vomited on myself, on my side. To my surprise, I felt Dina rubbing my back as I cried and continued to vomit. It was disgusting, and I lay in the vomit, unable to move or get away from it.

"Now that will get their attention," Dina said.

Lights blinded us and the Peacers came in. Dina whispered, "This will be unpleasant, Love, but you need to stay strong. Now they are going to see if you are diseased. See, that will get their attention in case you infect all the 'possible nourishment'. Once you are out, I will get a message to you. We are lucky this worked, because what we had planned was worse."

"What," I muttered as the top of the cage was taken off and then I felt hard shocks through my telegraphic. I screamed out in pain. "Please," I cried out loud, but the Peacers made no motion. I realized they put a blocker on the sounds I make in their telegraphics. However, I could see the Peacers felt for me, knowing who I was. I was starting to pick up people's emotional cues without a telegraphic, feeling so much less - I needed to pay attention. I could barely read their faces since the shocks hurt so much. I could barely stay conscious.

I was dragged past other cages, a different type of housing. It had cages made from plastic and the bubble material. The bodies of women whose hands were tied by plastic clasps behind their backs. There were hundreds of them in a row. You could see where the plastic dug into their wrists, they were red, and some were bleeding. Their breasts laid on a plastic shelf and were connected to a machine that was a tube into their nipples. You could see their nipples pulsing and contracting. The veins on each woman, you could see almost through her breast, they were tangled and blue. I could hear the breath of each woman, it came out heavy and withdrawn. The machines making whirring noises and sucking. I could see bruises painted all over their bodies, and especially around their nipples. As if someone kicked them into the positions they were in. A Peacer was watching all of them, shocking some of them if less of the white liquid came out. They cried out in pain.

I saw one Peacer brought in a littling. A woman on the nursing bench saw the littling and squirmed, screaming for the littling as it cried out to her. This lesser had not produced as much of the white liquid and a Peacer came over and put a plastic gag over her mouth. As she tried to bite him, he shocked her internally again. He fastened the plastic gag and huge tears, streams poured down her face as she looked at the littling held in front of her. The white liquid started to come out more. The Peacer took the littling away as it was screaming and the lesser fought the clasps and nursing bench trying to tear herself out of it as the Peacer pushed her head down and shocked her back into submission. All that was left was the vacancy in her eyes, snot coming out of her nose and over the gag along, spit falling to the floor, her head to the side again.

My gaze had left that woman as the Peacers rushed me past. I saw all those pumps, so many sucking out white liquid, the littling lifeforce - a long winded onslaught of insult to mind, body, and soul added to the injury of having their littling torn away from their mother's chest. All the women's heads were oddly supported on shelves that came up from the ground, as if the shelves became necessary when their necks broke from heartbreak. It felt as if they could not see me being hauled past them. I thought their eyes followed me, though, as if they were some wounded creatures, watching another wounded creature go to death at the hands of those who had coated their eyes in trauma. I will always be haunted by the image of their heads turned unnaturally to either side, a visual summary of their forced unnatural lives. They were just things that could be owned. Ahead of me, a lesser woman was brought out of a cage, her nipples bloodied and sores on her body. She cried in agony as they moved her, tears stagnantly trailing down her raw face of broken capillaries and broken spirit. She looked at me and, in that moment, it was as if time slowed down. I saw her blonde hair wave in the air slowly, looking like something that was wild, her eyes had such grief in those brown eyes, they were so bright, and her skin was white, like the whitest plastic we had. They ported away.

I was then thrown into a cement cell. I fell on the floor and hit my sores. My whole body ached. I could not believe that lessers were put into these for their entire lives. I was dizzy, and my body still smelled of vomit. I didn't even have a chance to look at my body yet since it was so dark in the farm, no windows. In the World Collective our telegraphics made it so that we could change the look of what we wore on our bodies. Though nudity was accepted, most people wanted to express themselves. I saw now how my blue and purple cheetah print was gone from my skin. I saw my sores and open wounds, and now more wounds. I was shaking uncontrollably on the cold floor, and seeing the wounds made me feel even worse. I looked as if I was diseased.

I stood up after realizing that I could. It was so painful. I have no idea how long I had been at the farm, but it took every fiber of my being to lift myself up standing, crying out in pain as every muscle stretched for the first time in a long time. *How did I not know how this felt?* I went through my mind thinking of how much I loved the taste of nourishment. Half of my mind was still justifying eating these... *People* I thought, almost throwing up again. These were *people just like me.* I threw up again on the floor, and it splayed out in front of me. I could see the color was sickly, with some blood in it. My chest ached as if someone had sat on it, and it was rotting, hollowed out.

The bubble blocking the entrance to my cell suddenly burst open and I panicked as I felt my telegraphic shocked me again. A healer came in. I tried intentioning, forgetting again my telegraphic did not work. He looked at me and looked surprised. I saw he was trying to intention something and then realized I could not hear him. I pointed to my head. He then did something, and I felt my telegraphic, lifting the block.

Atlia?

I knew that intention. Had I been at the farm so long that I forgot my own family?

His hair was neater than when I last saw him in the World

Collective. Usually I loved the state of his hair, it was straight but would form all different ways, sometimes when he woke up he had his thick black hair sticking out all over. His purple eyes looking at me with laughter. I had noticed how the laughter had left his eyes in the past few years. His tan skin had gotten lighter, his cheeks gaunt. He was so tall he often had to bend down to enter buildings when porting. He looked to be hunching over now, coupled with grief.

Telepa! I intentioned and he just stared at me aghast I could see he felt everything I felt, and I felt what he felt. He could see what happened and tears had fallen from his face. *You were not supposed to be in there this long, but every excuse I gave to them, they would not let me in.*

My poor Dalto. We were not direct, but we might as well be. He was my best friend other than Beleeka and when he started working at the farm I saw less of him, but I had no idea this was the reason why.

He had some rags in his hands, as if he knew I would be needing them. He cleaned me off gently, I cried out every time he touched a sore. He hugged me, and I stayed in the hug, wept and he let me. He then pushed me away *I need to see you* he intentioned and I felt his worry and sadness. He felt my happiness and sadness and everything. I could see he was trying not to cry himself as he looked me over.

There was a woman - so many of them. Telepa, these are not lessers, these are humans. They are like us, they may not intention, but they are people. I am telling you, Telepa, you have to do something I started to sob, *They have mothers, all of these mothers, they have them with these machines...*

Shhhh Telepa calmed me. *I know.*

I looked up at him feeling betrayed *You... you know?!* I could feel my anger raise. Something was not right in me anymore and I knew that instant. I was touching his hand at that moment and saw steam.

Ouch he exclaimed and took his hand away, it looked burned. Both of us looked at it shocked *I am sorry, I don't know...*

38

It does not matter Atlia, we don't have time. You saw what I did to these people when you walked past those women. I know what happened and I can't help it. That is why this is so important. That is why we did this he intentioned.

I looked at him blankly *Did what?* I intentioned.

Hold on. Then I noticed he was checking our channel. I realized it had been private this whole time, an illegal thing to do. *The Intentioneers can't hear us at the farm, but just in case I had to make sure we were absolutely private.*

I nodded waiting for more information.

You don't remember, do you? he intentioned and then groaned. *This was not supposed to happen this way. You are so stupid!* I never remember him using a tone or a word like that. We could express frustration, but we usually don't use old derogatory words as intentions.

I was shocked and said nothing - he could feel my shock.

You just had to do this, didn't you?

You think I did this? I intentioned and he could feel my anger. He was confused and then I could feel his understanding.

I need to tell you something he intentioned and touched my shoulder. *You did this, and you don't remember. You and Avia Carlo. You both did this.*

It took me a second but then, that is when I felt Telepa release my memory. The one I forgot. And everything changed.

7

MEMORY

I did not know how much memory was lost but then I realized my memory was not lost, I wrote over my memory. It was something no one ever needed to do, because who would want to make themselves forget? Only in some instances did experienced guides do this to possible lessers if they experienced accidental traumas. I did this, so I could be sent to the farm. I played my memory from the beginning.

It started from when I was a littling. My life started to fit together, the lost memories filling in places like pieces of a puzzle. I saw myself at the beginning age, very young, and I was in the garden and I was playing with another little human. I was not playing like a normal child, as we typically play in our telegraphics. I was playing with an ancient artifact my Avia Carlo kept calling a "ball". I was giggling as it rolled back and forth between us, she was giggling as well.

That human was Dina. I remember the smell of fresh roses, and the early morning rise. Dina laughed like how the plastic bells sounded in the wind, cheerful and light. I remember then a shadow stretched over above us. My Prime Avo, I will never forget the appalled look on her face, as if I physically attacked her. She intentioned me to stop, trying to tell me the difference between humans and lessers. I did not understand as she picked me up to pull me away and I grabbed for Dina as Dina cried. My Prime Avo scolded me in her intentions kindly, calling me a sensitive one. She then blocked my telegraphic to not feel pets. My Avia was there as well and felt awful. He tried to discuss it with my Prime Avo, but my Prime Avo said she would report him if he did not uphold the laws. That teaching me otherwise was treason. Later, as I sadly rolled the ball by myself in our living area, he came over to me and looked me in the eyes. I could tell, somehow, he understood. He took the pet blocker off when he felt how much I cared for Dina. He then secretly would let Dina and I play together in his sleeping area. We would have so much fun chasing each other, and not using our telegraphics so no one would know or feel I was playing with a pet. Every time she left, I could feel her fear and sadness. I would cry as I remember feeling another human, another girl I could feel her pulling Dina away to teleport with her, I could feel the invisible leash. And felt Dina's eyes saddened as they teleported away.

Dina, I knew Dina. Memories flooded in. Memory of growing up with Dina secretly and my Avia helping us see each other. I remembered teaching her the old language as I learned it and my Avia helping. He took off the blocks of Dina's telegraphic and connected her to only me and him. I started to know her more, as we intentioned and spoke the ancient language together. When we were able to be together, we were inseparable. I remember the first time I felt love was the moment when I was in my middle age, that when she intentioned her love for me and her want for me, I remember feeling the same for her. I remember my Avia feeling my love for Dina, and he intentioned how I could never share with anyone my feelings for Dina. I made a private channel for me and Dina, so he would not have to bear witness, though he could see it with his eyes when he checked in on us, how she responded to me when we were together, and how I responded to her in the old language. To him he said it was a treat to hear us do what the ancients called "flirting".

I remember being with her. Our first time. It made me cry. I teared as I remembered her - how could I forget her? She was funny, adventurous, silly, courageous, and amazing. We were at the lake, we had a secret spot, a portion of the lake that was a watering hole. We found it once when walking in the woods. We went there when my Avia felt it was unsafe to be together in his sleeping quarters. He suggested we explore the plastic woods, many people did not even go in them, it was thought to be the saddest place in the World Collective since the trees marked where the Greatest Battle was fought with the Southern Founders. We set up a picnic next to the lake, which was made from the water that fell through the dome. It was cleaned by the dome as it fell in.

We sat on a hammock that we made between two plastic trees as we ate the different nourishment my Avia Carlo got for us. He somehow found nourishment that was not made of lessers since I had stopped eating and refused to eat lesser nourishment since I found out what it was made from. I knew this was probably the toughest memory I had to overwrite so that I could complete my mission. Dina was feeding me, and I fed her, and we laughed at each other, getting it all over our faces. She then kissed me, where the nourishment had fallen right next to my lips. I felt her mischievousness as she intentioned *my master is gone for today, she is traveling to the north borders, we could simply sleep here under the dome, maybe even see stars.*

I intentioned laughter and happiness, and a little bit of excited fear. *We shouldn't, what if we get caught?* I intentioned. She felt what I was feeling, and I could feel her strength, love, and her devilish smile. *We can't get caught if they are not here.*

Dina had a pet's mask on, one that made her all white and she turned it off. I admired her body as she went into the water. When in consensual love, we were taught we could admire bodies in that way, but we were taught to feel people more than just act upon what we see. And I could feel Dina and the love I had for all of her, including her body. Her beautiful petite figure, her long arms and her breasts and hips adding a slight curve. She looked stunning, the light shining through the trees on her body and her smile. Her light brown skin looking golden, the sun kissing it. I wanted to kiss all over her, as the sun did, I wanted to be that close to her. And then she jumped in which shocked me and I felt the water splash up on me. She laughed and splashed me and I intentioned my *Oh really?* and went into the water with her.

I splashed her as she splashed me, and we came together wet and warm and I kissed her sweet, soft, plush lips. I could feel the way she looked at me then. She saw my orange freckles as something cute and kissed them, as she touched my pink skin, which, to her, looked like a shining sunset. I laughed and could feel her seriousness in her attraction to me. Seeing myself in that light, I could feel as beautiful as she saw me through her eyes. She loved my curly red hair and sifted her hands through it, feeling every curve. I felt her feel my curly hair and felt how attracted she was to its depth. I saw and felt her love for my thin eyes, which slanted upwards, a deep chocolate brown. My eyes were the only beauty I felt that connected me and my sister Beleeka, but to Dina, all of me was beautiful. I felt fire and sweetness as we loved each other. I felt her determined kiss back, kissing as if we only had moments, and she was going to make the most of them. She put her hand down, as if instinctively she knew where I would be pleased most, I followed her lead and we moaned together kissing. We would come together and away together, feeling each other's breast press against one another, our hands, our mouths. We were beautiful.

I felt her next to me as we secretly would sleep together after we both had released, drying ourselves from the water. We lay half on each other in the hammock, still breathing heavily. We slept there most nights, making it our home. We tried to ignore the world we lived in and agreed not to talk about what we were going through as I started to become a leader, and she fewer rights as she was a pet of age now.

That soon stopped, we could not ignore our worlds forever. She once arrived with bruises on her face and arms with tears in her eyes, shaking. I had seen her in horrible states before, but she usually would distract me. This time she collapsed to the floor, crying, holding her knees to her chest. I rushed over and felt what she felt and saw what happened.

She was put into a stone room, and she sat down in a squat as pets do. Her owner was there, and Dina could not feel the intentions of her owner. She usually ignored the girl who owned her and just tried to do what she said without enraging her. Something felt different this time and Dina was scared.

A man came in with a male pet who strode into the room. He was tall and well built, his eyes were slits, his hair was blond, and he had tan skin. Dina thought he looked like what World Collective people would think is a perfect yellow head specimen - the name for his breed of lesser being. There were hammocks for the humans to sit on and they did. The male locked eyes with Dina. I felt Dina's fear and her fiery anger within her. It was so odd, the humans just were watching, smiling sickly as if they were waiting for something to happen.

The male went over to Dina and pulled her up into his arms. Dina struggled as the man tried to turn her over. Their masks were shut off now and she was nude in front of the humans. As Dina struggled and got out an arm, she punched him in the face. Then I saw her face pain as her owner frowned at her. I felt her telegraphic sear with pain as she tried to blindly fight the male. He punched her in the face and she fell to the ground, face down. He pulled her up, and she was on all fours. He thrusted in her as she fought still with every fiber in her body, crying out. She saw the humans smile at each other in perversion and they lifted glasses, popped the nourishment bubbles into their mouths and intentioned to each other. Dina cried a warrior's cry as he kept thrusting into her. Telling them with as much as she could that she was not going to take this, and they would have to listen to her. I felt the pain between Dina's thighs and the sharp needles that she tried to ignore. She felt as if her insides were being scooped out by a plastic tool. Her human sent more pain towards her, she tried to cry out strongly and loudly at them, defiantly. He held her arms as he expressed himself and then pushed her down.

Dina tried not to cry and held all her sadness inside of her. With all her strength, she stood up and looked at them. They seemed surprised to see her standing, his seed spilling out of her. Her human looked upset and intentioned pain at her. The male pet slapped her again. She fell again to the ground.

His human laughed and clapped. The male pet smiled at his human. He then proceeded to force her down again. This time covering her nose and mouth, so she could not make any sound. She lay still, feeling as if she was suffocating, waiting for it to be over. He licked and bit her nipples until he was ready again. She tried to fight it, but again as she could not breathe except for moments when his hand slipped, he thrust inside of her on the ground, her back scraping on the stone floor. This time she just lay there. She thought about surviving long enough, hoping he would finish before she suffocated. I could feel her flee her mind. She noticed her human nodding in happiness. After he was done again, she lay there on the floor.

The male slapped her in the face again for good measure and his human motioned for him to get going. They teleported out of the cement cell. Dina lay there, covered in his disgusting sweat and seed. Her human came over and pet her head. She did nothing. She then teleported out. That is when Dina teleported to me.

She could not speak the old language or teleport, she could let aynone know she had these abilities otherwise they would send both of us to the farm. I hugged Dina close to me as she cried, and I picked her up and took her to the water. I bathed her saying and intentioning nothing. She could feel my love, how I loved her all my life. I could say nothing. I knew what this horrific act was, they were trying to breed her for more pets. I then dried her off and hugged her in our hammock until she fell asleep. My Avia came later as she slept and his was face widened in the abhorrence at what happened to her.

My Avia then went straight with me to Dina's owner and he tried to buy Dina. The other Avo of the girl who owned Dina refused. And she threatened to report us and banned me from seeing Dina ever again. She said we were disgusting and she knew that Avia Carlo was a "lesser lover".

I went back to Dina, who I felt was not ready to go, but I felt her strength that she would do what she had to do to survive. We both cried as she was torn away from me again, the invisible leash pulling. They must have found she got out of her cell and blamed Avia Carlo for teleporting her. Our intentions stayed close to each other as I felt her slip away from teleporting. My Avia felt for me and I felt how sad he felt. He felt how my heart broke, how I had become used to being one with her. He also felt my feeling of protection, how I would die to protect her from anything further, no matter the cost. Some of us only find one love while others find multiple. My Avia noted I was one of the few who do what it is called imprinting - where my love for Dina and her love for me was one already. You could see and feel it through the telegraphic. We were what people called in the ancient days "soulmates".

My Avia loved me so much - and that was the night he let me know he was a freer, someone who helped emancipate the lessers. I remember feeling saddened, angry, and scared for him, but how I understood. That is when I learned what they did to lessers that were not pets. I was told before what nourishment was made from, but I didn't know everything until then. I told him to tell me everything I ignored for so long. He told me about the terrors of the farms, the slaughter of lessers. It made me sick as he described the conditions. That all lessers, including ones at the farms, were the same as Dina.

My Avia let me know this is what happened after there was no more meat and that we used to do this to animals. That is the second time I got sick, my Avia had brought the eliminator in with an intention. My vomit disintegrated into the disk - it acted like a black hole. It only recognized non-living matter. *Animals?* I intentioned, those cute creatures I was taught about that existed.

Yes. They did not view them as people either. Yes, they are a different species, but they had lives just like ours and they should have lived free, to make their own choices. Though they were not as intelligent as us, that was the reasoning many ate them. Though they felt pain, had their own families, and had their own preferences and ways of relating to the world.

We are beasts I intentioned, crying. My Avia held me as he told me everything. How our ancestors committed the same violence to animals and how humans craved meat, thus the different "breeds" of humans were formed when all of the animals were gone so that people could still get their "meat". He told me that we had all the plants we needed still and that is what we fed the lessers. That it was the deadliest secret that the World Collective kept from everyone.

We are the lesser humans my dear, not them he intentioned and I realized that we were. There was no difference. We talked the entire night about this strange violent behavior of our ancestors and how it shaped what we had.

How could we be so cruel and why did no one do anything?

Many people felt passionate about meat my Avia intentioned *and it was a part of the culture, the culture became so twisted that even people who felt for the animals still ate them. A majority of people did nothing since the culture created cognitive dissonance. It's exactly the same way that we think of lessers, that them being not human and tasting good is a reason to murder and eat their flesh.*

I don't understand I intentioned and he felt my pain and sadness. At that moment, my Prime Avo ported into Avia Carlo's study. Her eyes were furious.

Carlo she intentioned her fury and betrayal. My Avia felt her and sighed. He could feel her love and anger as I could, but more deeply since they were lovers.

That is when I saw two Peacers come in. Then I felt the feeling of betrayal from my Prime Avo in my Avia Carlo. The Peacers took him. *I warned you* my Prime Avo intentioned and I could feel her sadness.

Don't do this. My Avia intentioned and my Prime Avo intentioned for me to teleport away, but I fought her intention as my Kamma taught me. My Prime Avo was surprised. I grabbed my Avia and teleported to the woods where Dina and I would go. I hid my tracks like my Kamma taught me. It would be awhile before they found us.

All of the sudden I saw Telepa teleport in. I was confused, but my Avia let me know that my Dalto was a part of the movement too and they had a plan. Apparently, Dina and I ruined that plan.

They have Dina Telepa intentioned and I felt shocked, terrified, and sad. I felt theirs as well. *She tried to get away when drawing a bath for her human. She set the temperature to boil and pushed her owner's face into it. She was caught, and for blinding her master she was sent to the farm.*

I fell to the floor sobbing, Telepa and my Avia could feel my pain. They rushed to help me, but I shooed them off, getting up and wiped off my tears *We must do something.* I intentioned *This was my fault and I will do something about it, tell me your plan.*

Telepa intentioned *Our plan was to frame Avia and have him sent to the farm to help get the lessers out and to escape, he was supposed to get caught until you teleported him.*

I could feel my Avia and Telepa both thinking for another plan.

I will do it. I will pay for it, I will get them out I intentioned.

My Avia and Telepa were terrified. *No* they both intentioned, but I stopped them.

I have to do this. It was my fault and now they know I am a part of this too - they will send me to rehabilitation anyway.

My Avia I felt agreed, surprisingly, and intentioned *We must go.* I could feel Telepa was not happy about it and intentioned *No* as we teleported to the room. Then, that is where it happened. Where I killed my Avia.

8

MURDER

When you teleport, it is literally like blinking. There are no movement sensations - nothing. One moment you are in one place, and the next you are at your new destination. I remember loving this feeling of convenience.

On this particular day I could feel my Avia was not pleased. He told me to meet him in the garden and that he had to go somewhere first, and he left me. I am not sure what he was doing.

I quickly teleported to the garden and pretended I was reading a book on Compassion by a World Collective leader via Eden in my telegraphic. It was almost impossible to act normal, my body shaking. I wanted to do something now, but I knew I had to wait for my Avia Carlo. Out of the corner of my eye I saw movement. Sure enough, it was the cutest little creature. It had a small nose and big eyes. I only saw them in my Avia Carlo's ancient books. It was a mouse. My Avia showed up behind the small mouse, making a high-pitched sound to it, and it climbed up him. I had never seen an animal in my life and I sent my intention of love, excitement, and wonder.

So cute! I chirped in my mind making a private channel with my Avia. It distracted me for a second, I was fascinated. My Avia laughed and sat down with me and the mouse came over and sniffed and then licked my hand. I laughed and felt wonder. I could feel my Avia's wonder and love at what he was witnessing.

They are back my Avia intentioned and I felt his excitement and yet sadness and fear. *What would we do if they are back - therefore we must do this now. This is what we were planning for. We know it could be any day that they move to these innocent beings as well. They would never give up eating lessers, and they would expand their slaughter.*

The mouse snuggled into my hand and fell asleep in it. *Little ones like these would be murdered for nourishment, the same thing that happened to this world will happen again and we can't allow that to happen, and we need to save the lessers - we have the army now* my Avia intentioned.

I put the mouse on my shoulder and hid it with an intention. *Take care of him.* I felt such a sadness and I felt my Avia's as well, and I felt something else... determination.

Atlia, I am going to ask something of you that is unspeakable, but it must be done. I thought they would just send me to the farm, but something has happened and your Prime Avo has sent order for my immediate passing.

Scared and saddened I intentioned *No, I won't let that happen!*

My Avia sighed and smiled at me, I felt his sadness. *You know we could live forever, we have the technology if we don't eat the lessers or any animals. You, Dina, and your Dalto changed my mind and I have participated in horrible acts that only I can make up for now. This may have been going on for more than one 1,000 years, but we need to change it. Your Dalto is scarred for life after he started working at the farm as a healer and I want you both to have better lives than we had. You must take care of the little one* he intentioned towards the mouse, and I tucked him in my hand.

I started to cry and was horrified, shaking my head as my Avia continued, I now knew where he was going with this *I am almost the third age, my time has almost come anyway. Atlia, I need you to be strong, I need you to do this and to bring change to this world. To make it truly peaceful for generations to come. I need you to kill me and go to the farm.*

He quickly transported me and the mouse to his sleeping

quarters, and I immediately felt others trying to transport in. *I need you to do it Atlia, I need you to do it now. And then I need you to erase your memory and send it via a private channel to Telepa. That way you are the one framed to go to the farm. I don't want to send you there, but this is bigger than you or me. We owe it to them to save all of them, and I think you're ready now.*

Before I could intention anything more, since my Avia could feel all my sadness and anger and stubbornness, he intentioned forcefully *We don't have enough time and it is clear I have to help. I love you and I hope someday, you will understand it.*

And then my Avia committed the biggest violation you could to any human. He took control of my telegraphic and I felt him and his hate for himself and for everyone. Hate filled his entire body and I could feel it killing different parts of him. I felt his body shutting down, one by one, until it reached his heart. *I love you* he intentioned. I could not stop it; my feelings joined his and I saw him fall to the floor. He was gone. I gasped, feeling him let go, the last bit of my telegraphic, the tears flowing down silently. My breath was ragged, and I could only feel the pain.

I felt the Peacers trying to port in, but I ported out to Dina and my place before they came in. I could not let myself cry, I felt so sad. Telepa ported in and intentioned *give me your memories, I know what happened* - I saw he was crying himself, trying to keep himself together. I did the same by gritting my teeth and sent him my memories.

This way Avia would not have died for nothing Telepa intentioned trying to soothe my heart with feelings of love, sadness, and understanding. *And we need to make sure that they can't verify that Avia had committed his own telecide - it is the only way we can get you to the farm.*

He knew I understood. I felt his unease *what are you doing* he intentioned and I intentioned back *I have to give you my memories of Dina too, I will remember what happened and can't do what I need to if I am thinking of Dina, make sure I get to her and send her the memory of Avia's mouse.* That is the moment I gave the mouse to Telepa. He smiled, and it is then I knew he knew the mouse.

I then created an intention for Dina, a message to go along with the memory. *I know you won't be happy, but I love you, I am coming, and just like the mouse I hope you can kiss me back into existence.* I tried to joke, but it felt more like a goodbye message. I had no idea how this was going to work.

You ready? Telepa intentioned. He felt I was, and he took my memory. He replaced the first part of going to meet my Avia with a different memory. Next thing I knew, I was in the room with Beleeka on my way to nourishment, with no memory whatsoever of these events.

9

AWAKENING

All of the memories were too much for my telegraphic, with the feelings and emotions that poured in, so much so it pushed me to the floor. I felt the pain and sadness, but I also felt hope and happiness. I stood up, ignoring my pain, and felt Telepa's worry.

I intentioned a laugh *I remember Dina and I have a very big apology I need to give to her* Telepa felt that and smiled *I see* he intentioned *we have a great deal to do, though.*

He felt I understood and intentioned what our plan was. Every night we would teleport the lessers, one by one, out of the farm to the secret lake. One by one was not that much for our telegraphic, so it would keep our escape plan under the Intentioneers' radar. Telepa set up a camp there and hid it with a dome, a small one that is like our city's, but it would make it invisible to everyone. It was Dina's idea.

Another idea they had, I was not too happy about, was that they wanted me to go back and get exonerated after we created a teleport system and unblocked Dina's telegraphic. Apparently, Telepa did see Dina under the pretext of examining her as a possible breeder, but instead he made sure the male pet did not impregnate her, and he sent her the memories. He still had her telegraphic limited because they did not give him enough time to do more.

The freers wanted me to frame others to have them experience a life of a lesser. I was happy to frame them, to show them how horrible it is for the lessers, but to leave Dina again would be difficult no matter the awful conditions we were in. I learned that Telepa had taught the lessers how to speak the old language, and I learned some lessers were like the ancient animals we learned about. Some were less intelligent, but sweet. Some could not speak or could not see but could think. Telepa told me in the beginning they started with those humans who were deemed "most like animals", not realizing their own hypocrisy that we are all animals regardless of how smart we are.

I intentioned I was ready to go back with Dina and put a blocker up so the Peacers did not know my telegraphic was active. Telepa gave me full access to my telegraphic so I could ignite Dina's.

We don't have much time, but when you did not have your memories, it may have been easier at the farm. We have to do this plan slowly, and it will be hard not to try to save the lessers from slaughter. Just know you are doing the best you can, and everyone is thankful.

At that I felt guilt, feeling like I wish I could do more. *I won't think about that right now, Telepa. I am ready to focus on the mission. Don't worry about my feelings, they do not matter.*

Okay, then Telepa intentioned. "I am sorry," Telepa said and before I could ask about what he was sorry for, he shocked me. It was painful, and I cried out. I felt Telepa's sadness and worry for me. He could feel my annoyance, but I took the pain and pretended to not have my telegraphic active. The Peacers came in and grabbed me.

Telepa looked at the Peacers and I knew they were doing something. In our private channel he sent me a sorry feeling and intentioned *what I must do next - I am so sorry - but I am required to do it in front of the Peacers, and I need it to be real.*

That is when I saw a tube they brought in with a pump. I struggled against the Peacers and was shocked again. It was then that I was force fed with a tube down my throat and I felt Telepa bring my telegraphic to another place, one Telepa made in his mind so I did not feel what was going on to my body. I could see my body react violently trying to get rid of the tube, choking on the food.

Well that was great. Thanks for no warning I intentioned to Telepa, and immediately regretted it feeling how sad he was to do it and how much he did not want to.

You don't know how many horrible things I have had to do to keep my position Telepa intentioned and I could feel the cold dread he felt from what he did have to do.

This is the best I could do Telepa intentioned referring to the space in his telegraphic he made for us. *It will hurt after, and I am sorry, but I have to show I show no preference.*

I understand I intentioned and he felt that, while I knew my body would be in ridiculous pain after. It did not matter, I was determined now with a purpose and mission. I was determined to make it so that nothing ever separates me and Dina again.

I was then pushed back into my body and felt the pit in my stomach, the ache from the tube had hit me like a blow. I groaned and cried loudly, and I found there were tears running down my cheeks. They had taken out the tube and the Peacers were taking me back to my cage now.

Even though my body was in pain, my head was alight. *Dina* I thought, and I felt the love and comfort even though I had not ignited her telegraphic piece yet, I knew she was waiting for me. I saw her look at me frightened, but I smiled drunkenly and hurt at her, I saw her sadness and annoyance in her face, which I knew was increased by my smile.

They threw me in the cage and it hurt as I groaned, but I did not care. I waited on the ground as Dina rubbed my back and glared at the Peacers, squealing. The Peacers could not hear anything, but I saw them laugh at her, though they looked sad and frightened at me.

Good I thought *be frightened because this will happen to you.* Dina could feel my intentions, but I could not feel hers. I then looked at Dina as soon as they left. I unblocked her intentions in her telegraphic. I felt her sigh *finally.*

I felt instantly at one with her again and my mind and her mind looked each other over for aches or pains and comforted everything with love, sadness, validation. I then grabbed her beautiful petite body and held her close to me on our sides. Even though it was so painful to lay down again on my soars, I ignored it and focused on the feeling of being close to her. I am tall and long, so she fit perfectly under my chin. She looked up at me with tears in her eyes and intentioned in the old language *Hello, stranger* and she kissed me, as she felt me protest how gross I felt after going through what I just went through. She did not care. If we were not in a tiny cage with ten other people, I think she would have loved me right there and then.

She felt that I could feel her intention and smiled her mischievous smile. *It has been a while my love and it is nice to see you fully now. I have missed you.*

I have missed you, too I intentioned. It felt amazing amongst all the aches and pains. I was with her and could feel her again, I could feel whole.

Why did you play with me when I got in here? I intentioned.

She laughed and looked at me pointedly. *I was angry with you and I could do nothing until you got your memories back. I decided to play with this very different Atlia who was the epitome of the "World Collective"* she smiled wryly at me.

I laughed at her, I missed her humor, and she was right next to me the whole time. She felt how embarrassed I was, and I felt her love and annoyance and frustration with me. We both felt how nice it was to be near each other, and we could feel neither of us wanted to argue about what happened. It happened and now we had a job to do. But until then, she and I wanted to just be with each other, holding each other.

We lay there in each other's arms for a while until we fell asleep.

10

ACTION

I woke up first to the warmth of Dina, and then to the pain I felt in my stomach. The cage was disgusting and even though we were in our own filth and blood, I was still able to hold Dina and that is all I could care about.

It is so disgusting they don't even remove our excess I intentioned to Dina - everything in the World Collective was spotless. I focused on the mission again, I intentioned for Dina and felt her wake up comfortably in my arms. She gave me a kiss, ignoring my first intention. I felt her intention of her knowing what we had to start doing. We planned to start at night to save the youngest lessers first. Now that all the lessers knew I was back, all of them were talking to each other in the old language. They could not risk me acting even stranger when the Peacers and farmers were in to grab people for slaughter.

We had lain there for a while. I know we had to be quiet until Telepa sent us our contact to start getting lessers out. Dina and I connected, intentioned, and laughed as the others talked. I met all the lessers as we shouted to each other from the cages. I heard the stories of the ones that could talk. The ones that could not speak, some of the other lessers shared their stories.

All of them were brought up in this farm and it was awful. They split families apart, everyone lived in cages, some standing and some laying. The standing cages were for "exercise" to keep them lean. I was surprised to learn that some knew the old language as it was passed down to them from their parents, and their parents' parents. They were taught brutal tactics to not be chosen for slaughter. They tried many times to free themselves over the many years, but so many attempts failed. Most had given up hope and tried to live as nice of lives they could.

Some even had ancient religions passed down to them, something you never see in the World Collective. Most religions got lost as they were associated with lesser beings. There were only two religions left in this farm: Buddhism and Judaism. I was fascinated by the rituals they had every day, and I was surprised I did not notice any before.

While we waited, the lessers taught me games we could play from our cages by calling out to one another, and we discussed many things from, philosophy to Creationists, some willing to learn everything I knew. Some of them knew more than I did about the ancient world and they taught me about how people used to do something called "text" each other and use facial expression drawings to express their feelings.

As Telepa said, though we tried to make the best of it, the worst times were what the lessers called the "killing hours". The first time it happened since I got my telegraphic and memories back, it took me everything in my power to not do something.

They would grab the lessers, some that I knew, and I felt so bad - but I couldn't do anything as they were forcefully dragged away, crying. This became a problem one time when the farmers came to choose - I was chosen. My cage was opened and I intentioned to Dina *I am sorry, keep up the cause.* As I heard her scream "No!" the Peacers did not know what speaking in the ancient language looked like, so they seemed to just assume it was a scream. She held onto my arms and I held onto hers one last time, tears falling from my face.

The whole place was wild now, I was their last hope. I had to figure something out. I felt the pain in my telegraphic that which made me collapse, the pain of the other lessers who had such fear in their eyes. They were wide, and tears were streaming as we were teleported into a place with steel walls. More lessers joined us. Everyone was crying and screaming, eyes lit with fear as we were pushed into a line. We looked ahead and there was a pot of boiling substance. I saw as a male lesser, in mid age screamed against being thrown into the tank. His skin peeling off as he screamed, his eyes wide with such fear. I was getting closer and closer, and I started to scream. I could not help it, it was the most violent thing I had ever seen in my life. Then, to my left I heard screams as well. The lessers who were taken out of the pot, some were still alive. They were trying to slice their throats one by one.

The first lesser was a girl littling, no more than beginning age, her teeth were not even all grown in and she was screaming and crying. I felt my heart strings pull for her, whispering, "No," under my breath. One man holding a noose around her neck started punching her in the head repeatedly. She first cried out in pain and then I saw her eyes start to roll to the back of her head with every punch. Then the farmer took out a knife and he slit her throat, and it too did not go all the way through. She gasped for air, her eyes rolling to the back of her head as a farmer chopped her again. She cried out again, and I prayed as I saw the Buddhists and Jews pray. I prayed for the first time that her life would end. I tasted the snot from my nose and the salty tears of terror as I saw her die, her body go limp. Suddenly I was pulled out of the line.

Don't look It was Telepa. He brought me through the slaughter house and I made myself see every lesser get killed. I made myself look at the horrors we, the so-called humans, inflicted on the lessers.

Why are they not blocking their telegraphics, why are they butchering them?! I cried in my mind to Telepa.

Because they thought it would speed up production and they did not want to fully enable their telegraphics in case they figured out how to use them to teleport and escape. Telepa responded plainly. I could feel his deep sadness at my reaction, and his numbness to the situation.

I sobbed as I saw all the carnage. So many times, they were

not killed fully. They had guns, which I thought were an extinct tool, to shoot them. Blood flooded the floors and slowly went through drains. They tried to electrocute them with a device, the people screaming. The sadness of the people screaming would haunt me forever. The ability to do nothing. I had no idea how Telepa could witness this, my heart felt as if it was heated by the fires from the Greatest War. I did not know what he was saying to the Peacers to let us through, but finally he could teleport me, the stench of burning, boiling flesh still hung in my mouth. I vomited on the floor crying.

You can't do this right now Telepa said with love, but at the same time with hurriedness. *You almost died. We need to do this now.*

That is when I felt a Peacer teleport in. It was the one that teleported me to the farm.

I am so sorry Katcha intentioned, another sibling of ours. *I was trying to point them to someone else.*

I could feel Telepa's fury with her, but it went away as I felt he knew there was nothing he could have done differently. *Tonight Katcha, I don't care what it takes - the freers will make contact with Atlia tonight.*

I felt sick and numb. Katcha I saw nodded and she teleported me back to the farm. She put me as nicely as she could in the cage, I said nothing. Dina held me, as I heard people give thanks that I was back and tried to ask me questions. My mind went somewhere, and I did not know what to do. I heard Dina tell them to give me some time. She hummed something as she caressed my hair. The little girl's face still in my mind. She looked at everyone, including me, before she died. Crying with loud bellows, it was like she wanted to scream - Please! Please! I don't want to die! I am scared! Please! as they chopped at her neck and she cried out in pain the first time.

I hid these from Dina, though I felt her try to pry. I did not want to cause her more sadness. I lay as she caressed my hair and I cried for all the people who were murdered for nourishment.

That night I started to feel better. Dina pleaded that I put a block on the memory in my telegraphic, so I could focus. I could feel she hated asking this of me, but the fact that I never experienced violence, she said she thought it was affecting me more than others. I put a mild block on it so that I would be ready for the contact. It was the first time I had ever been to the farm, and now I saw no difference between lessers and humans. Lessers were all too human. I was not aware that a Peacer had come in and she opened the cage.

She created a private channel with me and I felt her name was Ota, one of the freers. She reiterated that we had to be careful and could only choose one a night to free as to not raise suspicions. Our plan was to fill the cells with World Collective people instead.

I had to move on from what I saw. I solemnly asked Dina who we should free first and she suggested the old man. At first, I intentioned that I was unsure since he was frail and the first person we would free would have to set up the camp and take care of the smallest ones. The man somehow knew what I was thinking, sat up from the floor, and said, "I am stronger than I look, I can take care and build a camp. I am George, that's the name I chose for myself." This man had never introduced himself, and I thought he was one of the ones who could not speak.

My eyes surprised, I said, "Then, come along."

He laughed and stood up groaning. "You are now one of us kiddo. You saw what most of us only see in our final days." He got close to my face, "Remember it because it is your people - your guilt to carry."

"Leave her alone, she has been through enough," Dina replied looking at him with daggers.

"I know how that feels," I said, pointing to his slow maneuver to standing, trying to change the subject. He looked at me and shook his head.

"You have no idea - this is the first time I have been standing in two years!"

I was stunned into silence, feeling embarrassed, I felt Dina laugh lovingly.

"Now come on, do this teleport mumbo jumbo," he said.

I looked at Ota and she nodded. Holding onto the old man's telegraphic and Dina's, I used my telegraphic to port us to the camp. I saw only plastic trees, and we kept walking, looking for the camp. I walked by a familiar tall plastic tree and suddenly we were in the camp, passing through the invisibility dome, which had mirrored the surrounding environment. They had cleared apart most of the plastic plants and made cushions on the floor. We left the man there, I saw a woman was already there. I saw that she was tending to something and I looked closer. "Plants!" I exclaimed with glee and ran over like a child. I touched one and was in awe in how light and life like it felt. It was the woman I remembered when I was younger, the sibling who was sent to be a pet. I did not realize she was probably sent to the farm. She was an Avo now, I saw her two kids next to her helping as well. She was the color of the earth when it was under water, her eyes were a deep blue, like how I imagined the real ocean looked. Her hair was curly and tight to her head with blonde, grey, and brown streaks through it.

"I am Liat and these are my littlings, Dove and Leaf." I crouched down and they hid behind their mother. Leaf was taller than Dove and the same color as his mother, however his hair was a dark black and straight and his eyes were green. His sister was small and petite, with chubby cheeks and big round eyes. She was a mahogany shade of red brown, the same color as my Avia Carlo's desk in his study. Her hair was tight and curly like her mothers but with green eyes like her brother, except hers were so bright.

"Hi Dove and Leaf, I am Atlia. Don't worry, we will protect you."

"Not a bad one?" Dove asked, her light brown eyes shimmering up.

"No dear," said Liat, comforting her littling.

This saddened my heart to hear this child be afraid, Dina felt my sadness and she could feel my guilt. The image of the littling I saw murdered flashed before my eyes. I shook the bad feeling off.

"How did you find these plants?" I asked in wonder.

"They were from seeds, the collective has a whole seed bank," said Liat.

I looked at her blankly, "What?"

Liat laughed and said, "They collected seeds when the world was being torn apart, every last one of them, and they protected them. However, the ancestors chose to hide them away in order to punish the lessers. And since the animals were gone and nothing could grow until we created the dome, they ate the lessers. There was always an alternative, they just did not choose it. They chose the greed and lust for flesh over love and peace, which they tried to establish still after. That is why this society is deeply flawed."

This made me disgusted. It churned my stomach after my recent experience at the slaughterhouse and made me more determined to free these people. "Taste? I can't believe the ancestors would be so... naïve and evil."

"Well, then you will have to count yourself evil as well. How many lessers did you consume without a thought?" That statement turned my stomach more. She was right, I was disgusting.

Dina felt me, touched my back, and intentioned *you didn't know better, now you do.* And she let me feel her calm and love to calm my stomach. I sent her love and thanks.

George then said, "You best move on so that we can get things ready."

We went back to the farm and waited for the next night. And the next. The Peacers and farmers had no idea what was going on since they never looked inside or could hear what was happening. Also, with Telepa's and Ota's help at misdirection, they never even bothered to check, too afraid to become ill themselves. Telepa told them we all had a highly infectious virus that needed to go through our systems. Since we did not have our telegraphics accessible to the knowledge of the World Collective, it would take us longer to heal. Their want of cognitive dissonance worked to our advantage. We freed fifteen children, four babies and their mothers, and three pregnant women. The pregnant women we tried to free first, the ones that were nearly due so that they did not have to give birth in the filth or be brought to slaughter. Telepa gave us ideas of which ones to save first in case they came again for killing hour, even though he told them that we were all sick. He had some Peacers who were a part of the freers go along with the plan to agree that we had to "get it out of our system" until more slaughters could occur.

The pregnant women were grateful to be freed first, especially in their state. I was amazed that lessers would even want families, all of them living to a little above middle aged, that would be 19 or 20 years old in old language. I learned that most of the pregnant women did not choose to be pregnant and were forcefully impregnated by the healers, by my Dalto, Telepa. I am not sure how Telepa survived all this time, but I imagine it was hard to be put in that position, knowing if it wasn't him, it would be someone else doing it.

We created a center space where we all could meet and discuss things. Not all things from the World Collective were bad, and their government representation system seemed to work with our group.

"Can I propose something to the group?" I asked in the old language, which we decided to talk in from now on until everyone had telegraphics.

"We don't have time, we have to move on," George said looking at me.

I nodded, "Yes, I know, but we need to make a plan B, just in case. We need to see if we can live... outside the dome."

Everyone either scoffed or gasped in shock and George said agitated, "That is suicide. And other lessers could die before then!"

"Who would go and see if it was safe?" asked Teff, one of the pregnant mothers who recently gave birth. She cocked her head to the side, listening for her little one while also paying attention to us.

"Just listen, I think she has a good plan," Dina said, intentioning me comforting thoughts and love.

"When I am exonerated I will be in the rehabilitation center for quite some time. I can easily frame people of the World Collective because they are already on their way to being sentenced as lessers. Also, the center is near the edge of the dome. I can explore the outside with the help of others. My Dalto says there are two freers at the rehab center. Dina can continue to bring people to camp."

"Are you sure you can accomplish all that?" asked George.

"Yes, George. Don't you see by now I am very capable and will do my best to save these people. It would be wrong to say that I will, but I can say I will try," I responded to George.

Everyone was silent and somber for a second. George then clapped his hands and said, "Okay, let's do this."

We broke off in separate ways, Dina and I going to our camp. All the camps were made with plastic tarps and the plastic trees and flowers. Even though I was with Dina at our own camp, now it was hard not to think of the people we left behind every time we freed someone. So many people were still left, anxious and frightened. People sometimes started fighting over who could be freed next. I almost felt I was playing with their lives when I did not want to be the one choosing them in the first place. Dina was ready to free them because she saw everything I did and usually was the one comforting the lessers who were upset that they would not be freed before others. She saw how I covered my tracks with my teleportation just in case Peacers or Intentioneers sent feelers out for odd signals. Everything inside Kalea was recorded, all intentions, unless you went around the tracking algorithms. We luckily had some Intentioneers on the inside helping us hide our tracks, and my Kamma taught me the best ways to hide from the Intentioneers. I knew Dina was ready for this.

As we went into our tent and decided to bathe in the bubble bath tub, a creation from the World Collective that was easy to have in each tent. I bathed Dina, caring for her sores as she bathed and cared for mine. I got out of the bath and intentioned my telegraphic to dry me off. Dina held my hand and squeezed it until my knuckles were white. *My hand* I intentioned to Dina and Dina then looked up at me frightened. *What?* I intentioned and tears streamed down her face.

Promise me you will never do that again, that you will never make plans without me. I can't lose you again. What happened with Avia Carlo, I know you were trying to fix everything but that was still not fair to me. I know I may lose you because what we are doing is dangerous, but please let me be a part of the plan in the future.

I could not stand to look at that beautiful petite copper face her brown green eyes glittered with tears. I could not stand her tears, I kissed them away and held her close rubbing her back as she clutched onto me. I cried also knowing it was not just my rash plan that made her upset, it was that this was our last time together before I went to rehab. I scooped her up and carried her to the bed. I placed her down gently on the sleeping mat and kissed away her tears. Her tears had fallen down her face and past the curve of her breasts, past her belly button and I kissed down until I met herself with my lips. Her tears turned to moans.

I will never do anything without your approval again. I intentioned her as I licked her and that tiny spot of pleasure. I kissed and sucked and loved that area until her moans got so deep with pleasure that she held her breath as she released all her pleasure and a gleeful cry. Relief, half laughing, half moaning. She grabbed onto me and my body moved against hers. I could feel myself completely wet from her wetness, her hands all over my body, caressing and loving me. Tears fell down my face as I had felt her pain of being apart and I saw her face running with tears too, for being apart from mine. I was committed in that moment to loving her, to forget the pain, embracing the sadness, and giving her all the love that I could. I kissed her tears away as I caressed her neck and kissed the small part of her neck that I knew she loved, hearing her moans get heavy. As we moved, I could feel her breasts against mine, my hand started to roam as well to please her again, I felt the beating of her heart as she went faster. I licked her breasts loving them as she did mine and the tingle of pleasure was sent throughout my body, I was now moaning as well. We moaned together, this beautiful song of love and pleasure. Her pleasure was released, as we kissed each other and held each other close. We both breathed hard as one.

I was about to lay back when she intentioned *you are not getting off that easy* and kissed me until her mouth went down further.

Neither of us rested, as we loved each other throughout our last night together.

11

APART

The next morning, I woke up next to my love, feeling her body fit in mine. She smelled like fresh air mixed with the way it smells when it rains. I kissed the back of her neck and intentioned *good morning, beautiful.*

Dina turned to kiss me with her soft lips. Her eyes smiling and then dimming. At that moment I felt her sadness and I knew she felt mine. Today was the day that we would journey apart - again. This time I felt her hope, happiness, and determination. She felt my hesitation and I felt her laugh at me. *We are one again, Love, don't be so sad.* She kissed me as I rolled my eyes at her, something I learned from the lessers. She laughed again and smiled her mischievous smile. *Shall I love you out of your mood?* she intentioned and I finally laughed and kissed her back.

"Um, Atlia?" I heard my Dalto Telepa's voice. And stopped groaning inwardly, Dina smiled and kept kissing my neck as I laughed and tried to stop her.

Trying not to giggle I said, "Be right there Telepa," I said collected, keeping in my giggle. Then I felt Telepa via my telegraphic and Dina stopped suddenly, feeling him and everyone else in the camp. I felt Dina and the rest of the camp's embarrassment. I intentioned a laugh until I realized that the lessers did not have the same culture the World Collective had. They had never felt two other people's love for each other as if it were their own before.

Next time make a private channel? George intentioned, and we all felt he was laughing and laughed with him. Dina made a private channel with me and I felt her embarrassment heat my own insides, as if her residual shame of being caste in society as a pet mingled with little flickers of an angry flame. *I know your community loves freely in front of others, but we don't get it. We always hid our love and in the lesser world, love from another was never felt* while it was all we felt in the "human" world. I felt her intention, and her intention of anger was toward Telepa.

I intentioned my laughter and love for her, and scooped her up, filling our channel with my love and slowly feeling her anger wash away like how the sunrise washes away the night. I felt my brother trying to pull me away, and she did too. *Go* she intentioned and I gave her one last kiss as I went out of our tent, and in doing so took my place in the rebellion with renewed sense of awareness, fortitude, and purpose in the face of what was at stake.

I could feel Dina going back to fighting mode, her channel exuding confidence to the rest of the group. The group intentioned it together as we felt some fear, we also felt the love, hope, excitement, and readiness of the others.

I see you turned on everyone's telegraphics, couldn't give us a heads up? I created a private channel with Telepa and Dina. It was typical to include loved ones you were closest to in all communications.

Yeah Telepa, that was very observant of you. You could have waited to put them on the public channel? Dina intentioned and I could feel Telepa's embarrassment, which he brushed away quickly and turned it into confidence.

You should not have been so loud with your love Telepa teased, and Dina blushed. They had a friendship that was of a respectful balance of love and jealousy that made one laugh. Feeling my laughter, they laughed, and we stopped for a sobering moment.

You have to go Telepa sadly intentioned.

I know I responded, feeling then the sadness and fear of Dina, Telepa, and myself.

Arriving at the edge of the dome that enclosed the camp, Telepa and Dina hugged me wiping tears from their eyes and I did too, feeling their pain.

Dina took two fingers to her heart, a symbol I did not know. And intentioned in front of everyone:

Tonight, we change the history of the lesser. Tonight, we all face a different future. For some it may be lost, so that others may have one. Thank you all to your sacrifice and courage. May us be together as a new family and thrive. Dina's intention was filled with all her feelings her love, her fear, and her want for justice.

Everyone felt the same feelings, all of us were one and resonated, putting two fingers to their hearts, looking at me. I was uncomfortable with them looking at me, and I was not sure why, but I let it go. I turned my back to all of them, not wanting to feel any more of the sadness and wanting to look toward the future - my future with Dina. I pictured our own family, the future of their children. And then holding on one last thread to Dina, I teleported back to the farm to set up the greatest magic trick in history. To convince the World Collective that lessers were people.

I intentioned myself back to the farm. The other lessers shouted hellos excitedly.

"Hey," I said to Talia, another lesser who did not have her telegraphic installed yet.

"Are you ready?" Talia asked.

"Yes," I responded, laying next to her in the cage, in even more disgusting disarray since the Peacers had come by even more infrequently now because the lessers were still thought to be contagious. Moments later the doors burst open, two Peacers opened the cage and came in. The Peacers covered their mouths with plastic shields in case something went wrong with their telegraphics, to not get sick. The lessers around me squealed in terror, and I did too. They pulled me out of the cage and took me through the front. I pretended the light hurt and that I felt the shocks of pain, but my telegraphic was protecting me. I was in a cement cell again when Nurium let go of my arm and so did the other Peacer. I hugged her, and she hugged me, welcoming me back, my Dalta sharing with me how hard it was to put me in the cell in the first place. She told me that she got a position as a Peacer so she could put me in the cage with Dina. She typically was an Intentioneer, and a very good one at that. Before this she managed all of the Intentioneers in the Kalea. She had bright purple eyes, curly black hair, dark skin with orange freckles, her face concerned. The other Peacer was a man with broad shoulders, dark skin, and white hair. His green eyes smiled at me.

This is Logos. He is a freer too Nurium intentioned and I felt her love and happiness rejoicing in seeing me and she felt mine in knowing she was a freer.

I have heard of the infamous Atlia, Black Dove Logos intentioned.

I laughed intentioning *What a silly name, but nice to meet you. What family are you from?*

I am from the Locket family. Logos intentioned feeling my laughter as I felt his amusement to it.

The Locket family was as powerful as mine, the Clippers family. Our family's last names were formed out things that they found still around after the Greatest War.

Are you ready for the exam? Logos intentioned. The last time I had gotten an exam, I was force fed and my stomach hurt so much I could barely keep any food down. I was ready though, ready for a fight.

All I could grab onto were two words that sounded as ridiculous as I felt right now, pretending I had strength that I did not have, "Bring it," I said and when I saw their questioning looks, I intentioned *as they would say in the ancient days.*

Both nodded seriously, and I could feel their anxiety, as if maybe the ancients had no idea what they were asking for. I was determined to not be afraid, so I felt that righteous anger that drove me. The love for Dina, the discovery of the atrocities to the lessers, the fact that all of this could have been different if a few humans had stood against it instead of feeding themselves into a sick system.

I could see Nurium and Logos felt my anger rising and were a bit startled, but it seemed to help settle their nerves. I thought of how moments before Telepa sent out the memory I had hidden to the entire colony. How they would have received the memory and how my whole family would cry for the horrible mistake they made. Now all we did was wait for the examiner to be teleported in. I gripped my knuckles standing there. The examiner opened the door and walked in the room.

I realized they must have brought in someone from another dome colony in the World Collective, someone who did not know me, so they could do an unbiased examination. Like my Kamma taught me, I hid everything I knew in a secret channel so the only thing she would find was what I wanted her to find. She was a very plump woman with black hair. I never saw an unfit World Collective member before. Her meals must not be monitored. She smiled at me and intentioned kindly *The Peacers turned on your telegraphic I see, that is good. I am sorry for the inconvenience this may have caused. Your memory of your father passing passed through your whole community and now they know it was not you. I am here to assist you to see if you are still human and have not been influenced by the lessers.*

The examiner looked me over and as she did, a chill ran down the back of my neck. There was something eerie about this woman. She looked at me and I felt as if her piercing yellow eyes were seeing into my heart. I felt her in my mind searching for possible cracks. I said nothing, acting wounded, innocent, shocked and frightened at what they did to me - a human, at the same time I let her feel the feeling of what I first felt here, that I had deserved to be here because I had believed I was responsible for my father's passing. I also let her feel how strongly I previously felt and believed in the World Collective. She felt that, and I felt her slip, letting me feel what she was feeling. She felt sad for me and a little horrified that one of us could be sent to the farm. That is when I proceeded to have no doubts in my mind. I felt confident and ended up guiding her to the memories and feelings. The love I had for the World Collective and my family. I guided her through feeling triumphant. But then I heard the examiner intention *but there is someone missing!*

Telepa then came in and I could not be happier to see my

Dalto.

Everyone turned to look at him, including the examiner, who we all felt was annoyed by the interruption.

Sorry my Dalto intentioned. She brushed him off feeling his embarrassment. My Dalto opened a private channel with me so I could feel what he was really feeling was worry. His dark blue eyes filled with concern. Wow, I thought, my brother is good.

Felt you may need my help my Dalto intentioned. I intentioned back that I had been guiding her according to plan but appreciated his effort.

The examiner turned back to me and intentioned *I am so sorry for what had happened, and I want you to know that the farm you were in was unsupervised and this would have never happened had it been properly managed like all of the other farms. We have sent people to the farm to change it, as I see there were no open fields and the lessers were poorly taken care of.*

I intentioned my sarcasm to Telepa through our private channel and felt his agreement.

My judgment would be that you are removed immediately and put into rehabilitation. And you seem to have many other physical injuries that our experts at rehabilitation can help at once. I am so sorry this happened. We all felt her sincere sorry and her sadness and fear to how I was treated. I sent my anger from feeling this, annoyed at the duality, to Telepa, and he, surprised, sent calming feelings. I forgot how in the World Collective this emotion is usually toned down by our telegraphics.

The examiner then grabbed my arm. And nodded to the other Peacers and my brother. I nodded in return, ready to go. And then we teleported.

12

RESCUE

The rehabilitation center was designed for absolute relaxation and the "re-awakening" of your humanity. It was in a structure not too far from the main area of Kalea, but far enough that it would be impossible to escape. Most people's telegraphics were blocked here so they could not teleport. The only way to get away would have been by foot. The dome was made of happy plastic colors such as yellow, white, and pink. There was painted glass-looking plastic that made up the dome and let the light shine in. Fountains were everywhere, dropping water from the sky out of what seemed like nothingness, a beautiful creationist invention. Everything was designed to honor the World Collective, to show people what came from humans, not lesser beings.

I was in the rehab for a week before I felt my body move without pain. Our specialized sleeping hammocks were made for our bodies to heal faster since many in rehab usually hurt themselves and need a speedy recovery. My guides back into the World Collective were all supportive and warm, filling me with their love every time I saw them. I could feel my aches and pains being soothed as I went to each session, the mental ones as well. The guilt at first was hard to deal with. The guilt of losing my father, of me being able to be loved by these people while the other lessers were not even given the chance. It was hard to deal with the sadness, but I tried my best.

Sometimes, how loving they were being almost made me want to pretend Dina didn't exist, that everything was fine.

Other times I felt as if I should not live, for having these feelings. Thus, every night I made my own private channel and replayed my memories feeling the pains and fears I felt. I was almost immediately put back on my path from it, though sometimes my mind plays tricks between pain and guilt.

I felt no relief until Latla, my guide, exposed herself.

I was sitting in the rehab in a session the day I went to venture outside of the dome. I had imagined as much as I could of what Avia Carlo would say. He always encouraged us to explore and I remember him taking me aside once. *You are special, my little Atlia. You and your sister.* Beleeka and I were Avia Carlo's only direct children. *You must take care of your sister, help her grow. She won't want to do all adventures with you, that is something to accept, leafling. Some adventures you can do on your own. There is life outside of this dome.* He stopped as I listened, fascinated. My Direct Avo came in at that point when he stopped, and she stared angrily at him, I could feel her anger deepen for him. I shook off the memory. I understood what he meant about Beleeka, she always followed the rules. I would have to make sure she knew nothing, or maybe he meant for me to expose her to the cause.

I was waiting for my session with my guide as I pondered this. I figured I would feel out her thoughts. I decided to sneak out of rehab and explore moving forward our plans outside the dome, when my guide, Latla, intentioned *Are you ready to explore?* when she ported into the guidance room. Startled, I got up ready for action, breathing hard. I startled my guide, too, who intentioned shock, fear, worry, and love for me. *I am here to help you* she then intentioned and I realized she was my contact for the freers. She was a thin woman with bright green eyes, dark black hair that flowed straight down effortlessly. Her skin was a light brown, like the color of sunset when it is setting and the dark red mixes with the yellow of the sun.

She showed me her story. Her wife was considered a lesser, thrown into the farm, and was never seen from again. This is how she found out what the farm was.

I felt her pain and sadness and her disgust when she found that she could be eating her. She recognized the famous flower dish that was in fact a hand.

It was that night that she found the freers and my brother, Telepa and my Avia Carlo. The freers put out a line in the community to get notified when someone is disgusted and then they recognize the disgust (disgust is not common in our community) and talk with them and feel their telegraphics to see if they are a potential freer. She was then able to eat what the freers ate, a mix of something that Liat made from her garden. I had received mine delivered in my pillow every day from a freer infiltrator and usually hid my nourishment by outing it through the teleport eliminator.

I am ready when you are I intentioned a sigh with my telegraphic, tired of seeing the sadness and feeling it, but ready to do something about it. I could see she felt the same.

We will have to do something about that later, I feel the duality in you.

Then an intention interrupted her *Hi Dalta, I am in the visitor lobby* Beleeka intentioned and showed me where she was. Stunned, saddened, and surprised I intentioned *Arriving.*

We will finish later Latla intentioned. I did not look forward to addressing my guilt.

I teleported to the lobby where I hugged my Dalta the moment I saw her. She felt my pain and sadness of missing her. I almost forgot to create a private channel for my real feelings while hugging her, wanting so badly to share what I know. I have felt this way for a long time and it felt as if I would burst if I didn't. However, I kept control over my emotions and just hugged her deeper, knowing she would not catch the meaning behind it, not knowing the subtle intention of a deep hug that our ancestors used to communicate through. It was so nice to feel her touch and I could feel her intentions, her sadness in losing me, and her fear. Her tears touched my shoulder I laughed, and she felt my happiness in being able to see her, hold her, and she laughed too as I wiped off her tears. We went and sat down on the hammocks.

I am so sorry Beleeka intentioned holding my hands. I intentioned the feeling of how it was awful but how I am happy now and she understood.

Now you can come back to us, soon I hope! They know it was Avia Carlo now who had killed himself. What a tragedy. You must be so pained knowing this, it is no wonder your telegraphic had that problem. I felt her sadness for Avia Carlo and her pain as well.

I shared that with her comforting her with my own validity of pain that she received. She looked at me, her eyes wide with fear, and a little excitement. And then I saw her lose it, feeling shame.

What? I intentioned. Her cheeks flushed, and I felt her embarrassment.

I am sorry, I was wondering what it was like at the farm. I know we are not supposed to talk about it.

Shhh I intentioned in a new channel I made between me and her.

Her eyes widened again *But this is illegal! How do you know to do this?*

Kamma taught me I intentioned back. I felt her amusement and somewhat fear.

Our Prime Avo told us to never listen to Kamma. Our Kamma was our direct Avo's direct mother who was sent to the farm. She had lived with us when we were little, and she always liked my Avia Carlo. Before she was sent away she hid in Beleeka and my room. She made an invisible dome around herself and intentioned quietly to us. We pretended she was not there when the Peacers came to look. They looked through our minds, but Beleeka and I hid our knowledge in our private channels. I could feel Beleeka's fear but was amazed she was able to keep her resolve as well to protect our Kamma. Our Kamma smiled, her eyes crinkled. She had white hair and deep blue eyes like my Avo. She looked frailer, though, her skin pink and dappled with orange freckles. *My dears, I will be gone for a while, you know what you must do to protect yourselves. I wish I could have made this world better for you.* She disappeared, and we never heard of her again, except that she was found and sentenced to the farm.

She was one of the few who was found to be a lesser. That's what I was afraid of when you went to the farm. Beleeka sat for a second on the hammock, I could feel her thinking of what to next intention. I could see she was pulled between asking about the farm and her fear of breaking the law with our private channel. I felt her intention to give in to ask about the farm and her embarrassment and shame, but then excitement to feel about it.

I then intentioned what I felt when I was first there, my true honest memories when I did not remember Dina or anything. She saw the horror and the sickness and everything. Shocked, she let out a small yelp, when she felt the pain of the sores. I intentioned her to be quiet but felt her fear, sadness, disgust, and amazement.

How could they do this to these poor lessers? she intentioned, crying again. I sent her love and comfort and I could see she still had the telegraphic emotion controller in. That was good because I was afraid everything she learned would hurt too much and cause her damage.

We must do something Beleeka intentioned to me and she felt my agreement. She was my best friend, I trusted her with my life. I decided to finally tell her everything.

After I was done, she was overwhelmed. She said she needed a second as she went to the elimination area. She put up a blinder from her telegraphic, so no one could see her, as she shut off her telegraphic for privacy.

I sat there in silence, wondering what would happen. What if it was too much for her? What if she was a part of the Peacers or the Intentioneers? At this moment, I wished I could reach out to Dina. To feel her presence just to know if she is with me. I knew how dangerous that would be and I felt Beleeka feel me, she was not used to feeling me love so deeply another. She never knew that Dina and I were together, as Avia Carlo hid our love from everyone.

She came out of the eliminator area and intentioned sadness at how I felt about Dina and her confusion on how I could fall in love with a lesser even though she could feel my powerful love for Dina. I intentioned how we were the same, and even though she felt as I felt, she could not adopt my feeling. She intentioned how dangerous it felt, but also how she wanted us to be together and how she would help. I felt tears fall and felt her tears too as I hugged her. We then sat in silence for a moment gathering our thoughts.

You could become a lesser Beleeka thought and I felt one intention slip away of *maybe you are a lesser.*

My anger ignited, and I could see she could feel it since I did not have my emotion suppressor on. *Don't you see now, there is no difference.*

I felt her frighten, and I calmed down my anger. She felt my sorry and I felt her sadness. *I didn't mean to upset you, this is new for me* Beleeka intentioned.

I know I intentioned back, laying my head on her shoulder. She laid her head on my head. *What will you do?* I intentioned and I felt Beleeka startle and look down at me.

Nothing of course! What are you thinking. I need to help you Beleeka intentioned and my heart lifted.

She hugged me, and I hugged her back in the hammock.

Now tell me about the rescue.

I went into detail of how we would rescue all the people in the farm, how I needed to explore the outside, but then I was cut off.

Let me come with you! Beleeka intentioned and she felt my halting feelings.

It would be too suspicious I intentioned back. Beleeka felt me and knew what I knew - sharing with her how I felt.

Beleeka intentioned *Be careful and let me know what I need to do!*

I need you to start finding the people who are hiding all of this. I am not sure who it is, but the Prime Avo I am sure is involved. I felt her sadness as she felt mine as this was her favorite Avo.

I felt her strength and felt her agreement. I intentioned that we should open our channel back up, so no one would get suspicious. She agreed, and we opened it.

I love you I intentioned and felt her experience again, the fright and repugnance of the farm, but her belief in our justice. I was surprised to feel it still rang true to her. I felt the pull of another entering our channel - it was Latla, my guide.

I have been waiting. Nice to meet you, Beleeka she intentioned. *She knows* I intentioned to my Latla, and I felt Latla being stunned and she created a private channel with us both. *Please speak on this channel in the future, the rehab is full of spies* Latla intentioned. Beleeka and I internally nodded and she felt it.

Nurium then chimed in and intentioned *Yes you all need to be better about private channels, I moved to the rehabilitation center just to make sure you were all safe. I have been cleaning up the traces you just left behind.*

Beleeka and I murmured sorry and sent love and thanks to Nurium for her help.

Bye I said to Beleeka. I felt her hold me until she let go and I did too. I teleported with Latla to the edge of the dome next to the rehab. There was an immediate alarm that went off in our telegraphics, but before it could signal anyone Latla disabled it.

Have you been out before? I intentioned, guessing if she knew how to disable the alarm, maybe she went outside.

No she intentioned and I was shocked. With all these newfound rulebreakers, I thought someone must have gone outside by now, even if I had originally intended to be the one to explore beyond the dome. *That is why we are taking precautions. I set up a blocker at the edge of the dome to hide our telegraphics outside the dome. I also arranged for a pod here as there is only one exit out of the dome - through the underground pod.* She switched on the telegraphic extender and used the extender to open the hatch to the pod tunnel. The pod arose, and we got in. *Turn on your oxygen just in case it's toxic outside.*

I nodded and got into the pod, stepping through the bubble shield that was the top of the pod over us. I looked at the dome that had plant decorations on it, excited to see what was on the other side. I was also scared, not knowing if I would live or die from this experience. I sent a message to Dina via Telepa last night hoping it would get to her in case I did not make it.

I closed my eyes as the pod went down into the Earth, and we were shot across and then up. I hated pod rides and turned on my motion sickness remedy in my telegraphic. As the pod cooled down from the ride, it opened. The top popped open with Latla's intention.

Atlia, oh my Latla intentioned and I opened my eyes one by one. I opened my eyes to a forest brimming with trees and flowers I had never seen before. Real flowers. I got excited for a second and almost turned off my oxygen until I felt a pull from Latla *No* she intentioned *you are too important. I will do it.*

Latla, no! I intentioned as she turned her telegraphics oxygen translator off. She breathed in one breath, smiled, but then slumped forward.

"Ahh!" I screamed as I rushed towards her.

She managed to intention softly, a laugh. I felt her happiness and laughter, and it bubbled out of me too. I turned off my oxygen provider. I breathed in once, and it was like nothing I had ever breathed in before. I too got light headed, kneeled, and adjusted the telegraphic to auto-oxygenate to an appropriate level until I acclimated. I laughed, and she laughed, knowing I did the same as her and how it felt. So fresh and beautiful, it was clear I never felt pure air before. It felt so good. I felt an impulse to want to explore more.

I noticed both of our bare knees were scraped by the dirt. *Dirt!* I intentioned in awe and we looked and sifted our hands through it, laughing feeling dirt for the first time. It felt coarse to the touch, like little hard brown beads, but then some of it was so fine it fell off immediately. I then turned on my armor as Latla did hers since this strange world seemed to be a bit more dangerous than in the dome.

It added a shimmered barrier to both of our bodies. Mine was blue with a hint of teal while Latla chose a purple one with a hint of lavender. *Should we cover more in case we meet... people?*

Latla agreed and we made our armor less see through in case we would offend what other cultures lie outside of the dome. *There must be people out here, there must!* I intentioned with excitement and Latla nodded.

We set off through the thick jungle, admiring the red trees and pink and red flowers. There were some green trees still that were very tall and large. They stuck up like sticks, leaves close to the trunk, while the red trees were short and had flat red leaves as the vines were red as well. I saw so many creatures, too. I saw a massive creature fly in front of me, I almost fell back and intentioned to my telegraphic, asking what it was. Then I could feel the closest it could come up with was an ancient animal called a butterfly. This animal did not look like the butterfly that was in my telegraphic. It was about the size of my arm span and had no antenna. I named it in my telegraphic grandifly and Latla I felt agreed with my naming of it with some amusement.

It paid no mind to me, as if I was one of the trees it was passing by. I smiled at Latla and saw her marveling at it as well. It flew up into the trees and I could see they were covered with them. It was beautiful, all colors of green, blue, yellow, purple, and red. Some were flying while others stayed on the trees, as if they were stuck to them.

There were also small creatures that had fur that covered their bodies on the trees. It was hard to see them, as they were the same red color of the trees and the butterfly creatures were covering most of them. They looked smooth and sleek, with small black eyes. They looked sleepily at us as they moved along the trees. They had long tails that wrapped two or three times around the trees and had faces similar to the mouse Telepa had. Their noses were more rounded though, and bigger than a mouse's nose on their tiny narrow faces. I named them sleepers in my telegraphic.

Hello I intentioned for some reason, Latla looked at me and I could feel her laughter. I laughed too. The animals did not seem fazed, they were living their lives as if we were insignificant beings. *How do you speak to these creatures?* I wondered to Latla and felt her shake her head internally.

I don't believe they speak any languages, unless you know the ancient language. Still, they seem to not even notice, or care that we are here.

I nodded internally. *Let's move on then. We need to find a place to build the camp quickly.*

I felt that Latla agreed and we walked through the forest,

past these creatures that were new to us. It was hard not to stop and study them. We thought there were no living beings outside of the dome, and here they were, thriving after the Greatest War.

There were other creatures I can't name that I could just hear running away. If not for my mission to explore and find a campsite as soon as possible, I would have explored the animals more.

We had walked almost three hours until we stumbled upon a creek of clear water. We had to toughen the bottoms of our armor, we had not realized the ground could be so uneven. All of the ground, whether stone, cement, or plastic was even in the World Collective and smooth. There was something about this ground that I never felt in the World Collective, I felt connected to it somehow. As if my feet were meant to only walk on this real Earth.

It seems like global warming was the Earth's answer to parasites that were killing it Latla intentioned and I felt the irony in it. If we had just stopped all the killing, using, and everything that did not matter more than the Earth, we could have had a peaceful, happy world. If we had just listened, if we had just stopped. Why couldn't we have stopped? What mattered more than killing the Earth for generations and to annihilate almost all the human race? Why were they so selfish?

All these thoughts ran through my head as we planted tents in the area, being careful to pick places that were not covered by any living beings. We pulled out the packing bubble that carried our tents and unlocked it midair to produce the plastic tents we brought from the World Collective. It took us a bit to find a perfect spot to put them down since there were so many small animals in the dirt, we finally decided to put down a telegraphic barrier under the tents, so we would not disturb anyone.

Smiling at our triumph, we used the last of our energies to teleport back to the pod. I saved the map in my telegraphic, as did Latla.

Excited with our success we teleported back into Latla's

guideroom.

Our excitement soon wore off as we saw we were face to face with an Avo, this one a guide at the rehabilitation center. Standing there was Avo Laurili, she looked us up and down. I looked down to see I was still in my armor and it was covered in dirt. I made a private channel for my panic. I was amazed at Latla's face, her mouth was in a wide smile and she intentioned love and hello for Avo Laurili. Avo Laurili who first looked confused, intentioned understanding.

I see you had a pleasant visit to the concealer. I hope it helped, it was Latla's idea to have you spend time outside of the center. How do you feel?

Great I intentioned, feeling love and happiness, as I put my feelings of *thank the great Earth* in my private channel. I could not help but feel a chill on the back of my spine. They felt this and laughed.

Still cold I see Latla intentioned to me and I agreed.

I thought you were a good skier, I am sure Avia Carlo… Avo Laurili stopped intentioning and looked down I could feel her embarrassment and sadness. She did not mean to mention Avia Carlo. I could see Avia Carlo in my telegraphic the way she intentioned it, with his full smile, how he used to teach me, my memories and felt the sadness again as I let that leak to her. I hoped that would convince her to leave us be. It did.

She intentioned her sadness and said her goodbye to leave us to complete our guiding session. I made a private channel with Latla and laughed. Latla was not pleased.

We need to be careful Atlia, luckily, we also have synthetic dirt and they thought it was that. Next time we won't be able to get away so quickly Latla intentioned her frustration and fears. I agreed with her feeling her fear and my own. And then I felt her excitement for what we found again.

How much longer do I need to stay here? I thought it would take a long time to explore outside of the dome and possibly find a campsite. But now I am ready.

I know, Latla said, *but our protocol says you must remain here one more week and then be judged if you should be released.*

I stood for a second, shaking with annoyance. Latla felt it

and tried to comfort me. All I could think of was getting Dina and going to our new camp.

Now we can work on the hard part Latla intentioned as she sat down in a hammock and motioned for me to sit on a cushion on the floor. I sat down cross legged and she could feel my sigh, for I did not think it would help.

Let us start with the guilt you feel, it is natural to feel this way. They are people. It is hard to be a witness.

The hard part is not witnessing - it is knowing I participated. I snapped and apologized.

Latla was unfazed. *Good, that is a part of healing, be angry, feel it let it out. But also feel what I feel. I went through what you did. It will scar you, we must be accepting of our scars. With our guilt. Only time can heal what we feel.*

From there we dug deep into the feelings, the sadness, and most of all the guilt I had for not being able to save my Avia, and that of being born in a different circumstance.

The week went by fairly fast, though it felt incredibly slow during my sessions with Latla, as I felt every piece of myself come apart and be put back together. I acted the perfect reformed World Collective participant. I went to my sessions and talked about Avia Carlo to the other guides while being able to express my true feelings with Latla. I also kept my eye out for people we may be able to fill the farm with. During nourishment time was the hardest. They brought out the nourishment and I saw their hands being the "flowering" meat, and the baby fat meat covered in milk and cheese sauce disgusted me. I decided to start with those people, the ones who got excited about eating the baby lessers. It was hard not to stare at the nourishment sometimes, and multiple times I had to go to the elimination room after getting sick. Those little toes. Hands that could hold, love, feel. All these people - so selfish, not caring because they don't see what happens. They don't see how the nourishment are people just like them. If the lessers had a telegraphic, the humans would feel their pain as they were slaughtered. Their fear of going to their deaths, holding their loved ones crying for them when they are separated. These people did not care about their feelings. Was it the culture or was it pure selfishness? I am unsure, but sometimes I hated my people and hated myself more knowing that I was confusing sound judgement against atrocities with hate for my people and for myself in being a part of such gruesome, disgusting violence. How not seeing something could make us so blindly take part in the cruelty and suffering. This was my fuel, this anger and sadness and disgust at my own race. I kept a list in my private channel - the people I was going to frame. And one by one I started practicing that week. I started to do little things like leave plant materials in people's rooms. I also made private channels where I built out my feelings of the nourishment and the farm and I sent it to people. People did not know where it came from, but just having it was treason. I started to see these people change. When they found things they were shocked, scared, and withdrawn. Not having the ability to make a secure private channel, I was able to quickly condemn 13 people to the farm. Hearing their cries as they were taken away made me so satisfied. I shared everything with Latla at the end of the week, our last session.

I felt concern from her and I let my anger go. She stopped me and turned on my feeling suppressor.

What? I intentioned. Not clouded by anger, I could see how she was... scared.

You need to learn to control your anger without a suppressor. I can't let you turn it off - you will jeopardize our mission. It is out of control and you have to understand your anger is unjust, you were one of those who ate nourishment. You had the same excuses until you learned Dina could be one of them. Anger can be a good tool, but you need to learn how to focus it and break it apart by tempering it with love and understanding. Otherwise you will be no better than those you are angry with.

She made sense, and I could see what she saw in my telegraphic. I felt my hands get warm. I had to calm down, I had to turn the anger into love. Of course, the World Collective did teach us some good things. I calmed down and realized how I was not angry - how ultimately, I was sad. So sad. Sad about how mean and cruel people could be, sad that there may not be a better future. What if our plan didn't work.

Latla felt all of this and I was surprised she felt the same. *Let us work on this together. I am going to release you now, but please keep our private channel open.* She felt my intention of agreement. And I teleported to my own room, my teleporter now open since I was now considered a functioning member. I still felt uneasy about the anger I had, wondering if I could control this new power I found. There was something with anger that felt... dangerous. *For now, Nurium can do the rest of the teleports to the farm.* Latla sent to me via our private channel. I felt Nurium join our conversation. She had become a great confidant through all of this. As she asked for a new position at the rehab, I was able to see her for every secret nourishment. We shared all our feelings, from what we both experienced at the farm, and how we had to act in the "real world".

I was about to argue having Nurium do the teleports, but I agreed I needed to gain control of this anger. *I trust Nurium to let me know how she does.*

Of course, I will do my best Nurium intentioned and I believed her. I trusted her as much as I trusted Telepa or Beleeka.

Then it is settled. We have so much to plan for Atlia, we must plan the escape perfectly. I have the Smooth Square map, where Tartia will be held, when everyone celebrates the other humans in the World Collective. *We all have to stand in strategic locations to teleport everyone out* Latla intentioned, showing us the map that was drawn up for our greatest move yet for the cause. *We need you in the middle, can you stomach that Atlia?* Latla continued intentioning with no sarcasm, but real concern.

Yes, I will do anything to help I intentioned back though privately I know that it would be incredibly difficult.

We are ready then, I felt Nurium intention with excitement, fear, and drive. We broke off from our channels and I went from the guidance room to my quarters.

Beleeka was the first one to import in and then my Grand Avo, Telepa, Nurium, and my other family members. They congratulated me on treatment, hugging me as I hugged them back all of us with tears in our eyes, none more than my Grand Avo.

Avo I can't breathe I intentioned when she was holding me too tight and I could feel her overwhelming sense of sadness, happiness, and regret. She kept apologizing for what happened, and I felt how sincere it was. It was hard to remember that this was the woman who murdered Avia Carlo, who secretly was a huge believer in nourishment. She was my Avo, and I could not help but still love her, feeling the tare between love and disgust for loving someone who could do that.

I kept the negative emotions well hidden in my private channel while I hugged all my siblings and parents.

I have a surprise my Avo said and then a giant cake of nourishment was brought in. Hands protruded from the sides, burnt to made to look like flowers, the cake was a mixture of human meat and fat, adorned in felt and arms that were made to look like roots on a tree.

It's a tree of life my stomach turned horribly, and I quickly put all of my disgusted thoughts into my private channel and shared it with Telepa, Beleeka, and Nurium. They could feel everything I was feeling, and they felt the same.

It is your favorite, the tree of life for your homecoming. Eat my love and nourish, no one is stopping you tonight! My family cheered and, in that moment, I had such a mix of emotions, wanting to be part of my family, being one of them, but most of my disgust and sadness at how many humans were used to make this cake. Little innocent humans. I could see the littlest flowers being that of littling hands.

Grand Avo, let me see if she is well enough, she has not eaten good nourishment in a while. They need better nourishment at the rehabilitation facility. Telepa, my savior, quickly removed me from the party to the eliminator. We felt an understanding from our Grand Avo and her worry as we left. He rubbed my back and as I vomited, he intentioned *You need to have a better stomach,* plans of the camp, Dina, and all we had to do.

I can't do it, Telepa, I can't eat it. There is no way. You would have to take my memories again, but I promised Dina. I can't I intentioned. *Fine, I will figure something out* Telepa intentioned. He sent my family a message that I was too sick to come back and to enjoy without me. My Grand Avo teleported into the eliminator and expressed her worry through her telegraphic.

She is fine, Grand Avo Telepa intentioned and just showed that I picked up a small stomach bug from the rehab center, and I felt my Grand Avo relax. I sat moaning and intentioning feelings of being sick. I felt my Grand Avo comfort me like when I was a child, she caressed my hair and gave the top of my head light kisses, her sick blocker on in her telegraphic. Both Telepa and my grand Avo took me to bed, my Grand Avo caressing my hair and arms and kissing my head over and over again, intentioning her love for me, her little Atlia. Telepa intentioned she could leave though she tried to argue he intentioned I needed rest.

My Grand Avo nodded and sent us both love and then left.

I stopped intentioning the fake feelings I had and instead went back to my private channel with Telepa.

Thanks I intentioned to Telepa and Telepa shook his head. *Don't you understand we are going to war? You need to toughen yourself.*

It's hard I intentioned back, snapping at him, and hearing the excuse in my own response. I realized then I had to do whatever it takes to free these people. Even go against my Grand Avo. *I won't kill, that is one thing I refuse to do.*

I understand Telepa said, agreeing with me. *If it comes to that, leave it to me.* His purple eyes a steely gaze and I could feel his anger and how angry he had felt. It scared me. Feeling this, he controlled it and sent me love and soothing feelings. *You would be proud of Dina, she has freed almost all of the lessers at the farm, and we were able to put more humans into the farm. Good thing Peacers have blinders to the farm and people, otherwise they might have seen how most of it is empty except for the humans we started to frame.*

Dina, my Dalto, could feel my heart singing from hearing her name. He shared the view of other lessers of Dina freeing them and installing their telegraphics for the first time. I could feel their feelings of happiness, gratitude, and fear. I saw them at the camp, dancing and singing and lessers who never talked before being taught how to speak, the telegraphics helping them with speech and to grow the parts of their brains that were inhibited due to the trauma.

She is well and now we have to move everyone to the new camp that you and Latla found Telepa intentioned. I saw the camp he saw and the people moving there, with their thoughts and feelings.

I think it is time we have the World Collective of this colony in one room I intentioned and my Dalto agreed. In two days, it was Tartia. The whole colony gathers in Smooth Square to celebrate with nourishment.

Are the lessers ready to teleport? It will take too much energy for the few of us.

We have a Creationist Intentioneer on our side who can connect into everyone's teleporters.

It was then that Beleeka transported in. *I had to sneak out through the elimination room, how exciting.* I felt her excitement and matched it with fear and happiness and worry. *Don't worry I know what I am doing, and I am happy to help. Now why are you in the sick?*

She can't see the nourishment anymore, it reminds her of...

Feeling what I was feeling and what Telepa was feeling Beleeka intentioned *of course.* And she then intentioned her plans and what it would look like. We then hugged each other for courage and strength for our plan to put our people, our family in the farms.

It will only hold them for a while in the farms, Telepa you need to teleport to the camp immediately and then teleport everyone who is there to the new camp. Atlia, you need to help us teleport humans to the farm.

I will I intentioned and so did Telepa. They teleported out, but before Telepa teleported I sent a message to Dina, *I am coming my love.*

13

REVENGE

I kept quiet in my quarters, but it was difficult, especially the second night. Since I had missed the tree of life nourishment, my Avo decided to take me for a private "special" return dinner at her quarters. My Avo knew about Dina a little, so I knew she wanted to test me to see if the farm and rehabilitation had changed the way of my thinking. I did not need to feel her intention to know this was what she wanted.

I felt her invitation float before my eyes when I arrived home after a guide session and groaned internally. I released the invitation in front of my eyes, it floated in the telegraphic with lights red and green, the World Collective colors, shooting from either side of my eyes. Forming the intentions with light around them saying *Welcome Home, please join me for dinner in 60 blinks.*

I groaned more internally, that was only in a matter of moments, and I had no way to escape it. Like Telepa told me, I strengthened my resolve and ported into my Avo's. She had a grand room in her plastic house, filled with plastic flowers, vines, and some fountains on the sides of each room, falling from the ceilings. She had pillars made of green plastic that rose to the top, with delicate decorations of World Collective leaders. I remember when she had this room molded and made.

That was when I learned that excess from the lessers, who were creationed into nourishment, were heated with material that was found everywhere - plastics. The foundlings of the

World Collective discovered that plastic survived the Greatest War, and we still have it now to build out of, a material that will never go away. "Waste not. Want not," was an old motto, and the only old language my Avo told me when she taught all of her littlings about the World Collective in this room. All of the lies she shared in this seemingly beautiful but fantastically fake room. It made sense in a poetic way. I could not help but feel my anger burning at a low simmer, trying to keep it controlled. My hand getting hot again, a problem I had ever since I had burned Telepa. I was still confused by how that happened but did not know who to ask to help stop it - or at least control it. Maybe I could get something out of my Avo tonight, something she knows.

I sat on the bubble chair at the bubble nourishment holder, waiting for my Avo. She loved anything created by the Creationists of the World Collective and always displayed them. This was a creation of my own Dalta Beleeka, my Avo was so proud of her. She arrived, on time as usual and I felt her love in the room. I knew she was hiding something from me, as I hid something from her as well, my disgust for her, and anger.

She came over and kissed my forehead and then sat down on her bubble chair. *I have some exciting news, we are having quite a delicacy tonight.* I felt her excitement and let go some of my anxiety in a private channel, I was here living my own hell. What would it be this time? Littlings cut up in their mother's milk? Littlings together cooked with their parents? I did not have much time to wonder as the nourishment ported into the bubbles. The bubbles floated towards us. In the bubbles on a white platter, the ones we use only for special occasions made from lesser bone, were tiny little pearls. They were called the pearls of wisdom. I knew what they were and swallowed hard, intentioning my hunger for them when, in actuality, my disgust filled my channel and I held in my vomit.

I could feel her sharp blue eyes roaming over me, I saw her twist her hands together as she looked at me, judging me to see if I had changed. Like I had practiced, I let out my fake intentions of love for her and understanding. She seemed pleased, and when I thought I was not going to be tested further, I learned I was deeply mistaken.

Let me show you how it is made, and what makes this such a... delicacy. She pulled me into her telegraphic and I stood there waiting, smiling at her as I intentioned anger, fear, annoyance inside my channel. To her I intentioned perfect curiosity, love, and understanding that these were lesser beings than us. She showed me through the telegraphic of one of the Creationists. There, in the kitchens where only light shown in from the windows on the ceilings, I saw the before rooms, where some lessers were taken. There were lessers with plastic in and around their mouths, gagging them in separate pods made of plastic. Tears streamed down their faces, they were red and raw from crying. All of my real emotions were almost too much to handle, but I focused on my mission that we will one day save all of them, though I could not do it that day.

I saw the Creationist go to a lesser and pull them out of the plastic pod, through the half bubble. There was a table hammock and the Creationist put the lesser on the table slamming them down as they squirmed, taking each end of the lesser woman's body and putting it into clasps. The lesser woman had bright green eyes like Dina, but without the brown, and light brown skin. Now I knew why she wanted me to watch this and picked this lesser. The woman jerked against the ties and the Creationist tried to soothe her. I was crying inside in my silent channel with such anger, but in the channel with my Avo I kept the curiosity and love flowing. She sent me love too, and excitement at watching the process.

There is a real art to it you know, you have to get them right at their peak. That is when I noticed the woman was younger than me, I tried not to look at her this whole time to keep my emotions in check and not lose control. I turned on my filters at full force. The Creationist did not turn on her telegraphic as he got out an old tool, what Creationists used for cutting. I saw the fear in her eyes and wanted to look away, but used all my resolve, the thought of Dina, and saving the other lessers.

Keeping in mind what Telepa said, this is what I was compelled to do regardless of how I feel.

The Creationist cut into her while shushing her and I could feel his joy with his "craft" as she squealed through the plastic gag. I saw the blood, red like mine, gush out of the small incision he made. Tears streamed down her raw face. He got another plastic device and opened the wound, making her scream. I felt his excitement at opening her. It was completely sickening and even my filters had a hard time controlling my gag reflex. I felt my Avo look at me and I internally smiled with excitement, sickening myself in my own private channel.

At that moment, the lesser's eyes rolled to the back of her head and then he turned her telegraphic on to keep her just alive. There the pearls were, in her body. He took them out with some other plastic instruments doing things internally to her. I looked right above it and focused on that spot to not really see how he was doing what he was doing. I was already dying inside with this woman.

You see he keeps her awake until she naturally goes to sleep on her own, this way no chemicals via telegraphics have to be used so the pearls are pure. I wanted to vomit so badly but smiled back at my Avo.

It makes sense, I heard the little lessers even have better pearls. I swallowed hard at what I just said, keeping down my sick feelings with all my might.

I felt her satisfaction at my pretend intentions, and I was brought out of her telegraphic. There I was, looking at the pearls, the human eggs, I would have to eat.

Those are hers, that was a memory from earlier. Did you know it is hard to harvest these? We must selectively breed them for generations to find larger, juicy pearls, and then emit the hormones via their telegraphics to make them plentiful and ready to harvest.

I nodded internally. I needed to vomit, so badly, but I pushed the feeling down more, my filters holding it back. It was the worst feeling in the world, along with all the other feelings I had in my private channel.

Now, enjoy My Avo said as she popped her bubbles and the plate fell to her hand. She used the bone instruments on the plate to eat the eggs. She looked at me. *You first, spring* I felt her smile. Her final test. If I did not do this, I would ruin the entire mission.

I popped the bubble quickly and without any more thoughts or feelings, I took the plate and those instruments and ate the eggs, scooping them into my mouth, feeling them there slimy, and squishy. I gagged a couple of times, but pretended I was coughing because I ate too much.

Slow down my Avo said with such joy in her intentions. She finally, I felt, believed me. *You know it is not good to indulge in nourishment so quickly.*

I forced myself to swallow them and then intentioned water bubbles to be popped into my mouth quickly, feeling all the eggs go down my throat, feeling absolutely disgusted.

I smiled and said *Thank you Avo, for bringing me back, I have missed you so much.*

Awe, spring. She put out her hand to mine and I held it giving her my love as she gave me hers. I pretended in that moment, it took me everything including the little love I even had left for her, and I exuded it to make it seem like as true of an intention as I could.

I then emitted that I was tired and my Avo agreed. *Let's do this again sometime spring, I miss you.*

Yes I agreed and then left to the elimination room just in time to vomit everything I ate.

I was sick all night and Telepa and Beleeka took care of me, and Nurium hid our intentions. She covered for me with intentions that I was elsewhere such as guidance or walking, or at the Eve room when I was in fact sick and disgusted with myself. I had to move on quickly though, and there were other nights I could not escape nourishment. It became routine to eat it and then vomit after. I always tried to have the nourishment that had the least amount of cruelty, such as just the cheese dishes. However, I knew all of it was cruel.

I never thought I would be grateful for when Tartia came, but I was. It was the last day I would ever have to show any feigned interest in nourishment.

It was the day of the Tartia and my hands were sweating, the only thing to give me away. I did not look forward to having to witness the feast. It was a huge display of murdered lessers from around the colonies. Even though I had participated in eating the milk nourishment, I had avoided eating actual lessers up to this point, or even seeing them by eating with Beleeka, Telepa, and Nurium who ordered the same as me. Each colony a month before sends the other their most delectable lessers. We sent ours a while back to our sister colony, but today was when we received it from others. The ones I could not save. It weighed heavily on me that I could not do more, even more so that I had to participate. Here I was saving a few lessers and starting a rebellion, how could I know everything was going to change? I didn't and that is what twisted my stomach and made it feel as if knots were there. I tried my best as I chose my mask for my body today, I tried to choose one that seemed most fitting. The one with the trees and blossoms seemed to be the best fitting for today, for I was determined to bring back life to the lessers.

The Creationists of the kitchens loved Tartia and looked forward to it. I unfortunately a few days before passed by the kitchens - they were a structure made of cement, the only one. It was said that the lessers tended to smell bad before being cooked so they put cement around it, no window on the sides, or on top of the building. I now knew why there were no windows and I could unfortunately smell the burning flesh of lessers. It made me gag. Now I was going to where the feast was planned, and I tried to focus on the mission.

I could not hold out for very long, I was on the outskirts of the Smooth Square, avoiding the center, but then Latla grabbed my hand intentioning it was time in a private channel. Holding in everything I could we went to the center. There in the middle were four huge pieces of nourishment. They were flesh and bones and some were just flesh that didn't resemble the lessers at all, covered in sauces and adorned with plastic flowers. The one I was hoping to avoid that Latla led me to was the one of the lesser littlings. The babies. It was tons of cooked babies in the fetal position, they looked like what our ancestors used to call chickens. Folded inward from sudden death, their heads were cut off since our society was too sensitive for the heads unless the noses and cheeks looked nothing like what they looked like when they were alive. There were hundreds of them, stacked on top of the each other.

I love the juicy flesh one littling intentioned as their Avo sliced into one of the nourishment littlings and offered it. Seeing them sever the flesh there was unbearable, so I turned my telegraphic to high gear to mute my feelings. Even still as I released what I could in my private channel, it was me screaming in agony. Everyone was laughing and happy and chatting as if nothing was wrong, slicing off the flesh of these babies, talking about how good they taste and how happy they were to eat them.

I saw again that littling about to be slaughtered. How the farmer hit her again and again in the head and how she cried. How they tried to slit her throat and her eyes. I will never forget her eyes. Sheer terror, pleading, in agony. That moment, I wish I could have killed the farmer and saved her. The second time they tried to saw off her neck, her whole body struggling, shaking.

My anger was the one thing my telegraphic could not silence, that slow seething anger and abhorrence and repugnance of my people, my family. It hurt so much that is why my anger was so high. Just like Telepa taught me, I tried to let it go, remember my people were brainwashed, and they did not know better.

It could not have been a better time that my Grand Avo came to speak in front of the community, along with the other leader Avia and Avos. It was when she was about to speak that Telepa transported to the front. My Grand Avo was stunned and stood there, we all felt her and everyone else's surprise.

This is a disgusting charade! Telepa intentioned and then sent out all the horrors he witnessed at the farm. *This is what the lessers are and how they deal...*

Stop My Grand Avo intentioned, appalled. Before she could

do anything, I felt the signal to help teleport everyone to the farm. I felt me and another person, and another, all of us connecting to teleport everyone. I felt each freer as they felt me, amazed how many we had. I felt Nurium as I connected to her, whispering quickly via our channel, holding her hand mentally as we did this extreme violation.

We teleported into the farm, all of us. Telepa made sure everyone was put in the cages, the freers acting as Peacers. We heard terrifying screams and agony from the people. In that moment I had to ignore them, though it tore at me too, my family, being put into the cages I was freeing people from. Someone grabbed onto me, it was my Grand Avo.

Spring, why? she intentioned.

I looked at her frankly, with sadness in my heart *You know why.*

I teleported back to the Smooth Square, not being able to handle seeing my family in crisis. It was as if no one had ever been in the Smooth Square, it was quiet and all that was left were the corpses.

Beleeka arrived and Telepa where Latla and I were. *We don't have much time...*

But the babies... I shared what I felt in my channel. *We have to do something.*

I will bury them and grow trees from them to honor them Latla intentioned. *After all, my wife is very good at growing.* I saw, in her intention, an older version of the woman she showed me earlier and I realized it was Liat, the lesser with the kids from the camp. I was happy to learn that Liat was Latla's wife and trusted her to honor the babies. I then felt I could leave, my stomach still in knots and the overpowering feeling of sadness still there. But I could not afford to let those emotions rule me, so I focused on what we had to do next.

I closed my eyes and intentioned to the camp outside of the dome. As soon as I arrived I exclaimed, "Oof!" as I felt arms around me squeezing the life out of me. I turned around into a kiss that Dina pulled my face down into. That steadied me as we looked over each other's minds through our telegraphics.

Seeing the pain, hurt, fear and what happened. Dina got quite lucky and did not have the carnage I had in my mind. We held each other for a good moment. Just breathing. Together, we turned around still holding hands to look over the camp. The shabby plastic tents amongst real woods. I saw littlings playing with sticks and parts of trees, smiling and laughing. It was the direct opposite of where I came from. I staggered, and Dina held me up. I felt her worry, but I brushed it off. The rest of the people were walking and talking with each other. It looked like an entire village, they got out so many people! The ones who were disabled were taken care of by other lessers and freers. People set up stations and they switched stations every day - Dina's idea.

Look at this world we created Dina felt this intention and I felt her love back. My feeling of sadness was swept away with a feeling of hope. Hope of our people. These people. Dina showed me through the rest of our little village camp, showing me how Nurium and some other Intentioneers who were part of the freers were monitoring the telegraphic technology that we had connected to, totally separate from the camp. I was amazed to see how many freers there were, and happy as well. Half of our society was in this camp.

Happy you made it out I heard a wry intention for the first time and saw George looking at me. He smiled and hugged me, and I hugged him back.

Thank you for helping Dina, sounds like you saved her a few times.

George laughed and said out loud, "Dina was the one I followed, I just helped a little."

We did it! I felt Beleeka's intention and saw Telepa with her. I could not help but smile and hug them both. Even Telepa who was mostly solemn was smiling.

I need to show you something Beleeka intentioned and then teleported us to a beautiful place with...

How did you... I stared in wonderment inside this wooden structure that was built and full of books... My Avia Carlo's books.

Tears were in my eyes and Dina rubbed my arm, Beleeka

rubbed the other. *Yes, I got Avia Carlo's books and Dina, with some of the others, cleared this old structure and made a library, just like Avia Carlo always wanted… It is in his memory.*

I kissed Dina in thanks, happiness for everything.

That will be hard to get used to I did not notice that George had also teleported with us into the library. His mouth though was still agape in awe. *You will have to teach me how to read these things later, sapling.* He looked at me. Dina and Beleeka laughed, in our language sapling meant young or naïve. George laughed at my face and then I saw Telepa had stopped smiling.

We need to plan I felt Telepa and he teleported us to a different structure. It was made from some kind of stone and had leaves all over it. There was some of the community, standing and forming a circle.

We need two moderators Telepa intentioned, but his intention was quickly overwhelmed with questions and statements. *Why will we do things like the World Collective, they were monsters! We don't need moderators, we need a new system. We are not going to do things like the World Collective…*

Please Dina intentioned, a powerful intention. *The World Collective was cruel, I agree, but they still have many practices that worked and were peaceful amongst their people. Now we can modify what they did to suit us. Let us hear everyone's concerns later, but right now we need to have a plan to protect this community. Let us all put in our judgement and have two moderators, one from the freers and one from the lessers.*

Everyone silently agreed with Dina. And between our private channel I sent her *My powerful woman* she waved me off in her mind and still sent love and a sly nod of acceptance.

George was chosen for the lesser moderator and Nurium was chosen as the freer moderator. We discussed for what seemed like hours and our moderators were well chosen. The lessers I found were harder to understand and had more violent tendencies. Liat, who was a part of the discussion, also helped the moderators by adding in the neutral perspective, educating the lessers on how their trauma played a role. With our telegraphics we could feel their trauma and they could feel our sadness, shock, and horror. This helped in our discussions, to be able to feel each other so that the lessers knew most of the World Collective had no idea what the lessers were going through and were ashamed not to do something sooner. Once we healed each other, coming together was still hard but it was easier. We all agreed on no violence unless absolutely necessary, and Telepa had planned to train lessers how to use their telegraphics in all ways, including telecide - the last resort and a way to kill other people with telegraphics.

Latla was put in charge of managing the freer guides to help the lessers heal with trauma. We also elected a main committee to speak for the people.

It included only 12 members, I was surprised more did not want to be a part of it, but anyone who had any other thoughts would always be welcome to say something and be heard and acknowledged. It was made of half lessers and half freers. It included me, Dina, Telepa, Beleeka, Nurium, George, Latla, Liat, and new people I did not know including Hatia (a lesser), Dati (a freer), Faro (a lesser), and Rachel (a lesser).

We sat down on the floor with our legs crossed in the old building. We sat in silence for a moment until Telepa spoke out loud. "I think we should be ready for them to attack and we should speak in the old language so they can't break into our telegraphics, or know what we are saying."

"I agree," George said and everyone nodded.

"So," Telepa continued, "I know the World Collective will come at us, and they will come hard. They won't use force with 'humans' but they will try to control our telegraphics. That will be their first attack."

"Agreed," said Nurium, speaking in the old language, but you could see speaking did not come easy for her. She continued, "I know how the Peacers and the Intentioneers think. I know what they are planning. We need our Intentioneers to also get ready for battle. They will try to take down our dome shield, and then they will go after the intention spot that we set up to protect our telegraphic from them. We can't let them take it. Once they do they could set up blockers on all of our telegraphics."

"Who will teach them to fight with it?" Liat asked, the last person I would guess to ask that question. "We need to teach them not just to defend, we need to teach them to fight with it."

"I will," the lesser Rachel said. We all looked at her, never hearing her voice before, it was low, like a hum. She was a mousy looking girl, with a prominent nose, her eyes wide and brown like that of an old rose bush's stem, her skin lighter than Faros but more like a light color of earth. However petite she looked like she was a fighter, scars on her cheeks and on her arms. She went on, "I will also teach them the old telegraphic tactics should they try to take away your telegraphics"

"You mean violence?" Latla whispered, the people from the world collective gasped as those from the farm looked on silently.

"But violence does nothing," exclaimed Beleeka, her eyes wide. She felt that I was shocked too.

"Violence just creates more violence, everyone knows that," Datia said, a freer from the World Collective. "Why would we result to such, excuse my language, but stupidity?"

"It is not stupid," Rachel said, "We would be stupid not to. They know violence, the Peacers know violence, I am sure even Telepa can tell you how violent our world has been even if your world was saved from it. We don't live in your world right now. We need to get to our own version of peace."

"How do you know how to fight with a telegraphic?" asked Latla.

"Not all of us had our telegraphics turned off. Faro and I have been training from our parents since we were little until this day came."

"But it needs to be a last resort," George added. As he spoke, the lessers listened. "We will create again a world without violence and we need to do that through nonviolent action. However, if it is to save someone or to save others, that will be the last resort."

"Let us take a vote," Telepa said. "Who votes to teach the old ways of fighting?" All the lessers raised their hands, including Dina.

What are you thinking?! I intentioned to her, knowing that nothing ever came from any sort of violence.

It is the only world they knew, and it could come in handy if we need the upper hand Dina intentioned back, as if she were made from stone. My heart broke a little hearing those words, that violence may be needed. She could not know that the old way was so much more painful than the telegraphic way to die. That it was so much less... humane. But that is what she knew.

"Then it is agreed that the old ways will be taught," said Telepa.

"What if we refuse the old ways?" Asked Latla, Liat laid her hand on Latla's.

"Then that should be respected," Liat said. No one disagreed with Liat.

There was a solemn silence, with the feeling of dread that no one wanted to result to any violence, but the feeling that may change history was deafening.

"I think we need to make laws, and rules around how we choose to defend," I said, still using the word defend since fight sounded like such definite violence.

Everyone agreed, and we made the laws of defense. First, we would bring the ones who were weak or small to another camp, further from the World Collective. Then we would set defensive locations up around the perimeter of the shield dome in case they try to come in from the outside. If they came inside we would then sound the alarm through the telegraphic and tell the warriors to hide in order to catch the World Collective by surprise.

We were about to finish the meeting when I felt a pull on my telegraphic. It felt like my mother, the Grand Avo.

"What?" Dina said out loud, feeling that something was very wrong.

"The Grand Avo is summoning a conversation," I said, trancelike.

"Should we hear what she has to say?" Telepa asked the group, and they agreed.

I connected all of us into a private channel, and then I allowed her to cast her image and audio in only.

We all saw my Grand Avo sitting in her chambers. Her eyes were filled with tears of happiness when she felt me, but then they went grave when she felt the others.

Hello those that have deceived and endangered the free people of the World Collective. We are saddened to see such violence and deceit when it was unnecessary, and the rest of the world leaders have chosen me to deliver the message. I felt her genuine sadness and some betrayal as did everyone. It made me, just for a moment since she was my Avo, just one moment, wish that I did not have to do the right thing. I strengthened my resolve, Dina feeling my true feelings in our private channel sent me love. *We will not be pursuing you. We want to have peace. We believe that to achieve that we will not be attacking you and ask that you do not attack us as well. We want to have peace between us both.*

Before she could say more, Rachel intentioned *Peace? What is peace if you keep murdering our people.*

Such anger, you must be a lesser you poor thing My Grand Avo sighed in sadness. Liat and George had sent Rachel calming and suggestive telegraphics, as if they touched her arm.

Remember Rachel, we must speak together George intentioned. Rachel nodded and stayed quiet.

We must still eat nourishment as it is the only way of life my Grand Avo continued and she as we all could feel the raw anger from the lessers and disappointment *however, to create peace we are open to discussions to creating a way we could create nourishment in the ethical fashion you feel. After our trip to the farm we realized our errors and saw what we did. We will not have our nourishment live that way anymore and have in fact set up housing for them with us. We will know our nourishment as they will know us. No longer will younger lessers be used for nourishment until they are the right age. We hope this will satisfy you until we find another way through collaboration.*

George set up a private channel amongst us. *Something stinks about this* he intentioned. I felt the lessers agree.

But she is saying they will change Beleeka intentioned. *Should not we give them the chance to? This has never happened in our history before.*

These people are plastic, we should not agree to anything intentioned Rachel in her low soothing thoughts.

What if there is hope through this? Hatia responded, a lesser who was timid.

We should make them feel what we felt Faro responded with his gruff intention, he was one of the tragic lessers who saw his whole family taken for nourishment. He was thin with broad shoulders, a great beard and mustache that were brown and grey, his hair was smooth on top of his head, blond dappled with grey spots. His eyes were a deep brown and his skin was tan, like that of the brown wood my Avia Carlo had in his study. His body was riddled with scars, including one that disrupted his top lip, as if it had gotten hooked on something. I could not help but wonder what he had been through, he must have fought against the Peacers every time they took a family member away. I realized it was his daughter who was taken to slaughter, when I first arrived. He was so subdued then, though he fought as much as he could. That was the last of his family.

Is it not up to us, the lessers, to decide what we want to happen to the people of the World Collective? asked Dati.

No, said Liat, the calm amongst the storm.

We should try collaboration, it is the best we can do and maybe no one has to lose their lives. Maybe we can teach them the ways of the plants.

They don't want the ways of the plants Liat, they had that all along, they want pain and suffering Faro responded.

Feeling Faro's pain, even I could admit I would want the same as him.

No Liat intentioned again. *We must not lower ourselves to their level. Tell us Atlia, Black Dove, what should we do?*

That name was given to me by the people as a way of honor for setting the plan that helped them escape, even though I was mistaken for having a blackened soul, it was a way to honor the sacrifice of my Avia Carlo. George came up with it, apparently, he told stories of doves bringing peace to the lessers all the time. I did not know it came with such weight. All of their intentions, weighing on me.

I believe my Grand Avo, though not fully. I do not trust her personally, but I trust the people behind the World Collective. If she was in charge she would have attacked us, she knew this entire time what was happening.

Then it is settled Telepa intentioned and we went back to the channel with the Grand Avo.

We accept your terms I intentioned to my Grand Avo. I felt her relief *On one condition. If there is any indication of your betraying us, then we will take that as an act of violence.*

Yes my Grand Avo agreed and I felt she was happy. *Can I speak to you privately?* She asked to me in front of all. I felt the others bow out of the channel, Dina was the only one that stayed. I felt my mother's annoyance, but she ignored Dina. *I wish we had not ended up this way my little one* she intentioned her love and sadness and disappointment.

I intentioned my disappointment in her, which I felt she was shocked to feel, as well as my sadness and my hurt. *Avo, you betrayed me, don't you see that yet? You knew this whole time and killed Avia Carlo...*

In order to avoid this civil war, and now we are divided! I felt my Avo's anger at this and sadness.

You still think you are right, don't you? I intentioned to her.

Don't you? she wryly intentioned back to me. *I love you and will always love you, that is the love of an Avo. All of your Avos and Avias miss you. Won't you come back.*

Not until nourishment ceases to exist I intentioned and I sent my love of Dina as well.

I wish you did not choose this path my Avia intentioned and then was gone. Tears were falling down my face and I did not even notice. Dina held me as I cried. The lessers looked at me puzzled, and the freers sent me love.

Crying was strength and feelings were strength in our culture. I could feel it was odd for the lessers since they did not typically have this luxury. Dina kissed my tears away. And I sat up and sighed, tired from everything.

You need rest my love Dina intentioned.

But then I did something I didn't even expect, I smiled. *Dina, we won* I intentioned.

She smiled and held me back. *I know.*

14

RECLAIMING

A month went by and it is as if we had reached paradise. We came together and built a town, all of us working different shifts to feed, love, and nourish our town with no discrepancies. Dina and I often chose to sleep under the stars, looking up and really seeing the world for the first time. The big red trees, the dark blue sky.

Everyone still trained who wanted to fight the old ways, just in case we were attacked, the vote was for being safe and prepared in every way. We did not make weapons, using the telegraphics as our greatest tools, and our hands if it came to a battle without telegraphics. Faro taught most of the old ways of fighting, taught to him by his family.

Religion was thought as a lesser trait and I did not know how many religions there were that still existed, until I saw mosques and temples being raised. I saw everyone praying side by side, as they said they had done as lessers at the farm for centuries, usually learning from one another. I enjoyed all their stories and lessons, while Dina seemed suspicious of them. Some had many gods while others just had one, it was interesting to learn about what they thought connected all of us, beyond our telegraphics.

I learned more than I ever had in my life, more than Avia Carlo could have taught me, as I learned from each person about their cultures they had, and George taught the history of the lesser, real history that was passed down to him. Each family chose a tribe name, a new one having to do with what we found in the outside world.

We went out into our new world and explored as Avia Carlo would have recommended. Dina and I did this together, it was what I guess you would call a date, to us it was just spending time together. We were walking through the forest once and I felt Dina have a mischievous idea *What?* I intentioned and she took one look back at me, her brown green eyes lit.

Catch me and then she ran off into the forest. I laughed and ran after her. All of the sudden I saw her stop in a clearing, it was a field of pink grass. I walked over to her and grabbed her from behind *You're easy to catch* I intentioned as she intentioned *be quiet!*

Taken aback, I stopped holding her and surveyed my surrounding for intruders, my heart beating. *No, it's safe* she intentioned and took my hand, and pointed ahead of us. There were these huge, beautiful creatures in the clearing. They were sniffing the ground and eating something. They were huge, maybe two humans tall, cat-like animals, some were blue with white stripes while others were purple with blue stripes, with soft fluffy hair. They had slick fur, with rounded ears where hair fluffed out. It seemed as if they had two fangs, but the rest of their teeth were flattened. Their eyes were like that of a dog. It seemed as if all these ancient animals were present in this creature. One saw us and sniffed the ground, slowly moving toward us.

Dina, afraid, was backing away slowly *Don't move* I intentioned. She sent me an intention saying I was not in the right mind – I honored it and did not move at first, but then I moved slowly forward, and it came to me, looked at me. Its golden-brown eyes, assessing me. It came over and sniffed me. And then I felt a huge wet thing go up and down me.

Dina laughed at me as I stood their intentioning *Yuck.* Then the creature put its head to my head lightly, and I pet its side, feeling its extremely soft fur. It retracted its fangs. She had blue and purple fur that was light and fluffy to the touch. She had dark purple patches around her eyes that seamlessly blended into blue on her face.

I am Boon I felt a low intention and looked surprised into its eyes. I saw its eyes squint as if it was laughing *You humans, always assuming you are the only ones to evolve. We have our telegraphics too. All of you?* I intentioned in awe.

We are the kinderling, the ones that are most close to you. The others can intention but are not as intelligent as we are. We know your tricks human. I have not seen a human in a long time, I thought you were extinct.

I laughed nervously *No, not extinct. So, your ancestors passed down the knowledge of us?*

We felt the kinderling laugh *No, I was there.* The kinderling intentioned and both of us were amazed.

How, how old are you if I may ask? Dina stuttered out in an intention.

I am as old as the war was, we were created by humans, the first animals to live the longest. Humans found a way to longevity, but their violent tendencies always got the best of them. I was a young kinderling when the destruction happened. We hid in a vault our creator built for us, though our creator did not survive the Greatest War. I could feel its sadness at this.

I intentioned sympathy, and the kinderling laughed again. *It was not you, humanling. You were not there. We have been watching you for a time, you are all different. I saw one of our cousins, a mouse I believe you called them. You take good care of him. His telegraphic I feel is blocked though, you should be able to turn it on.*

Animals have telegraphics too? I intentioned still in awe.

Yes, the humans started it, but mother nature followed. She is clever. We hear all telegraphic thought. The kinderling intentioned mother nature with a sense of honor, almost like how the people in the camp prayed.

Mother nature, who is mother nature? Asked Dina, confused.

In ancient times, she was considered a goddess, I am not sure what you are referring to kinderling, I intentioned.

Of course, you have your gods, humans, as do we. She intentioned mysteriously.

You human, I have decided to be bonded to you. She said suddenly and kissed me again.

I laughed *I accept that, ancient one. I would be honored.*

Dina cleared her throat and intentioned via private channel

Bonded, what does that me and don't I have a say?

Yes of course I intentioned to Dina, feeling some of her jealousy, curiosity, and annoyance.

I felt her settle *I too accept, yes you can be bonded with a kinderling.* The kinderling looked at Dina and went over to her, she lowered her head. Dina touched it as I did. *Thank you for letting me bond to your loved one.*

Yes, of course. I mean it's all right she ended coolly, though we could feel her feelings of awe, annoyance, jealousy, and want for her own.

Yes, you can be with one of us as well Dina, I feel one of my herd wants to connect with you. You must be careful with him though, he is full of fire.

A kinderling came trotting over. He looked fine, like the most muscled out of the lot. He had bright blue hair and white stripes that continued onto his face. His face was longer than Boon's and more narrow. He came over to Dina.

I would be honored to be your kinderling Dina, I am Raph, guardian of the kinderling. I hope you know by us bonding, I will be watching you Raph intentioned.

Dina nodded, *As will I.* He cautiously gave her a kiss and she laughed to our surprise. I looked at her sternly, not sure if that was offensive to them. *It tickled* she intentioned begrudgingly and we laughed.

Why would you want to bond with us? I asked Boon out of curiosity.

It is what we are meant to do, is to bond with humans, and guide them through life. We feel a purpose to protect you.

Protect us? We would like to protect you! I intentioned back.

I felt Raph chuckle, *Like you could protect us, you are puny little beings.*

I definitely could protect you intentioned Dina, with the fire she had inside her. We felt it match Raph's in agreement.

We shall see puniest human Raph intentioned, we laughed, and Dina did too though you could see she was annoyed at his gall, she also found it amusing.

We brought the kinderling with us to the camp. Not all the

kinderling chose to bond, but many did, and surprisingly so more with the lessers than the freers. We welcomed them into our camp and built them homes, though they protested they could build their own, we did it out of love and to honor them. They became a part of our daily life of dancing, singing, eating, playing. They ate what we ate, and they thought eating other beings was appalling as well. They taught us the ways of the forest, what new plants were safe for us to eat, and introduced us to other animals.

They helped us turn on the mouse's telegraphic, Telepa was excited to have him be able to speak.

Finally, oh my god it has been ages since I spoke. So nice to meet you Telepa, you are my human and I am your being. Anything you want, just ask. Anything at all. Let me sniff you because I think you are sweating a little.

Hi little one Telepa intentioned smiling regardless of all the intentions the mouse gave him *It is nice to meet you.*

Telepa you have so much pain, so much pain. There is so much to do for you, I will help you, one with so much pain. The mouse intentioned and then started kissing his ear.

Well you met Curly, I guess he has bonded to you. Boon said as I stood beside her, petting her fur, I felt her happiness and pleasure from it smiling inwardly.

Telepa laughed *Yes, he is quite a sweetheart.*

I am happy to help, always happy Telepa I love you Telepa. He continued licking his ear.

I think we can be on a private channel Curly so as not to disturb everyone with too many intentions Telepa intentioned and could feel everyone's amusement, including Curly's.

Oh yes, that is probably best I have so many things to tell you, secret things. Curly responded still licking his ear.

Then we did not hear Curly anymore, as we saw Telepa nod and walk away, bonding with his new friend.

All of this beauty was going on and I wanted to feel happy, but the nagging feeling of unfinished business haunted me. The faces of the lessers who were probably at the farm right now were in my nightmares. I often woke up sweating after trying to save them, they always perished. In a fire or teleported out to slaughter. Dina often woke up with me, comforting me, as I had for the nightmares of her own before she had her telegraphic control her dreams. I would not let mine, I wanted to feel the pain. The pain of what was left undone, unfinished. I felt responsible since it was my Grand Avo, I thought over and over again how in that one telegraphic session, how I could have changed her mind. The things I could have said.

This is not good Dina intentioned, I felt her worry for me. I sighed and grumbled and went back to sleep usually. One night it was so powerful though. A little lesser girl was crying on the floor backed up against the stall. A Peacer came in and forcefully installed her telegraphic as her mother held her screaming, holding onto every last piece of her child. The Peacer then ripped her out of her mother's arms, you could hear her shoulder crack as her mother sobbed trying to hold on so hard. She was screaming at the top of her lungs fighting to get to her child as other Peacers held her back.

Dina saw me convulsing in my sleep and she quickly moved my shoulders and shouted my name, I woke up with a start and ran outside, confused and distraught. I had looked at the Peacer holding back the woman but it was too dark to see anything. I could barely make out who they were, I just heard their voices.

"No, I... I... Dina," I said in confusion looking at my hands they were shaking. Dina took my hands and shushed me. Beleeka, I did not notice had teleported in and put a blanket around my shoulders. "I... I ..." I could not say anything the pain of that moment so clear like a memory. Dina sat me down in the tent and had her telegraphic warm me. I stared into the darkness, not saying anything.

I could not move, as if paralyzed. Boon came in and nudged me. Telepa soon teleported in as well and I could hear them talking about me in whispers. Telepa looked me over and sighed distraught.

"There is nothing wrong with her, why can't you convince her to turn on her telegraphic," Telepa said.

"Don't you think I have tried?" Asked Dina, annoyed he would even ask.

Boon sighed and lay down next to me.

It is up to her to wake up Boon intentioned and then just lay next to me.

Beleeka sat beside me and said nothing, she just hugged my shoulders and lay her head on my arm.

I sat like that frozen. I think what they did not know was that I had learned something, something important. That was a memory, my dreams were real. All of this was more important to me than if they knew I was happy, I had to stay in that painful space. I had to remember. I am not sure how I got these memories, but it was a piece to a puzzle, a piece that I had been missing. What had I not been seeing.

I saw the little girl, I saw the mother. Again, and again in my head. Who was that little girl? I knew I had to go to the World Collective, I had to find out what I was missing. My Grand Avo had invited us a little bit ago to come and see the new ways they were taking care of the lessers. I knew I had to go.

I tried the whole time I was silent to figure out who that girl was, replaying her in my mind. Finally, I knew I had to use my last resort.

Dina I intentioned in a rusty way, my brain raw from replaying what I saw.

I then noticed she was right beside me. *I am here my love, what happened?*

I am not sure but there is something I must find out, I think Avia Carlo left me a message through my dreams.

Through your dreams? Dina intentioned I felt her skepticism, love, and worry.

Yes, I need to go to the World Collective.

You can't be serious! I felt her anger and annoyance. *You will never be happy, will you? Until they kill you or something.*

I scooped up her hands *Doing nothing is killing me already. I need to finish this.*

She may have to go Boon intentioned, and I felt Dina's annoyance because she agreed with her, though she was not used to someone else chiming in opposition in our conversations.

Raph was about to intention something, as he came in too, but Dina asked to speak.

It is going to take a long time Dina intentioned to me, *You have to be patient.*

Do you love me? I intentioned her.

How is that even a question?! Dina asked I felt her frustration and hurt.

I laughed at her hurt intentioning how silly it was that she should be angry because of course I knew the answer. And she also knew why I asked it.

Yes, I love all of you, even the insane parts, and Atlia, this is insane Dina intentioned. She sighed. *Well, I guess we have another ludicrous adventure ahead of us. Should we summon the others?*

Yes I intentioned.

We gathered the council and they had agreed that I would go along with Dina, Rachel, Beleeka, and Faro. Telepa chose not to go, it was still too hurtful for him, and he was still healing from being such a huge part of the violence in the World Collective. The kinderling came to consult, though they did not want to be a part of the human council, we considered their wisdom. They told us to go to see if they Grand Avo had changed but cautioned to not believe her.

I said goodbye to Boon and Dina said goodbye to Raph, both kinderlings wanted to come but we showed them how dangerous that would be if people knew about them.

We teleported to the outside of the dome and erased the trail in our telegraphics to make sure no one could tell where we had come from - our camp.

We ceremoniously held hands in a circle. "Mind if I say a prayer?" Faro asked kindly in his gruff intention. His intention was typically low and sounded like plastic wheels rolling on gravel, but he had a lightness to his intention just then. We nodded but I felt Dina's annoyance. She felt my acceptance and intention *We can take all we can get.*

"Please watch over us oh great one, and that you may give

us comfort in our mission, love in our hearts, and understanding when it comes to violence." Faro then trailed off and we said, "Be well", the saying all said after a prayer. I was more anxious now.

Let's go Dina intentioned and we all teleported to the meeting space. It was in my family's grand cube, where we typically ate nourishment. All sitting up and down the spiral staircase was my family and the leaders and... people I had never seen before. They had white straps around their necks. Most looked like everyone else except they did not have a mask on them while others were hunched or blind but looked content sitting. My grand Avo was at the top looking down.

My littlings! She intentioned to me and Beleeka and teleported down to us she hugged me and then Beleeka at the same time, tears in her eyes. I could not help that feeling of love and hate in my heart, constantly at battle with one another. I wanted to love her so much but how can you love someone who does not see lessers as human, who does not support you?

Dina felt my feelings and I felt her sadness for me, feeling how deeply wounded I am. *I love you and you are strong* she intentioned via our private channel. I pushed my Avo away then and looked her in the eyes, letting the tears fall but not distract me.

We are here to see what you have done with the community and what you have to offer.

I felt her intention waver and her annoyance come in as she felt my feelings, as she felt how betrayed I felt. She backed away.

Yes, please nourish with us. As you can see we have changed everything, now lessers are a part of our family, we take care of them until they are of age to be nourishment.

How can you eat people at any age? Faro intentioned and for the first time I saw my Avo's eyes widen, she could feel the hatred Faro had for her and the World Collective. Faro did not hide it and neither did Rachel.

Are we at war? intentioned my Avo.

No Dina intentioned politely *We are not, though as custom we will not hide our true feelings of you, as we despise you, I will hide mine out of respect for my love.*

My Avo paused for a second and then laughed. The whole cube laughed with her. *Ah, yes, you must learn your telegraphics you poor lessers. You will learn. Now come and nourish with us, out of respect we have plant nourishment for you while we have our improved nourishment for ourselves.*

When my Avo felt that all of us refused this notion, my Avo agitatedly intentioned *Since you can't accept any other culture than your own and since you are all so self-righteous, then I guess we will eat plant nourishment as well if that satisfies you.*

It does Dina intentioned smiling and I could not help laughing in our channel. I love that woman.

We then were teleported up to the top with most of the leaders. We felt how they were disgruntled eating plant nourishment and relief on many of the faces of the lessers. I could see they might have liked the plant nourishment. It seemed that the nourishment Creationists took the plants to the next level using a white sauce made from a plant called hemp, and some plant meat they made from a plant called barley. We saw each name for each plant in our telegraphics, looking down at our food, verifying there were no lessers in it. It tasted delicious, creamy and rich, better than any of the lesser food we ate. We could see some of the leaders were trying hard to not enjoy it, though it seemed they could not stop eating it and you could see the smile of satisfaction on their faces. Then when they saw us looking they would stop and pause the food bubble about to enter their mouths.

Then the leaders shared how we could strengthen our community. We listened to them each tell us their different opinions, how we were being silly and should come back to the World Collective, how we should never go back to the collective, and how they should go to war with us. At that point we created a channel amongst ourselves, so the others would not know how we felt. At the end of hearing all the perspectives as we ate (including the perspective of how awful the plant nourishment tasted compared to lesser nourishment), we paused to relax. It was World Collective custom when negotiating with other territories to let all the opinions be heard from one side and then have some time in between to decompress so the other side could express theirs. Most of us did not eat the nourishment just in case they tried to poison us, though I told them that our telegraphics would point it out and if there were toxins they would help the body find them and flush it out. I ate the plant nourishment, could taste the plants in relief, my first meal here that was not made of bloody violent means.

I freely talked with my family and caught up on family matters, how well my zias and zios were, who partnered who, etc.

For a moment I saw myself wishing this was all a dream. Nourishment was not real, eating people was not real. I was shocked back into reality, the eyes of the little girl from my dream haunting me. *Help me* the lesser intentioned. I jolted forward breathing hard, Dina next to me.

I was breathing fast and the next moment my Avo was next to me rubbing my back.

How long has she been doing this? She intentioned Dina, for the first time talking directly to her.

For a while, she has not had much sleep and refuses to turn her tel... Dina stopped

I am fine I wheezed out and continued to breath steadily. I felt the worry of my whole family, I missed that connection to my family. I breathed out everything and in a separate channel sent what I saw to Dina.

The girl again Dina responded, and I nodded.

My Avo sighed heavily and asked for how long it had been going on.

Congratulations spring, you and Dina have brought a consciousness to this world. You are pregnant.

I was startled. I knew this could happen. Dina was turned into a giver as a pet (it means she was made fertile with bits of her consciousness through her telegraphic, that she could give and form new life inside of another, though they chose not to do it that way anyway as her owner chose to do it the "old fashioned" way because people wanted to enjoy the spectacle). When we loved each other that is how it passed and was created, amongst both of our consciousness. My Avo always told me how I was ready to have a consciousness once my body chose to. I was speechless. This was the way all beings became pregnant since the telegraphic was created. The Telegraphic made your body respond and start the inklings of having a child.

I smiled at Dina and we embraced. What an unfortunate world to bring a consciousness into. Some of the members of our family I felt disgusted that I would be with a lesser. I did not care at that moment, I was so happy and so was Dina. We kissed each other, and our people cheered while the others looked as if we were mad using our primitive voices.

She must get care My Avo said, looking at Dina.

No said Dina, intentioning. *We can't trust them.*

I must. I need to make sure we are all safe I intentioned to Dina and gave her one last kiss, pausing the negotiations at the moment. We teleported.

My Avo came with me and though I was perplexed as why Dina did not teleport with us I was immediately put into a conditioning room. I felt my telegraphic was turned to neutral and I realized I had made a mistake, but it was too late.

What you have is unnatural and you did not listen to me. That consciousness that demon put in you is a demon as well. I struggled against my telegraphic as the Intentioneers sat me down. Tears fell, that they could not control.

My dear little one, I did not want to have to resort to this. The Intentioneers then proceeded to poke in my telegraphic, I could feel them trying to find that spark, that little consciousness in me wanting to be born. I screamed inside of my body.

Don't fight it, it will be over soon my spring, we need to take it out. I fought with every fiber of my being as I felt them pull her, it was a her, out of my mind. I screamed internally so much I felt the walls shake, though they did not.

You will be right again, we are fixing your telegraphic. This is not just for negotiations my dear, this is for everyone. Looking at my Avo's eyes I saw who the girl in my dreams was.

It was not my littling, it was my Avo. She was the girl haunting me, the one the Peacer pulled away. At that moment I realized the Peacer's face, it was my Avia Carlo. My Avo could see this and was not surprised.

Yes, I lied like a lesser to get you down here, you did not have to get checked out, the demon was fine. I knew your Avia planted a memory in you once I saw your reaction. I knew it was of me. Now he made it a part of your core and I love you little spring, no matter what you did to me. I will fix this mess.

At the next moment everything went blank and I had wished I had known what I did now to have been able to fight back.

15

POWER

I woke up and felt my littling inside of me, I was happy. My Avo told me I had become unconscious and that I had to stay in the World Collective to be available for other procedures for my littling. I was so happy, it felt so euphoric. Everything my Avo said I loved. I love her so much.

We teleported back to the cube. My Avo smiled and hugged me congratulating me. I sat back next to Dina and smiled drunkenly at her. Before she could ask anything my Avo intentioned for the negotiations to continue. She asked me to go first.

I stood up and staggered a little, laughing, my Avo looked nervous. Dina looked at me worried, I realized then I could not feel her intentions.

I don't understand why we hurt my family. I think they are no threat to us anymore and realize error of their ways, you can see the steps they are taking to take care of the lessers. We should come back to the World Collective. Those are my thoughts.

I sat down. Dina touched me. "Why are you not connected to me," she whispered in the ancient language.

I looked at her confused and thinking *Why should I be connected to you, you are a lesser.*

A voice inside screamed, deep within me, I held my ears and fell forward on my knees.

You did something to her! Dina interrupted Rachel who was giving her thoughts about everything. Everyone silently watched me as my Avo teleported over to me.

No you stay back, you evil thing! Dina motioned her arm

outwards and I heard my Avo cry in pain. Dina was using the telegraphic fighting technique. Everyone came in front of me and we were teleported out of the room back to the edge of the dome and then back to camp.

I did not understand what was happening as my head kept ringing. *Lies, lies, lies* I felt over and over again. Dina brought me to Telepa.

Boon ran over and put her head to mine. *She is lost, we have to wait again.* She curled up next to me.

Boon, what does that mean?! Dina intentioned, though Boon was silent to her. She stepped aside as Telepa started working on me. Raph teleported in next to her and tried to console her as she ran her hands through his fur, lost in frustration and desperation.

Beleeka was sobbing *It is my fault, I am sorry.* Faro took Beleeka aside to talk to her as Telepa and Nurium and other Intentioneers and healers looked over me. I felt as if I could see my body, as if I was floating. I could see everyone around me trying everything. Boon was there with me.

Hi Boon I intentioned.

Hi, my humanling I felt her fur as if I was petting her. Both of us looking at my body.

So, I made a mistake... I said to Boon.

I know humanling, I know. For now, let's just watch. Boon replied with love in her intentions.

"The littling is gone," I heard Telepa sigh in the old language, and I heard Dina's sobs. She was gripping my hand so tight.

"I don't care, just bring her back to me. We will mourn our little one later," Dina said in a stern voice stopping herself from crying more.

Everyone was working around me. I saw myself frozen, a statue of myself. I saw and heard everyone around me, I could travel anywhere from one telegraphic to another, I was free.

When I observed what Dina was hearing I lazily floated around. It felt so good not being stuck in my body.

"She is not in her body anymore, we will have to wait until

she comes back." said Telepa in the old language.

"If she comes back." I felt Dina's whole body in grief. My poor love. It felt like a dream though, so I was not angry, though I felt sad for her. I felt content.

You should connect with her Boon intentioned encouraged. I did miss feeling Dina in my mind.

I don't want to harm her, I intentioned to Boon, she nodded internally.

You won't she intentioned knowingly. *Goodbye humanling, see you on the other side of your journey.* Boon vanished. I reached out to Dina.

"She will," Telepa said touched Dina's hand and I felt the warmth. Then I felt her. She stood up straight.

"She is here, she is in my head," Dina said, I laughed at this. Of course, I was in her head, I loved her, where else would I be? I thought lazily floating.

"She can't face the reality yet, it makes sense she would be with someone who is the most comforting. But how she is, I have no idea. This is beyond anything I have ever seen telegraphics do. All we can do is support her and give her a break as her telegraphic heals too. I wish I could kill the Grand Avo, for what she did was…"

"Please Telepa, don't say it, I can't think like that right now, especially if she is in my head. I need to do what you said." I felt her gripping Telepa's hand now, making his knuckles white.

"Perhaps you need to relax," Telepa said and I felt a side channel be made. Telepa was very good at side channels and no matter how much I tried to budge they would not let me. I pouted and sat down in her telegraphic.

"I can see her now," Dina smiled, and I saw Dina, a version of her sit with me. Telepa left before I could say anything to Dina. She hugged and kissed me.

That felt nice, but I pushed away. *Aren't I supposed to be alone?*

Dina looked at me and intentioned *You are not supposed to be anything, we went through so much, love.* She touched my cheek and I saw she wanted to cry but stopped herself.

You can cry I intentioned to her. *But I feel amazing, I am not sure I want to go back. I am so happy.*

I know love, a few tears fell down her face into nothingness. *We will just stay here for a little bit and see how you feel later.*

That sounds nice. Where do you want to go? We can do anything in here.

Dina smiled and bit her lip.

Anywhere, just tell me. Don't be shy, I smirked.

She laughed and intentioned *the beach?*

Sure I intentioned back and the next moment we were at a beach with sand that was so fine, it was like the white of the concealer, and the water was an aqua blue color, palm trees were lined behind us.

There my love, see? So simple here, here we can be happy. I intentioned my happiness and felt hers. I made a little tent out of real things like the trees and what I imagined that ancient stuff called fabric that the ancients wore. We wore no masks and lay on the sand feeling the sun. We played in the water, and loved each other over and over again, the water bringing us back and forth to each other. We laughed and played with ancient toys like a "ball" and a net. During the day sometimes, we would make things and share stories that we made up. Dina always had very exciting stories while mine were about romance and betrayal. She listened to my stories and often we would end up loving each other, she was so romantically excited from my stories.

We lay in a bed of fluff, I made our bed a cloud and we would sleep and love each other there. I am not sure what time went by since time in a telegraphic was different than time in the real world. The more we stayed, the more anxious I got about going back. I loved our place, but I could feel Dina every time we slept she joined the "real world" and I could feel her wanting to get back to it.

She never pushed me to go back, never even said it or intentioned it, but I could feel her feelings. I knew I had to do something. When Dina woke in the morning I looked at her and intentioned *Are you happy?*

Dina paused for a moment. *Yes, but I need you in real life as well. I am not ready to move on and I don't know how often I can visit if you are.*

What if I come with you? Maybe for a day to feel if I am ready. I love this place, but I love you more. I will follow you wherever.

I know, my love Dina was tearful, *But you have a very harsh reality to come back to, and I would never ask that of you.*

I held her hands as I felt my feet in the sand next to hers, our toes cuddled as I pondered our predicament.

I will come with you. I decided finally, and I felt relief from Dina.

We have a plan for you, you won't have to get back into anything until you are ready. Dina intentioned and I felt her hesitation. I felt great though and thought why not? How hard could it be? She felt this and sighed.

That night I stayed up and walked with her in the real world. It was day time there and the sun looked beautiful through the real trees. Dina I could feel was sending me all the good feelings from the real world. Dina went into one of the old buildings that the trees built back with their canopies and there was Telepa next to my body that was lying in a hammock. It looked blushed and life like, but like it was sleeping.

I look so peaceful I intentioned to Dina.

Dina ignored me and talked to Telepa. "She is here and would like to try to connect her consciousness with her body again." I could feel her excitement at this, relief, and a little bit of worry.

Telepa smiled and laughed, "That is great, what good news to hear! I will get you connected with her. Just sit here and touch her hand," he pulled over a piece of wood and Dina sat on it.

I have no idea if this will work. I felt him intention to Dina. No one could figure out still how I was capable of this.

"Now, touch her hand."

As Dina touched my hand I felt a pulse and pulling towards my body. I felt what Dina was feeling as I left her, I felt as if I was being sucked back into life. I was then in my own body breathing heavily. I sat up feeling all the aches and pains, everything coming back to me.

In a cloud I heard Telepa saying, "This is normal, and you are going so feel some pain, Atlia,"

"Put me back!" I shouted and grabbed my ears the pain of my littling being pulled from me filling up everything. I felt Dina in my telegraphic now she was feeling everything I was feeling. Then I felt my whole community, everyone – their love and support and sadness for me mourning with me. I felt Boon who was there again, filling me with the love and connection she has with me. When I wailed everyone did together as one and it lifted the pain, made it lighter.

At some point I was strong enough to put all my pain in a private channel to mourn with Dina, Telepa, Beleeka, and Boon.

Dina was stunned to feel Beleeka there and I felt her annoyance and Telepa's intention of *We will tell her later, she needs this.*

I was in the healing hammock for almost a month as I was learning to walk again. My body and mind had been separated for so long, that my body did not feel like my own. It felt as if I took on a machine as my body, and it did not all connect all the time. Boon laid beside me every day. She kissed my forehead and cuddled me to sleep. I could see Dina was not jealous but thankful to Boon. I learned it had been quite a bit since I went on my vacation which felt like years. The camp was even bigger, adding two circles to its original loop. Everyone was happy talking to each other, doing tasks, living freely. It grew so much and so did many different places for plant nourishment everyone adding their own twist to it. I was walking with help from my telegraphic as I was looking at all the new places that sprouted up. Everyone took turns in each place, giving like we did in the World Collective.

How did we grow? I asked my family channel, the ones who helped me deal with my pain.

Actually, Beleeka helped us grow Telepa intentioned and I could feel Dina's silent fury, trying to keep everything in her private channel.

What happened? Why is everyone furious with you Beleeka? I intentioned my Dalta.

Can we meet, in person? I felt Beleeka meekly intention and before Dina could lash out her fury, Telepa intentioned *Yes that would be wise.* Dina nodded internally though I could feel she was unhappy and she teleported us to where Beleeka was. She was sitting in the Freer Square, where we hosted most of our camp events though during the day it had wood tables and chairs made by the fallen purple trees. She was sitting at the table drinking at tea Liat had made - Liat made a little tea den and taught everyone how to make this ancient drink. The cups were made out of leaves, and invention from Liat and held the hot tea nicely. Beleeka sat by herself which was uncommon in our society.

She smiled and hugged me solemnly intentioning her love for me, and sorry. Confused I intentioned *Why are you sorry, what is going on?*

Yeah tell her what you did, you greeder (the name we came up with to call the World Collective people since greed was the worst thing you could have). I was shocked at her language but felt Beleeka agree with her.

Beleeka started to explain *Please know I did not mean this to happen. I had...*

Just tell her Dina's fury interrupted her.

She told me through tears how she had never stopped talking to our Grand Avo. From the beginning, she was not sure who to follow. That she loved our Grand Avo too and how she reached out to her separately when we all ran to the camp. *I did not know what to do, I was not sure who was right, I could see both sides...*

There is only one side to this, you killer, we both felt Dina's fury again.

Stop, please my love I intentioned to Dina *I need to hear all of this.* I felt Dina relax and her sorrow for me outweighed her anger for Beleeka.

She told me to watch you and I did and when I knew you were pregnant

I was so excited I told her. I felt your little one before you did. She then gave you the invitation. I thought it was to make amends, she told me it was to hear her side. That was it the next thing I know she took you away. I would have never...

Stop I said to Beleeka feeling even more pain in my heart. I lost my Avia and Avo, but now my Dalta, the one I am closest to decided to go against everything I am, everything those people are, for her own selfishness.

Beleeka I can't forgive you and I am not sure I ever will.

But I did get the other lessers out, for you! She exclaimed *That is why we have more people once I realized what had happened. I immediately went to my friend who was an Intentioneer and wanted to get out too, we teleported all the lessers we saw in the cube out.*

Beleeka I intentioned *I can't do this, do you understand? No matter what you do, I don't think I can ever forgive you, at least not right now. She killed my littling. Do you understand???! I still feel her, I feel the ghost of her every day. That pain will always rip me apart forever now.*

Beleeka was crying sorry in the ancient language. I could not take it anymore, so I teleported us home and I could feel Dina's love and how proud she was of me. She came into the hammock with me and held me as I cried and told me one of the stories she told me on the beach, it felt like forever ago. How I longed to be at the beach again.

16

WAR

Negotiations had stopped with the World Collective. My Grand Avo wanted to go to war, but they still had not declared anything. Our spies there sent back reports of what was going on. Beleeka helped with the spies though she had to include Faro in every intention she had, as that was the new law we passed if anyone betrayed our society for the World Collective.

Boon and Raph, as well as the other kinderlings, did not understand war, and cautioned us about the last war. They told us the stories of how the bombs and other man-made toxic weapons destroyed everything. We listened and agreed that the war we would have would only be a telegraphic one. Also, we were sure our opponents were dramatically opposed to the old ways, after all, they would be found lessers if they did approve of the old violent ways that ruined the Earth. They did not see as being violent to lessers, since lessers were not considered humans. We were not lessers, though we were humans, so they would be cautious by their own twisted moral standards.

Our people as well were not sure how to proceed as half wanted to go to war and the other half did not. Most of the time it was split between freers and lessers. No one really wanted war but the greeders wanted to chastise us, which of course made our people wanting to go to war, Faro and Rachel at the forefront of that movement.

I got stronger every day, as my new family helped. Many people made the sign of the Black Dove as I walked by and I would nod my head and thank them.

They made a nice area next to the fallen people and world collective members who were killed during the last few months. Our spies (some were caught) were sent back dead and some of the littlings were so sick from the World Collective, they just did not make it. Our village had grown bigger since other states had freers deflecting as well, moving so many people to our village. That was the one good thing, was beyond the graves you could see the thriving village, that I would call a city by now. I looked down at the little space they made for my lost littling. The area had the name "Coralina" on the stone, the name that Dina and I came up with for our littling. Flowers and tree bark surrounded it. Liat planted that small garden there in honor of her.

Every day Dina and I went to our daughter's memorial and held each other. Loving our daughter, sending love to wherever her unique consciousness may be now. As I got stronger, I decided to learn the arts of the fight from Rachel and Faro. I was reluctant before, but with my recent experience I wanted to be able to protect myself.

Boon watched reluctantly with Raph from a distance. She was not a fan of violence either but was happy we were fighting this way versus past ways. We prepared ourselves in the battle circle. We created a circle where there was nothing but the dirt. We sat on the dirt "grounding ourselves" for the beginning.

First, we will practice the battle of wills Rachel intentioned to the group in our private channel she created.

In the channel we felt a burst of heat, at first it was small and then it felt as if it was burning. We saw fire too, I heard some people gasp as others cried out. I gritted my teeth, a little heat I could take, I felt I could take anything after experiencing the worst loss in my life.

Good use your loss Atlia I felt Rachel via a side channel, guiding me as she was guiding all of us. I withstood the heat though I felt my flesh burn. *Stay strong* I felt the intention and felt others fall off our battle channel, the pain too much to take. I welcomed it, wanting to feel it. I felt Dina's unease and though I blocked my pain from her for this training, I felt her worry, as if she knew what I was doing. I knew Dina was fine since she had been training since everyone decided to learn the art of telebattle.

The burns I felt in my stomach, my hair singeing, I could smell my flesh burning. I welcomed all the pain inside of me until I screamed back at it letting all the anger, sadness, everything I felt towards it. I did not hear the cries until I felt Dina shaking my arm and her intention, *Get out of battle! It's over, you hit Rachel!*

I had not realized I did anything and snapped my eyes open to see Rachel on the ground holding her head in one and putting out an arm outstretched.

I heard clapping and turned around quickly to see Faro laughing and approaching the circle.

That was fantastic! He intentioned to everyone.

What did I do? Is Rachel okay? I intentioned and Faro made a silent channel to me smiling.

She will be fine, she was quite impressed, we both were. Not many have the strength that you do Atlia, you have what we call the rage. You need to be taught how to use it properly, so I will teach you.

Faro, are you sure that is wise? Asked Dina, who was a part of our private channel already, being my chosen and all.

You have the rage too; don't you think it was helpful? Inquired Faro, and I could feel Dina sigh and agree.

You are more violent than you think Faro intentioned and my first reply to that was a huge intention of *No,* but I knew that was not true and Dina and Faro could sense it.

The training is more gruesome, you can take how intense it is. When we get to the battle sequence, that is when you will be truly tested. That is enough for today, for we start tomorrow. Faro left us, and I looked at Dina quickly.

I felt her extreme worry. *I just don't want you to get carried away with it. I felt how powerful you are without your filters, your will is very strong, stronger than most. Most with that strong of will go mad. I need you to learn something else along with your studies.*

She teleported me, Boon, and Raph to the hall of knowledge where all our books are, along with Avia Carlo's books. Raph curled up into a corner and murmured to us how he did not like to learn stupid being's history. Boon followed me as Dina brought me over to the books. *We have added more and recently found on our last journey, Beleeka got these books that were hidden in the Grand Avo's rooms. They are the history of battles.*

Shocked, I ran my hands along the spines, surprised to see books, newer looking ones. My fingers felt how smooth they were, almost like the stones they made structures out of now. My eyes fascinated by each title, how I wanted to drink their knowledge. The Grand Avo must have had these made for herself. I felt something tugging at the back of my mind, something I had forgotten about my Avo that horrible night...

Boon rubbed her head on my back and I could feel her touch, comforting my sadness.

These were made so that no one in the World Collective could download them via Eden and since most don't read the old language, it was safe, until we found them. It tells of the many battles with the southern regions. They have telegraphics too and there are many stories of using their telegraphics to battle. The rage was only found in a few individuals from the south, and most of the people who battled never came back the same and could not control the rage. They killed entire villages of their own people. The World Collective thought they could control it, so they tried to use them as weapons, which is why the northwest region was wiped out.

Wow, I intentioned and began to read the books of knowledge.

I could tell you all of this, but I like to hear your mind read. Boon said as she stood beside me.

Dina laughed *Really? She reads so slowly.* Dina intentioned amused.

I looked at Dina sideways and took the book from her *I do not... always,* she felt my small amount of hurt but I laughed feeling her amusement.

Dina teleported us to the tea garden as I read. Boon curled up next to me as Dina read another book called Huckleberry Finn across from me with Raph curled up next to her. I felt Boon and her feelings as I read, knowing she went through most of this, it was hard to read. She knew of the rage though she never got close to the people, she and her herd stayed away from them, feeling their rage. It was an extremely sad story for both sides, battling over the last few thousand years. I could see why Dina wanted me to read it. The story was of Remmi and Ofro, also imprinted like Dina and me. They were both capable of the rage but Ofro could not control his. He tried and sought out the best telefigher in the realm Rana but even she perished at his hands. Ofro told Remmi to stay away, but Remmi could not leave him. One night, Ofro had such an intense battle dream that he did not know that he silently killed Remmi who was trying to wake him. When he saw what he did, he disappeared into the nothingness, and was never found, leaving trees behind his wake, reminders of Remmi.

I was fascinated by this history, and humbled by it.

Are you afraid of my rage? I asked Boon in a private channel, the one I created with just her since I was sick.

No, you are my human, and I know you human better than you know yourself by now. Boon replied sleepily. She went back to sleeping with a slight snore as I rubbed her belly. *That's the spot.* I heard her say as I turned my attention back to Dina.

Dina felt me read the story and I asked what she thought. *I don't think that is you or me, but we need to be careful. That was before we created telegraphic filters, so hopefully we can learn to put those on as soon as we can.*

I nodded but could not help but feel the goosebumps on my arm. I could not imagine doing that to Dina, ever. I kissed her abruptly, and deeply. She felt my emotion of sadness from the story and how much I loved her. Raph intentioned that Boon and he were going to leave us to our privacy and teleported out. I kind of waved bye as I kissed Dina not wanting to ruin the moment. I felt her love, deepening the kiss as she teleported us back to our cottage. This was a cottage Dina built while we were on the island, it helped her focus during the day without me. It was made of leaves, so many leaves that grew all over the house, it was beautiful. Dina brought me back quickly from admiring the house as she touched the side of my face. She kissed me and felt my wetness and I moaned in anticipation and desire. She continued to kiss my neck and down to my navel. I bit my lip hovering on shivers and feeling warm.

I felt her intention of protection, how she wanted to protect me and love me and gave her the same, gently feeling her neck with my fingers, caressing it as she went to my wetness and matched it with that of her mouth. I curled my fingers in her hair and matched her movement moaning as she went in circle deeper and then lighter and then deeper. She slid her fingers inside of me touching that spot of pleasure deep within me and knew how to feel it, the way I loved it. I double checked to make sure our cabin had the silence control on, so no one would hear, and we were in our channel. I felt her pleasure and excitement mounting with mine. She came back up to my face and kissed my longingly, I felt the intention via her telegraphic touching mine, and I felt it touching that place deep inside of me instinctively, feeling every inch of pleasure and I did the same to her as I felt her hard nipples between my fingers. We rocked back and forth together, our intentions growing in each other's telegraphics, feeling each other's pleasure until we released together moaning in each other's ears and sighing and kissing each other we lay, her fitting her petite body in the curves of mine.

Our breaths fitting each other's she felt how exhausted I was, still recovering. She held me as we went to sleep, though the thought slipped past me, one second of worry, that maybe we would be like Ofro and Remmi.

My dreams were not back to normal after I had returned. My mind felt as if there was something important, something I was missing. This particular night I had the same dream I had before the terrible event that ensued the next day. Again, it was a girl being pulled out of her mother's arms...

I sat straight up screaming, Dina woke up with me - *What is it??* she intentioned.

Boon teleported in, feeling between our bond that something was wrong. She came over and sniffed me as I pet her.

I know, Dina. I know what happened. I shared my dream with her and Boon and the memory of my Avo finally uncovered, what happened when she killed my little consciousness. We watched her intention *Yes, I lied like a lesser to get you down here, you did not have to be reviewed, the little demon in you is fine. I knew your Avia planted a memory in you once I saw your reaction. I knew it was of me. Now he made it a part of your core and I love you little sprig, no matter what you did to me. I will fix this mess.*

I felt Dina process this and her anger grow as did mine, along with the pain and betrayal, I was still happy to learn that I had remembered finally. I felt Boon's worry for me, and her anger at my Avo as well.

What do you think happened? I felt Dina intention and she could feel I was working something out. *The Grand Avo is a lesser, she did not want that to get out, but I am not sure how or why she is doing what she is.*

Maybe she felt she was not a lesser, or your Avia Carlo rescued her for a reason we just will never know.

No, Avia Carlo wanted me to know, there has to be a way to find out. She was the lesser pulled from her Avo's arms. The realization had hit me that the Avo I saw was the younger version of my Kamma, the one she sent to the farm. *She must have a reason she is wanting to keep the World Collective this way. Avia Carlo must have left me more clues somewhere. I think this will lead to how we can win this war.*

Dina sighed but agreed and we told the rest of our people apart from the leaders. They were shocked to learn she was a lesser and the lessers felt more uncomfortable with the fact she was one. The freers did not seem surprised and some actually thought if she was not the lead, that there would not be the eating of lessers.

But eating lessers goes back one thousand of years as the books describe. I was sure she had something to do with protecting it, but I was unsure as to how. As I was taught how to use the rage in battle, my mind was often preoccupied.

I was first being taught to control it but would often let it slip when my mind would wander in the battle of wills with

Faro. *What is in your head, Dove?* He would intention impatiently, as I would get consumed by water, or be stabbed until my will was done from all the feeling of stab wounds.

You must have absolute will. You must clear everything from your mind. I will teach you an old art called meditation. This is what humans used before we had the telegraphic controls, before we had the telegraphic even.

I was taught to still my mind, which was quite difficult, as I could only do a couple of seconds first, Faro getting annoyed with the clumsiness and clutter of my mind. I sat there for what seemed to be hours trying to still it. I tried to watch as thoughts moved past in my mind, but sometimes I was so preoccupied trying to figure out why my Avia did it. Faro became so frustrated he told me to section my mind off, so that those thoughts would not interrupt my meditations. I was able to learn to control everything I felt, going to at least four hours a day. Faro made sure I was not interrupted during this time.

As I trained, we finally got a response from the World Collective. Our Telegraphic war date, as specified in the war guidebook for the World Collective. It was to be a month from that date. We would connect via an accepted invitation and from there would enter the battle of wills.

Many people, including me, did not feel like we were ready. They had Intentioneers who spent their whole lives learning telebattle.

We gathered at the place we learned to battle.

Many of you know that we are not ready, but that does not affect the spirit we have Rachel intentioned to the group *We will fight and defend our people as well as hope to create change in the World Collective. We might not win. This will not defeat us though. We have already won. We have stood up and lived so far. We created this amazing community. Soon, everyone will see we are one.*

Everyone then intentioned cheering *We are one!*

We doubled our efforts, now Faro sped up the lessons to the first battle sequence. Test one, where your opponent would create a psychological test of sorts that felt real in your telegraphic that you would have to complete to move on. The problem was in order to win you had to think as your opponent would and win as your opponent would. There would be three sequences and you had to win two out of three.

Faro created the first test for me. I did not win the battle of wills and was sucked into his test. I was placed into a forest, it was beautiful. The trees gleamed of green flowers, and the sky was a beautiful pink blue color. I was astonished by the beauty and saw these little animals flying, they had little scales, see through beautiful wings, and gorgeous large eyes. One flew to my shoulder and I looked at it, adoring it. More started floating down beautifully hanging on the trees, looking down at me, painting the trees with their wings. I was about to pet it when it bit me. The bite felt like a thousand daggers and I screamed in pain.

I started to run through the forest but felt the bites of all these creatures, from my shoulders to my back crying out in pain. *What am I supposed to do?!* I intentioned to Faro, annoyed and in pain. I felt the blood from the bites fall everywhere. I then saw a river and I jumped into the river.

All of the sudden I feel my flesh tear and I scream and look to my right, a large animal with huge teeth was biting off my arm. I screamed and tried to intention something, trying to use my rage or will. None of it worked.

I woke out of the battle screaming Faro hugged me. *You are safe, you are here.*

What were you doing?! I cried out in our telegraphic sending my feelings. I could feel he felt sorry for the way I felt but he also felt like his purpose of this exercise was done.

Battles are not easy, you can't just jump onto a river, you have to assess your opponent's mind. Push for clues to open with your will and they will. Are you ready to go again?

After a second I closed my mind. *Yes* I intentioned. And then I was shot back into Faro's forest. This time right away I used my will, the will of the rage and as the creatures descended I could feel Faros thought. Where he put a blocker, I noticed if I ran forward through the bushes the creatures could not follow me, he did not create a space there. It was blank. *Good!*

Faro intentioned and appeared.

Most people think of running left or right, very few think to run forward through the bushes. Be aware that some are good enough to trick you with their will thoughts as well.

Go again. I intentioned, determined. He put me back into the forest and this time when I willed it, I felt him intentioned nothing to the right. I ran forward again but this time behind the bushes was the river, and again the creature with teeth got me.

You have to learn the mind and learn its tricks.

It is impossible, how am I supposed to will your thoughts when I can't?

You must try harder. The lesson is done for today. In your meditation practice your will.

I did and for weeks I was put into Faro's forest until I learned his mind.

This is taking too long! I intentioned once to Faro, frustrated. *Now I know your mind, but how will I know others?*

You need to learn to feel it as it moves and changes. You must keep pushing your will until you see a way out.

I don't think I can...

That is not your will speaking that is your cowardice.

No, it is not! I intentioned angrily.

Good, now use that! Faro intentioned and it only made me angrier.

This time it was a new setting, cliffs that were steep and shallow. I was balancing off the edge of one about to fall into a deep ravine. Immediately I intentioned myself to stay and balanced perfectly on it as my rage spread through his mind filling the crevices, to see the clues. One was the wind that was like a current, two was that there was no sun, so he must have been hiding some way to get out. I looked at the other cliff and knew what I had to do was to jump. With everything inside me all my rage and will with the current I jumped. I used my arms to keep myself up, wind milling. My foot touched the edge of the cliff and I willed myself forward tumbling onto the cliff my face it the ground. The impact hurt but I laughed knowing that I had defeated Faro.

Impressive when you use your rage. You found a shortcut I didn't even know existed. I could see he was worn though and felt how the rage had hurt him. *Now go so I can rest* I felt him wheeze. I felt Boon sigh. She was watching from afar the whole time. It felt like, disappointment.

I am not trying to be violent I intentioned to Boon, feeling the rage still sear inside me.

I know humanling. She intentioned mysteriously and vanished.

I did not feel bad for Faro, well, maybe a little, but I felt ready and angry. Dina could feel me when I teleported in. I was still filled with the rage, it filling my body.

Meditate now and turn your controls on. Dina ordered, and I did as I agreed I would do with her. I have the rage simmer and my happiness control come on though spurts of the rage tried to poison my mind as I meditated. I had to let it out, I was like a boiling kettle, those ancient tools that people used to heat water, holding the steam.

After I was apologetic, and Dina did not talk to me. I could feel her worry and annoyance. I came up behind her as she was angrily laying out our table for nourishment and kissed the back of her neck. *Maybe I need some deeper meditation,* I intentioned to Dina. She sighed and caressed my head behind her, on her neck as I kissed her deeper.

She turned around and I pushed her up onto the table. She bit my shoulder as I kissed her neck, sucking and licking it at the same time I stopped to intention *Ouch* but in a good way and she felt it. On the table we loved each other releasing our fears and anxieties. She was biting me, roughly as I groaned and nibbled on her nipples, she groaned.

It felt so good to get out the anger and love together, feeling hers as she felt mine we roughly loved each other until we both came, multiple times.

Finally, we lay panting in sweat, with some blood and bruises but feeling released.

I guess the table is ready now I intentioned to her and she bit my shoulder again as I laughed and fixed the place we had loved each other on.

17

BATTLE

I woke up the morning of battle groggy from the night before. I did not sleep well and was going through the training in my mind. Boon lay beside me in her big heap. I was glad to see she was not upset with me. Though she never intentioned she was I felt she was disappointed. I pet her on her head as she woke up going against my hand to press down more.

Good morning, Love I said to Boon.

Good morning humanling She responded lazily and spread herself out to be pet more still sort of sleeping.

She could feel my anxiety and exuded calmness as I thought about the battle.

I went over and over it so that I would be ready. Dina was doing the same though she was more relaxed since she had more training than me. She was also petting Raph who was kicking his leg out making a low hum sounds meaning he likes what she was doing.

We both said our goodbyes again to our kinderling. We gave them hugs as they sent us strength.

Remember I am always with you Boon intentioned via our private channel. *Please come back all together this time.*

I did not realize that my life affected hers. She felt this and laughed. *We are bonded humanling, that is the price we all pay for love.* I hugged her again, my newest and closest sibling.

We gathered outside of our camp in case we failed, trying to never show our location. I squeezed Dina's hand as she squeezed mine. I could feel how anxious everyone felt, we were not sure what to expect. They could change their laws at any time, we had to win the battle of wills first.

The invitation was sent, and we received it. *Hello* the Grand Avo intentioned we could see her from her rooms along with others in the battle room. *It is my sadness to say that we are now at war and it will commence shortly. Please pick four people as we pick ours. Choose wisely as I know you have some unqualified people.*

In our private channel Faro and Dina could feel my rage building as I could feel theirs, I felt fear from others in our group and definitely anger from Rachel. In our channel Dina, Faro, and Rachel, and I all offered ourselves. The rest of the group chose to watch anxiously, though most felt relieved that we intentioned forward.

I felt four more intentions. All were my siblings, Aria, Tiago, Reze, and Yalka. I felt their feelings of sadness for me but how sure they were in their fight. They were stone cold, and I knew my Avo did this to distract me. I would not be distracted by the fact that my siblings had fallen, in fact it only made me angrier and more focused.

In a separate channel, all four of us connected together as people watched us in a cloud channel, one that would not be touched by what we did to each other.

Begin was intentioned and right away I used the rage and I felt Faro, and Dina using it as well. Faros was expert in the way he was using it but we felt so many things at once at one time we were without oxygen, another time our bones were being broken one by one, another time a shrill horrible sounds was making our ears bleed, and lastly was when we were being roasted as if we were in an oven smelling the flesh... flesh of people. Tiago was the first to go out screaming, then Dina, then Rachel I held on using my rage, finding it almost too easy to use and not concentrating on how many of us were left.

All of the sudden the four of us found ourselves in the desert, nothing for miles.

They were cheating Dina screamed through the screeching wind via our telegraphics.

Yes, they used something I never felt before Rachel intentioned. *We don't have time for this!* Faro intentioned and we could feel my four siblings we poked them with our will to find clues. A masked man appeared in front and started to run. We followed trying to keep up, he was almost too fast. We had to keep up our will to push forward, Dina, Faro, and I using the rage, Rachel still not too far behind using her will. Rachel started slowing though, her will being too frail. Faro, noticing Rachel was slowing push his will into the minds of our opponents and saw we all had to complete this sequence together. He ran back and picked up Rachel, hoisting her on top of his shoulders and then used his will to run faster it was draining him I could see so then I went back to hold Rachel on my shoulders.

It seemed like we were running for hours after this man, no time to think and to push our will into the opponent's further, no time to stop. I pushed my will as much as I could as Rachel was almost falling off me. I was distracted by the reality created and I did not notice a door suddenly appear to our right. Faro made it first to the door, then Dina. I willed as much as I could to get to the door, but I had already passed it. Dina and Faro and Rachel were intentioning anxiously to get to the door. I willed as much as I could but the next thing I knew we were back in the battle channel.

We breathed heavily, our hearts pounding. In the channel, we could feel the fatigue still from the battle before. Our opponents intentioned they won the first sequence. I felt the frustration and sadness from my people, that we lost a round.

We had to win the next one so that we could win the battle. My Avo interrupted before the next battle and intentioned *Since you lost the first sequence in the next one we get to choose who is able to go into that sequence.*

What, there are no laws that state that! I intentioned, she could feel how I felt and I felt her happiness to my anger, and some fear.

You and Dina my dear are picked to go through the next sequence together.

Fine Dina intentioned, *We will go through the next one on one condition. There is no third sequence. If we win this, we win the battle.*

My Avo thought for just a moment and then replied *Done.* The next moment Dina and I were swept up into the next sequence. We were by the lake, our lake.

What twisted thing do you think my Avo has in mind? I intentioned to Dina.

I have no idea, she replied cautiously.

Suddenly the plastic trees became alive and one tendril of a tree latched onto Dina's leg.

Don't move I intentioned to Dina, quickly trying to figure out what to do next, using my will to pry through the intentions. I felt Dina doing the same. *Leave her.*

I felt the intention strongly in my telegraphic.

Dina felt the same, her mouth agape as the plants slowly entangled themselves around her.

I won't! I intentioned to Dina and I could feel Dina's fear as well as her confidence. She nodded at me. *Do it, it is not real.*

No, I will never let you die alone, even if it does not last, I will never leave you.

I tried touching the plastic plants that had snaked their way around her arms now and tried to free her.

My hands burned with a searing pain, feeling the intention *Leave her!* Getting stronger. *No!* I screamed and I let the rage consume me, and with my will I pulled back the tendons off Dina and she screamed as I did, knowing the rage was not in my control anymore, she could see my eyes were distant, and I fell back with a scream like roar. Letting out all my pain.

Dina felt it and as the whole place went white I could hear her intention *My love, you are hurting me.*

Let go the intention felt like it spanned beyond space and time. It was Boon, I felt her force me back into my normal range of emotions.

I was so lost in the rage but her pain I felt it in my heart and let go. We were back in the battle room. We had won. My Avo I felt was upset that I did not win the way she wanted me to win and also had fear on her face.

You have the rage, my spring, that is not something that should be here anymore.

She is a curse upon this world, a leader watching mentioned and others agreed.

We should go Rachel intentioned and with one second before our telegraphics were seized we went out of our battle sequence and woke up in our battle area. We then quickly teleported to the camp and hid our tracks.

What happened?! Latla asked *We were watching but it all went white.*

I am not sure Dina replied, intentioning to me that she wanted to hide the fact that the rage existed.

Did we win? I asked weak, Dina and I leaned on each other. Faro and Rachel held the other sides of our arms up.

No Faro said, *that has never happened before, I am not sure what they will do.*

They are probably mobilizing everyone, not in the World Collective, but in the International Unity. Rachel replied. We all looked at her *I read in the battle of the Norths when Ofro...*

Let's discuss this later as Dina and Atlia need to rest, they are heroes! Faro interrupted, and everyone cheered although confused at what will happen.

Dina and I took that as our cue to leave and we teleported to our cottage. I first ran to Boon who I saw was on the floor, looking withdrawn. I hugged her and gave her all my intentions of love. I felt her, she felt weak in her telegraphic.

I am fine humanling, I am centuries old, I will recover your rage is not the first that I have stopped, though it is powerful Boon intentioned as tears ran down my face falling on Boon.

I never want to hurt you please don't ever do that again I intentioned *I have to if it threatens everyone, but you will learn humanling, just hopefully in time enough that I won't have to do anything about it again. Now let me rest, your humans are packing for you, it seems we have a journey ahead of us.*

There was Beleeka and Telepa... *Packing?* I intentioned and both looked up at us. *We heard what happened* Telepa intentioned and he could feel my confusion *They know about the rage, you have to move, I know what they do to people who have that, the whole world will hunt you down until you are annihilated or used.*

But Faro and Dina... I responded

Yes, but their rage has never been uncontrolled, and they have not lived with it uncontrolled. You have which makes you a target. Rachel intentioned.

I know you are tired, but we must move now Telepa intentioned.

She is not coming Dina intentioned to everyone, included Beleeka - indicating her. We felt Raph beside her intentioning agreement.

It is fine, I forgive her. I need to in order to move past it, I am so tired now, can we go? Feeling my weak intention Dina was concerned and then everything went black.

I woke up to warmth and opened my eyes to see we were in a tent made from real trees and leaves. It was a large one and we had a local televice with us to make it warm for all of us. I assumed we had an invisibility dome around it as well. Dina hugged me so hard when I awoke and started kissing me right away. *I need to breathe* I intentioned to her and I felt her laugh and her love for me and her worry.

Back to life I see George was with us, the old man was doing some sort of stretch, I am not sure what it was.

I could feel everyone had felt my embarrassment at that moment and Telepa started, smiling *We did this for you yes, but also it gives us a chance to explore too! Who knows what could be out here.* It was the first time I felt excitement in Telepa's voice, the first time in a long time.

How many people are here? I sat up groggily, unsure how to sit on the hammock, it felt like I had too many of those grass drinks, what George lives on. And then I felt around everyone's presence, Nurium, Faro, Rachel, George, Telepa, Beleeka, and of course my Dina, Raph, Boon, and two other kinderling Lila and Raka, George and Faro's kinderling.

There are more people outside I felt Dina say and I felt half of the members of the battle group, the rest of the kinderling herd plus some healers, and some others.

Wow, this many people wanted to explore? I asked Dina surprised. *Do they know?*

Yes, Dina said, *All of our people know about the rage now but we have protected our tracks. All of the people here follow you...* she smirked a little before she said *Black Dove.*

I smiled at her and fake attacked her with kisses while she was laughing at me and saying "Stop" but intentioning *more.*

We then stopped to join the group and I caught up in the center of the huge tent what the plans were.

Boon followed me to the middle of the circle along with Dina and Raph.

We are already moving south; the World Collective won't dare to go into the southern territories. Faro intentioned.

The southern territories I intentioned *Wow, I can't believe that you all are traveling with me. What is our plan?*

We hope to go south and claim our own society. We can grow there away from the International Unity, it is the one place they won't go either Dina intentioned.

But isn't it all... dead? I intentioned the question, but I felt others wondered that too in our group channel.

I heard there is magic there, they don't use technology and are all deformed from the Greatest War Rachel intentioned and I felt others internally nod.

That is ridiculous... I was about to intention when Boon cut me off.

There is some sort of old magic Boon confirmed *And the southern borders will be fine as long as we are with you. We know the southern borders and there is a herd of us beyond it. It is a different land though, and all of you must be prepared for the humans. They are the only ones you need to worry about.*

Magic. There were so many books about it, fake books my Avia told me, and he would then wink. It was never confirmed, but he said that was mostly the fake books were in western culture. In other cultures, magic was an accepted part of reality. It sounded ridiculous, but I trusted Boon, no matter how unbelievable she sounded.

She felt my thought process and sighed to me in our private channel. *Yes littling, we know this is a great deal for you to understand, humans have always wanted to prove things via human methods. This, magic, is what we animals understand. Don't take it lightly, it can cause you harm if you underestimate it.*

So why are we going there again? I intentioned to everyone, and Dina answered *Because we have to, my love, and maybe we can make peace with them, maybe they are a misunderstood people as well.*

I sighed, and we went onto our plans to move south and then west. We were already close to the borderlands and all we had to do was hide a few more days and have our map team try to teleport by miles, which was risky since you could end up anywhere though the telegraphic would create a dome ball around you, it is still not pleasant to get stuck over lava or in the middle of the ocean. Boon wished to walk the way and said she and the other kinderlings knew the way but refused to teleport.

You should want to see everything of this world. She would intention. Kinderlings did not understand the expediency of having to move fast. They believed whatever happened would happen and in the end, all will be well.

What if we walk the way there? I intentioned and some people gasped and groaned at this old way of transportation. Walking was only to keep healthy, not to transport ourselves.

I will do it too Beleeka chimed in and I could feel Dina's annoyance but only via our channel.

The kinderling laughed at us that this was even a discussion for they preferred to walk everywhere and thought humans were so odd to want to "speed up life".

We gathered a group and decided to go out of the tent to walk around in the south. Our telegraphics had their oxygen translator on in case when we got to the border the levels changed though Boon scoffed and confidently walked over muttering *Humanlings.*

As I exited the tent I saw huge plants that covered the area. They were beautiful with petals that stretched out over us, bright yellow, blue, purple, and red. These trees were gorgeous and looked like a mix between some old flowers I recognized of sunflowers and hydrangeas with tall green stems as their trunks. We walked through and were amazed at what we saw. There were these little animals that were sleek and looked like the extinct animals, the dolphins that were a dark purple and hopped up in and out of the ground blowing soot out of two holes on the top of their heads, they had instead of fins wings that flapped out to go longer distances. I loved the way they moved. It was almost trance like.

Don't look at the grounders I felt Boon intention. *That is how they deter their hunter, by dazing them. You will be walking in circle for days.*

There are animals that hunt them? I queried to her in the channel Dina, Raph, and I had.

Humans Raph responded. *The humans here are different, they are no better than those you called your family.* Dina hushed Raph, ever since they had been bonded, he always defended Dina to me, sometimes treating me like I was not enough for her.

Oh, so what will we do when we see the Southern Founders? Dina asked.

Luckily, I studied them when I was... I trailed off my intention, feeling Dina squirm, thinking I was a part of the leaders of the World Collective. It made me squirm as well, *In any case, we can offer them our nourishment, they like offerings.*

I just hope we don't see any George intentioned.

You don't want to intentioned Lila, George's kinderling.

We felt the kinderling chuckle, apparently it meant something to them.

Where shall we camp? I intentioned to Boon.

We go, two streams to the front of us and then we should reach my herd. Keep in mind humans, all the animals here may be different than we remember. We were here around 300 years ago. Be cautious of the plants too, let your kinderling smell them as you are close by to make sure they are okay for humans. Your telegraphics have not expanded to knowing this region. Boon intentioned with happiness and excitement to seeing her herd again, and caution for the rest.

As we set up camp I heard a rustle in the leaves. That is when my vision cut out as I felt a sharp pain in my head.

18

RUNNING

I woke up, my head splitting. *I really need to kick this habit of going unconscious.* I thought to myself and Dina, but I could not feel Dina. I saw the light shining through the trees somewhat. That is when I noticed I was upside down and hanging. My feet were numb. I groaned and then I heard a hushed intention.

In the bushes I saw Boon, Dina, and Raph.

What the...

Shhh Boon intentioned more sternly in a private channel with Dina, and Raph.

She can intention to you, but don't intention out, your telegraphic has been poisoned Dina intentioned.

"Poisoned?!" I said allowed in a whisper. "Who did this?"

We are unsure, Boon found you right away though, they must not know we have kinderling.

"It's the Southern Founders," I sighed. "I read this is something they could do, to make sure we are not spies from the World Collective."

You did not think that was worth mentioning ahead of time?! Dina intentioned. I felt her worry and annoyance with me.

Of course, your species would resort to this when they are wary Raph intentioned self-righteously.

They don't know better. Boon intentioned to Raph, soothing his annoyance too as did Dina by petting him.

So, what are we supposed to do? Intentioned Dina.

"I don't know, just hang out? I feel great," I said out loud.

That is the poison speaking, Boon intentioned to Dina who I felt was annoyed, my woman of action.

Dina, I felt wave this off in her mind and before she could do anything we heard someone say out loud, "A quien tenemos aquí?"

It was a man with bright blue eyes, tan skin, and black hair. He looked so strange, like old humans did, he looked as if he was right out of the Southern Founders book I read so long ago. He had brown simple cloth that wrapped around his chest and baggy pants.

I was rusty with other ancient languages, so I asked to change, "Habla usted Inglés?"

He laughed at that. "Yes, I speak English. I am happy to speak any of the real languages us humans should be speaking. I saw your telegraphic is very active. I assume you are from the World Collective?"

Southern Founders spoke in old tongue, so no one would know their intentions.

I laughed and said, "Yes, yes, we are here because I was from the World Collective..."

Stop! Dina intentioned, but I felt as if I had to tell the truth.

"And I have the..." I heard a bellow and Boon came forward breathing heavily standing in front of me.

Seeing Boon, the Southern Founder had his mouth agape in awe and quickly kneeled to one knee, bowing his head.

She will be released I felt Boon intention.

"Whatever you say, greatest entity." He kept bowing and I felt the hold on my telegraphic stop, all the poison leaving my system. The other Southern Founders came out and untied me. Dina caught me as I tried to stand *Hi* I intentioned drunkenly to her.

Yeah, yeah, yeah, She said and shook her head laughing.

Boon took the Southern Founders to our camp and before Faro could release anything on them she let everyone know they were welcomed.

We have a truce of sorts with the Southern Founders, they view us their givers of life as we saved them and their ancestors from destruction. Please welcome them.

We sat down, and I asked Boon *Why did you not just tell us this?* In the private channel with Dina and Faro. *Because I was not sure what kind of people your people were fighting, they may have changed over three hundred years. Jared* she motioned to a tall man with pale white skin and orange freckles *has been around almost as long as I have. I taught him how to nourish and heal his body with his telegraphic. And so they are still around, unless the World Collective has kept killing them.*

Excuse me Jared intentioned as we share our food and got to know the Southern Founders. *Now I have learned you are the ones who freed the lessers. Half of our camp is lessers from all over the World Collective. We call ourselves the Freedom Founders, or you may know us as the Southern Founders. All we want is peace with the World Collective, but they send an army now and again to kill all of us. We could use your help to fight them.*

The World Collective does not kill people Beleeka laughed nervously in the channel.

They do, said a navy eyed tan man. *I know it seems like they don't, I was originally part of the World Collective as well, but they have so many terrible secrets...*

We are just happy to be here to get to know likeminded folk. George intentioned and Lila rolled her eyes.

Why did you try to warn us about them? I asked Lila on the kinderling channel.

Because they are so annoying they treat us like gods. She intentioned and I felt George laugh at that as did I. That did not sound like a bad thing to me.

Throughout the week I saw what she meant though. The Freedom Founders tried to give everything to the kinderling, always fussing over them, and trying to make sure they were happy. Raph was in heaven and Dina was amused and annoyed half the time as all the humans were petting and feeding him.

Boon internally laughed at Ralph as she herself told the Freedom Founders to leave her alone and would hide behind me. *No thanks* I would signal to them.

We ended up going to their village to live there, though the kinderling set some new ground rules so they could be left in peace more. The Freedom Founders bowed and tried to not to do anything, though it seemed hard for them.

The village was nestled into the mountains. Currently it was nice at their village, they called the time of the year Spring. All of the tall flower trees bloomed on the mountain and many people lived in the stone and earth carvings in the mountain or in the flower trees, there roots leaving a natural hole that people could live in. All of the founders had cloth on, they gathered them from these tall plants called ilias that were in a field. They were so tall, flying high above your head. People climbed them with the fibers from the ilias to get the plant fiber and made what ancients called clothes. Most people wore the same baggy pants and cloth over their chests though of all different colors like the flowers they were surrounded by.

I loved them and put them on immediately. *Don't think I will be wearing those things anytime soon, they seem very uncomfortable* Dina intentioned and I laughed at her. The founders explained to us how to make them and what clothes they wore during each season. Many people made their own clothes though there was a group of people signed up for the task of making them. They were more intricate in the winter time thought in summer they went nude or used the pants but no tops. They did not use their telegraphics and wanted to be different than the World Collective. Respect wise they were not very different, respecting each other's bodies and having the same law of attention only given when they felt the peak of interest was mutual.

Jared led a group of us on a tour of the mountains which I had never seen before and taught us about all of the flowers we could eat. There were huge flower trees that surrounded all of us. They were called florias. There were all types of florias, the closest I could relate them to were ancient flowers in my telegraphic called hydrangeas, lilies, and geraniums. They ranged from bright pink, to yellow, to deep blue, to bright red, to teal green. Walking through the flowers I touched their thick trunks. All of them had different trunks, all were smooth. Some were twisted with leaves running up the sides of them, others were knotted and had flowers hidden in the holes of the trunk. I touched the smooth trunks with my hands as I always had been drawn to nature, real nature. I felt the trunk and sighed as I moved my hands up and down them. They had a smooth but catching feeling, as some of your fingers got caught on the trunk. They were not grossly perfect like that of the World Collective plastic flowers.

They had small holes where some of the smallest animals moved in and out. The animals on the flowers were just as beautiful and diverse in color as the flowers. All of them had bright colors that seemed as if they had lights on them. Their shells were hard though some had soft underbellies. They stopped if you felt their shell and would roll onto their shell to have you scratch their underbellies. I would do this at time to time to satisfy them, these little cute bug-like creatures. We called them gleepers. They had huge black shiny eyes that blinked at you when you did not pay attention to them. They were as big as my hand, long with barely any body shape, and they seemed to be the smallest creatures around the mountain.

Dina would laugh at me, playing with the nature, so connected to it. I felt she was close to it too but was not as forthcoming as I was to want to touch every part of it. *Sometimes, you could just leave it alone.* Dina intentioned once. I laughed *I agree if it wanted to be left alone, somehow, I am just drawn to them.* I said to her, touching the trunk of a tree once.

And they to you she intentioned when she saw a small army of gleepers around me, rolling on their shells waiting to be petted. I laughed and agreed to give them love. I felt a rumble go through their body, purring like ancient cats did.

We were to only go through the forest near the village though I longed to adventure more. I could feel that pull of wondering what was up the mountain.

Dina once took me there, she did not listen to anyone's authority, including Jared's.

Dina I intentioned to her once I realized we were going beyond the forest up the mountain, she shushed me. We went up through the forest to a field of blue tall grass. We went through the grass to a flower tree with a hole in it next to a small swimming hole. I laughed and knew right away this was our new secret place. Dina always had to find one everywhere we went, always needing a place to ourselves.

We swam in the fresh teal water, it was so beautiful to feel the water outside of the dome. It felt so smooth, but also was not perfect like the dome water. It had all different types of green, blue debris that floated and fell to the bottom as we walked into it. I watched it sparkle through my fingers. If I did not have the World Collective coming after me, I probably would have appreciated it more. Dina's eyes matched some of the colors of the water, the water changing colors from the sun peering through the flower trees that painted parts of the water with green, blue, pink, and purple.

Dina was easily at home though she refused the clothing and was her own authority in many respects. Jared did not seem to mind though, he said all people were free and that his rules were just crucial suggestions. Anytime he saw Dina and I going off to our secret spot, coming back wet in what the founders called spirit water he would sigh and let it go. He said out of everyone he trusted Dina and I to take care of ourselves.

Dina was not always trying to rub against Jared's authority. She surprisingly got into creationing nourishment, she is more of an eater in my mind, but she loved learning from Jared. He had roses, as we discovered my Avo's garden was not the last of the roses in the world and to Dina's delight Jared taught her how to cook with them. Dina loved sweets and made a creamy dessert with roses she called "creme de la rose", which she made up in old language.

Jared knew so many things and told us about what happened. How they were in another underground bunker and the kinderling had found them and let them out. By then all the war had happened, but the kinderling found a place they could live that was not touched. It was up north and southeast, so they made the long trip.

Jared at one point sat us all down to tell us his story.

I was in the south at the time, we had many different colonies and many different names. Our people were always at war, while in human history it was considered the most non-violent time, what made it more violent was the weapons. A horrible weapon was founded called the nuclear bomb. It went off in a place called Japan years earlier, and people saw the awful destruction it brought. We also used the Earth without care for her, though there were people trying to stop it, not enough believed or acted on it. Over time the leaders of this world were replaced with more violent people as climate change took over, and they blamed this or that, wanting more jobs to live in places they were destroying with these invisible made up entities with more personhood rights than people have called companies.

At the same time, there was hope. Alison Singer (he intentioned the image of Alison, her eyes blue and her skin was white with red hair) *created the telegraphic, and it was first installed in 2023. The first time humans could feel each other's thoughts, feeling, emotions.* (We could see the first humans she installed it in crying at the feeling of another person.) *She created it because she hoped it would change the way people think about each other. They would do more things for others naturally and it worked.*

Most people wanted it for selfish reasons (because it was a new technology that was more convenient than their current technology called a cellular device). What she did not expect was people putting up the blockers themselves. They felt uncomfortable feeling each other's feelings and just wanted to use the technology to teleport, communicate and work, play, or control their surroundings. She made it from a mix of biology and technology, so it would grow with us and be passed on to our children. Before the telegraphic, couples who were of the same sex could not have their own children, this made it so. It was extraordinary, the power the telegraphic had, but it disheartened her that most did not use it to connect more with each other. She and a group of others tried to pass laws to keep the emotions turned on.

They were dismissed, and things escalated. Wars were soon all over the world, being fought by other countries in poorer places. Once they were out of those places to fight in, the fight was brought to homes of the large nations. That is when the hydrogen bombs were released. Five of them nearly destroyed half the planet. The fighting stopped when climate change sped up from the fallout. Huge storms of cyclones, volcanoes, hurricanes, and tsunamis wiped out almost all the people. Everyone who could be underground was already from the nuclear fallout, but climate change is what cleaned up the rest.

To protect everyone she knew who had the same ideals as her, Alison created the dome before all of this, just in case, the worst-case scenario. Those who believed in her grew as things had become worse and the World Collective was born. It was protected from everything the Earth was doing to try to fix itself, while keeping humans alive. They saved the seeds because at the time they did not believe in eating animals.

The animals that they did have were taken from them during nuclear fallout, this was before she built the protective wall so that specific telegraphics could not get in. Before she ran, she told the people to bring peace to the world, and that in one million years it should be healthy again to habitat. Little did she know that without humans, the Earth healed herself faster than anyone could have imagined. Within 15 years from climate change flushing everything out, and normalizing the toxic materials, it was safe. They did not know in the dome, and people started to challenge Alison. She did not want people to eat others, but a new man from outside of her believers had come in. They had taken groups and groups of people in who were not original believers to save them from the outside world as long as they lived by the rules. These people decided that the ones who had been tied to what ruined the Earth should be punished. These people were voted in, due to the brainwashing of others, sharing how killing them could be humane, and using the anger of the believers who were too weak.

Alison left the community, and they allowed her to leave, feeling as if she was needed no more and so did her believers. By then Alison created a way to travel within the telegraphic without being infected by the world outside.

I met her after I heard banging on the latch. I had never known of Alison before, but she knew of our group. We were there before the war trying to fight to bring back the peace - the southern countries versus the northern ones. We used peaceful means and lost in the end. We made our bunker before the wars, knowing this may happen some day and our sustainable community we moved underground. We looked through the peephole, and I could not believe it was the Alison Singer on the other side. Her believers still live among us though she went out to find a better place in the world for us, and never returned. For years we sustain ourselves underground, anxious to get out until the kinderling came for us.

We thought the World Collective captured and killed Alison, and we heard that the rumors were true, they made other humans into lesser beings and started to eat them. When we got to the surface we vowed to take back the World Collective from the people who took over, but they kept their violent agendas to themselves and would brutally kill many of our peaceful protestors outside of the dome. We found it to be too dangerous and though we try to defend ourselves, we are never sure when they want to attack us. They think we are deformed and deranged, but we look different because we are old, we live longer than they do as Alison shared her secrets of how to live forever. Jared ended the story, all of us taking it in.

You don't look that old… Beleeka intentioned. We felt her nervous and could have sworn I felt some interest there, but the next thing we knew we were filled with Jared's laughter.

It doesn't get easier, let me tell you, but you do get wiser, I would like to think. Jared replied in good jest.

It was odd though, he looked like we were in his mid age, like me. In old language, I was twenty years old. I felt as if I could not trust him, though I could feel his whole story, see it from his eyes. As we broke I saw Beleeka go up to talk with Jared and noticed her body language and laughter.

Looks like someone can finally leave us alone I felt Dina say, she felt my disappointment, knowing she was still not over what Beleeka did.

I will never be over it Dina intentioned and I felt it, that she felt she never would be. *Maybe we should… try again?*

I felt her intention and she felt my shock and sadness at this.

Right, too soon, I am sorry love. I felt her love and shook off my initial reaction and gave her my feelings of love and acceptance.

No, you are right, we need to move on, I am just not sure about bringing another consciousness into this world.

You are not sure about this place. Dina responded she could see and feel my wariness of this new village. I felt her sadness at this.

My love, I will move past it. Don't worry, I will try to try. I sent my loving intentions to Dina and felt her excitement and love back.

She kissed me and I could feel her love.

Boon then teleported to where we were walking, on the way back to our cottage nestled in the side of a hill.

Boon, what are you doing teleporting, and your fangs are out, what is wrong? I intentioned.

We have to go Boon intentioned.

Why? Dina asked in sadness.

Because Jared is not who he says he is. Jared is Ofro.

19

OFRO AND REMMI

I could not process the intention that Boon had shared with me, I stood there like a statue.

Fast, humanling, we need to get you out of here! And the rest of the people, it is not safe She intentioned, pulling at me with her teeth gently.

I thought you knew him I intentioned.

I did, and he has tricked me for a long time, but during that story I felt who he truly was, he never let so much of himself out. Through stories, it is easy to see who the story teller really is. I felt Boon's experience of betrayal, but intentioned her love.

This is good though I intentioned

Good? How! He is a mass murderer, I felt Dina's fear in her intention.

It looks like his community welcomed him back, what if… he can teach me? He is the only one!

Ofro the one Ofro is gone humanling, there is no way he can come back from that. Responded Boon.

How do you know that? I asked in desperation and I felt Boon's anger rising though I never felt her anger before.

Because he was my humanling! I felt Boon burst out in sadness and anger.

Both Dina and I were shocked, and Boon felt this.

I am sorry humanling, I should have told you. I felt her sadness and while I should have been angry at her not telling me, I could not help but feel sorry for her and I shared that with her.

She had lowered herself to my eye point at that moment and I took her big face and looked into those dog-like eyes. *Oh*

Boon, I am so sorry. And I hugged her, as I felt her weep. Nowhere in the books did it talk about Ofro or Remmi having a kinderling.

What can I do? I asked and wiped her tears away kissing her head. *I thought you said you only bond to one human.*

At a time. She responded and stopped crying. She looked at me. *You are different humanling.* She licked my face and I laughed. *You are coupled with Raph, does that mean he was with Remmi?* Dina intentioned with a very different feeling. She was angry if this was true and if Raph had lied to her.

Yes, but... before Boon could finish Dina teleported away, I could feel her anger and want to confront Raph.

Boon, I know you, I know you must have a good reason. But I need to learn to control my rage if I am ever going to defeat the World Collective.

You want to defeat the World Collective? I felt her curiosity.

Yes, I can't leave everyone there behind, controlled by my Avo. I sent her the images of everything I went through at the farm.

I also have still not figured out what Faro made me push aside so long ago. Why my Avo is a lesser, and what my Avia Carlo meant by sending us that memory.

Boon was quiet for a moment and I could feel her thinking. She sighed *Oh humanling you will put me in an early rest, but I will support you. It seems he may have learned control but be careful.*

I will, how did you know he was Ofro?

Ofro was young when I was his kinderling, we met right after we freed them. Ofro then was just a typical man. He had not discovered how to fight with the telegraphic yet. No one even knew the rage existed. He was younger then, and it has been so long, I had to make sure it was him. We remember things, but I chose to remove my memory of him only to be sparked if he ever looked at me. It appears he recognized me as he told his story. My memory came back and I could only wait for the ending to tell you. He is different now, he must have changed his looks in his telegraphic. But I will never forget his eyes, there is something lost in them since Remmi. Her eyes looked as if they were glazed over, as if she was in a trance. She bounced out. *Old memories humanling time to make new ones, let's talk to "Jared".*

Boon teleported us to "Jared's" tent. There were two

Freedom Founders I felt who were ready for a telebattle, but "Jared" paused them with his two fingers.

Leave us he intentioned and the protectors of Jared vanished. *Hello Boon, it has been a long time.* He intentioned with great sadness. His smile melting away to a thin strip.

Hello, Ofro, why do you look like Jared? Boon replied matching his sadness.

Ofro intentioned *Jared passed a while back and this was a way I could conceal who I was.*

He went over to her and she knelt her head cautiously down and he put his head to hers, tears streaming down both of their faces.

He broke from her as they had a small conversation in their private channel, Boon nodded at Ofro.

Ofro sighed *I know why you are here, but I can't help you. I have hidden that part of myself for a long time. I don't plan to visit it.* He intentioned sternness but love and compassion towards me.

That is fine, you don't have to show me, you can tell me about it. I intentioned thoughtfully, I felt Boon listening to us both intently.

Then Dina showed up *What did I miss?* She entered our channel. Her hair was all over the place and she had scratches on her. Raph was next to her and had scratches on him too.

What the... I intentioned.

What did I miss? This is important Atlia! Dina intentioned and the in a private channel she sent *I am fine, love. I will explain it to you later.*

You missed nothing, Atlia here is vying for me to help her. Ofro continued *Though I am not sure I can.*

What do you want in return? I can do anything, I need to get this under control and fight the World Collective again. I stated passionately through my intention.

What about settling down? I could hear and feel Dina's frustration in our private channel but then her next thought, a sigh, saying *You are right, we need to help all those people.*

Anything? He said thoughtfully.

I saw Boon give him a look and I could tell they were

privately chatting as well.

He sighed *Fine, Boon,* he laughed a little. *She was always the strong one, she will fight for you, you know.*

Raph growled at Ofro, he then turned his attention to Raph. This whole time he was so worried about me it seemed as if he forgot Raph was there.

We all felt his great sadness. *I can't begin to talk about Remmi Raph, I am so* Raph then vanished... *Sorry.*

Ofro shook his head, sadly. *I won't forgive myself either. I am not sure you should ever use the rage again. It is too dangerous, just, just leave me please.* Ofro intentioned with great sadness.

But... I intentioned and Boon had already teleported us.

Well humanling, you tried, now he can't help you, you might as well forget about this rage business and settle down. Boon intentioned

Why does everyone want me to settle when you know I can't! My rage ignited they felt my sharp intention. *I am sorry, Dina.* Dina left the room shaking her head in frustration.

Ahhhh I screamed in my mind shattering things around me. I looked at the damage shocked and crumpled to the floor. *I need to do something Boon, I need to learn to control this no matter what, or I might end up like Ofro, and I need to save those people. Please.*

Boon shushed me and curled around me. *Oh, my simple humanling, it is not that easy. You will find a way, us kinderling we know these things.*

I let myself let go surrounded by Boon. *We need to do something.*

So, we shall. But you have to get Dina first. She is scared of you.

Scared of me? That saddened me greatly and I exhaled and teleported to Dina using our tether.

She was sitting at one of the village tables with Raph.

Hi I intentioned to Dina.

Hi I felt Dina begrudgingly intention back.

I'm sorry. I let Dina feel how sorry I am and how much I loved her, she let me feel her sadness and her fear and her annoyance and love.

I know She intentioned back. I sat down next to her on the stone bench.

I kissed her on the back of the neck and she sighed as I held her.

I am going to figure this out, I am going to fix this. I need to learn from him, so I can be safe and help our people.

I know you think you are doing that love, but I am not sure if this will work. If you will get better or worse. I felt Dina's fear and worry.

I am adamant to stop if it gets worse, but my love, doing nothing would be worse than trying. I felt Dina's agreement even though I felt she did not want to agree.

How will you get him to help you? Dina intentioned.

I don't know. I replied. *By the way, what happened to you and Raph?*

It's a long story Dina replied laughing. *Let's just say we worked out our issues.*

Okay I intentioned to her quizzically. I held her close, happy to just feel her, that she was not totally scared of me. But I had to do something, and I was determined to make her feel safe.

The next day Boon and I hatched a plan. I would become friends with Ofro and then would ask him to help. I started by volunteering for every task at hand. Cleaning the elimination rooms, making nourishment, gardening, watching the younglings. Everything he did, I did, and I could feel his annoyance, though I tried to wave "hi". I hoped by showing initiative he would learn more about me. It just seemed to make him agitated.

So much so he asked to port into our house on the fifth night. Dina and I accepted, and he arrived in fury.

Fine, I will teach you, I can't stand to see you everywhere. I would rather teach you and have you leave my village than see you as the reminder of what I am. I felt his anger, but it was not the rage. It was in the normal range of emotions.

He and Dina felt my excitement. *Great, when do I start?*

Tomorrow, 3 hands before the sun rises. He disappeared.

Three hands, I breathed out in sadness Dina could feel my annoyance at that even though I was more excited about working with him. Dina giggled knowing how much I enjoyed sleeping in.

What are you laughing at? I asked her with mock anger and love. She could tell I was wanting her in that moment.

She widened her eyes still laughing and said *Nothing, nothing at...* at that moment I picked her up and brought her to the hammock.

Nothing? I intentioned as I kissed her neck. I saw the hotness in her eyes and mischievousness. My goal was to have her mischievous fly from her eyes to see her true intentions, her want for me. It worked *Nothing at all* she moaned.

The next day my telegraphic woke me up. I was so tired I had to turn on my awake enhancers which I hated to do. They made you feel jittery sometimes, more so than feeling awake.

I went to the spot inside the mountain village, Boon at my side. Tall stone and dirt pillars held up the inside of the room. It was the great room where you could see everything, the whole history carved in the sides in stone and earth. I admired this room every time I went into it.

Ofro was at the end of the room, sitting in a cross-legged position. His eyes closed in meditation. Boon sat not too far beyond him and curled up to sleep more.

Sit he intentioned with sternness. In just a few days he became such a different man than the one I first met, always smiling, sending love. He now felt tired and old.

I feel you calling me old, I don't appreciate it. Ofro intentioned.

I was surprised *How did you know my inner thoughts.*

I will teach you many things people don't know, many things Alison taught me herself. He intentioned to me.

Alison, Alison knew about the rage? I intentioned back.

Yes, she studied it. It was the one reason she was afraid of making the telegraphics a part of our biology, a new biological weapon. She did not realize this until she discovered she had the rage itself. She had a theory, though it has never been tested before. It will be hard though. He looked at me sideways then waiting for my consent.

I internally nodded, intentioning I was ready for anything. He laughed *You have no idea the pain you will have to go through to control this.*

Let's just get to it already I said skeptically.

It is called the insight. This is what Alison thought may temper the rage. If you use the insight you may just be able to do it. It comes from love, compassion, and empathy which can be extremely painful when you are put in difficult situations. Are you ready?

Yes I intentioned. And the torture began.

20

TORTURE

Ofro pulled me into is telegraphic. *I need you to empty your mind of everything. Try to be at peace.* I did this by pulling up a stream, a river, where I typically went to when meditating. Watching the leaves go downstream.

Nice Ofro intentioned. *Now hold onto this.*

I did and in a matter of seconds I felt extreme pain in all my body. As if each bone was being broken. I saw each bone snap with a pop and the blood come out of it, feeling such extreme pain as it came out of me. My red blood I saw coming out of me made me queasy and I felt a humming in my ears. Images of people with fangs as teeth yelling in my face, scratching me all over came upon me. I felt each scratch as if knives were cutting me slowly, methodically, waiting for me to break. I screamed in agony, feeling each break as my muscles tore apart slowly.

Tap into your insight now Ofro intentioned. He could feel the rage building. I could not control it, I was in too much pain. He stopped, and I fell to the ground.

I can't help you if you are not trying.

I am trying I bellowed and slammed my fists down in his telegraphic and bounced myself out.

Ofro was massaging his temples, clearly angry. Letting his anger go through his breaths he said, "It is not safe for me to do this. You are not ready. Meditate at least 20 times a day and then come back to me."

He vanished. I could not help my anger and hit the real floor this time. It physically splintered under my hand, blue smoke coming from the broken earth. I jumped up, scared I could do that outside of my telegraphic. I studied the floor where my hands had just been, and ran my hand over it. *Oh my...*

The rage is changing you humanling, I suggest you do as he says before it consumes you and me. She intentioned and came over to me and lifted my head up with her nose.

Tears of frustration ran down my face and I let go of the rage. How was I supposed to even know how to use this insight or what this insight even was? Boon felt me think this.

It is there in your chest, you feel it for me, for Dina, and your people too. Just as much as you feel the rage. Sit humanling, let me teach you.

I sat down cross legged an closed my eyes. Boon came into my telegraphic easily and guided me through my mind. There was a dirt road and fields of bright pink and yellow flowers on either side. They were roses, all different types of roses. As we walked down the road I felt my love starting to grow as I saw moments of pure love. Dina laughing, I loved it when Dina laughed, head to head with Boon, love for Telepa, Beleeka, Nurium, Dina again, making love to her. We reach a grand structure built of pure gold light that changed and warped as we looked at it, sometimes it was a flame, other times pure light, a powder or a smoke. We went inside. All different colors reflected off a fiery hot center of pure white light with hues of blue, red, pink, and every color you can think of light shooting off around it. I went over mesmerized. With one finger I dared to touch it, I could feel its strength before I had even entered the room. A burst of smoke, pink and gold encompassed me, and then a gold powder fell from the sky. I felt love, empathy compassion, it filled me up so much with such a warmth my body was buzzing. I did not feel myself on the ground anymore. I opened my eyes, frightened from not feeling myself on the ground and fell to it, caught by Boon, I was almost six feet up.

I slid off of Boon and she licked me, and I laughed, filled with joy.

That is the insight. Both have manifested in your body now. Now you have more power beyond anyone known to man.

I felt the weight of this, but I could not really feel bad about this weight compared to the glee of experiencing the insight.

So how do I use that? I intentioned to Boon.

That is what Ofro must teach you. He uses his insight though he was a poor instructor to showing you yours. I believe he has a different way of teaching, one I do not approve of, but he knows more than me about the rage. All kinderlings have the insight and only the insight.

This gave me so much to think about and I thanked Boon and sat down again. I wondered why I had not heard of the insight until now. Boon told me it was because my rage was too strong, she thought my insight would be pointless against it. I meditated 20 times that day, in the hall I took turns with meditation and the ancient practice of yoga. Dina came and went, bringing me plant nourishment quietly with mock silence pretending to be extra quiet and then when distracting me smiling at me and winking. I would kiss her and felt her approval and she would leave the plant nourishment and disappear. I focused on that place inside me, controlling the joy was hard, I could see how you could get lost in it as well. It almost felt so good you might explode with gold light. I started to temper it with the rage little by little and then came down to a medium. Though I did not know how to temper the rage, I got more confident that it was possible I could temper it.

The following day I arrived early and meditated, feeling the insight. Ofro ported in and I felt his surprise, my awareness being around me now that I had the insight I could feel everyone their thoughts and feelings. I felt his unleash as well, filling me up with joy. He smiled.

I see you found it. But not on your own, I felt his annoyance as he intentioned to Boon. Boon lay quiet sleeping ignoring him.

Are you ready now?

Yes I responded in a zen state. He sat down, and I felt him pull me into his telegraphic. We stood there for a moment and then I felt the bones break again. The screaming faces with fangs. I felt my rage build but tempered it with the insight as I practiced. My rage was still more powerful than my insight and it almost took over, but I pushed it back, crying in agony. This fight between my rage and my insight lasted for what seemed like hours, neither winning. My body felt so pulled it was about to give out when my insight won and I broke out of his telegraphic breathing hard. I felt his satisfaction.

Good, again. He pulled me in again as I felt Boon's disapproval at his tactic of bringing me in again wearing me down. This time I was in something black, like sludge and it was gooey and I felt it suck me down and I could not breathe. It was sticky and felt like melted plastic, cold and hot to the touch. I could feel my skin burning off as I tried to move in this matter, gritting my teeth against the pain. The flesh of my skin peeled off piece by piece. The stench smelling of that of the farm. The memory of the farm started such fear in my heart, my rage flaring. My arms flailed, and I tried as hard as I could to not let the rage build, feeling my insight trying to bring that love and light and warmth. I felt like I was burning and drowning for eternity, my body fading, my mind pushing me forward. I felt Boon intentioning him to stop and I then could not control my rage, the anger. It flowed out of me through the mud but at the last second, I felt Boon's insight match with mine overpowering my rage and bringing me out.

I woke up on the floor coughing, still feeling as if I was drowning, my hands flailing. I then felt Boon and Ofro were arguing on a private channel I could see them through my slit eyes as I lay down on the floor, in pure exhaustion. Ofro intentioned begrudgingly to me *Fine more tomorrow, rest now.* He vanished.

Boon came over to me and wrapped around me, healing me with her insight. Dina ported in asking Boon what happened. Boon explained, and I could feel Dina's anger. *Please stop your anger it hurts.* I intentioned feeling a massive headache. Dina intentioned me home as I was too weak to. She put me on the hammock and lay beside me, putting her head on my chest. She caressed my head as she sent me love.

Rest my love she intentioned and I fell asleep.

The next day as I got ready to go I noticed Dina was ready. She wore the cloth now just like the rest of the village, not wearing the mask her telegraphic had like she did in the World Collective. It was made up of baggy light pants that were tailored at the bottom and the top was a band around her breasts.

I thought you hated the cloth I intentioned.

Well, maybe it is time I fit in. She intentioned back. She wore the green and teal outfit well, the green matching her green brown eyes.

It distracted me for only a second. *Wait why are you in cloth?*

I am coming with you to learn about insight.

That is when Faro appeared. I hugged Faro, it was a long time since I had seen him.

We are ready? Faro he said in his gruff intentions.

Wait, what is going on? I intentioned back.

We are learning about the insight, we may have not gone overboard like you, but we want to fight with you.

You can't it is too dangerous! I intentioned love, annoyance and fear. They felt this, but I felt their determination.

Fine we will see what Ofro says. I said annoyed but accepting.

We ported to the great room Ofro was there. Raph came this time with Boon and they went to a corner together and curled up.

I see we have more seekers of insight I felt Ofro. He welcomed everyone in with a smile and I frowned at this. Dina felt my annoyance in a private channel and gently intentioned *Maybe he is mean to you because you are so much like him.* This did not help my feelings toward Ofro.

We sat down and Ofro showed them where their insight was. I followed them to see theirs and observe with Ofro.

I see you are angry with me Ofro said in a private channel.

Why are you helping them I asked and felt Ofro's love for once.

Because you need them more than you think to take down the World Collective. They also have controlled rage unlike yours.

I felt sadness and hurt at this and he felt it and sent me love and support back. *I am sorry I was hard on you, but I was hopeless, you have restored my hope.*

I felt this and happiness from it. I practiced my own solo

practices he gave me with my insight and rage that were lighter as I tried to balance them on a silver scale at my stream as I felt Dina and Faro got through the brutal tests that Ofro put me through.

Faro seemed to be an expert at insight – he was one of the last people I thought could be balanced after what happened to his family. Quite a few times with the help of Raph and Boon I sent Dina my insight to save her. *Maybe you should break.* I intentioned as she sat cross legged on the floor next to me.

No she intentioned, and I felt her intention Ofro, *Keep going.*

Ofro sighed intentioning to me *She is a tough one* he felt my agreement.

She went again and though it pained me that she had to go through that pain, I knew it worked. I could feel Boon's disapproval every time, but she offered no alternative.

After a couple of weeks practicing, Dina, Faro, and I having off days, I finally felt like I got the hang of Ofro's first tests.

Now for the next test. Ofro said to me and I felt his sadness knowing how it would be difficult. He intentioned me to a blank space. It was just white everywhere. Dina was sitting in a hammock chair. Then I saw walls around her start to close in.

Is that really Dina?

Yes, I felt Dina and I ran towards her.

How do I stop them? I asked, pressing the walls with my rage might, but it was not working.

Dina, run!

I can't she said, tears streaming down her face. I could feel her trying to use her rage, but Ofro sealed it off.

My rage grew, and I tried to temper it with the insight, but it was almost impossible. I let out a huge scream and before rage could take me Ofro ported us back to the blank space. I held her and cried. *What the fuck were you thinking?* Using an old word that some of the founders used quite frequently, but here I felt it was the right usage.

I never felt fuck intentioned before laughed Ofro making me even more angry.

Stop. Boon quieted me and sent annoyance to Ofro, while soothing me as I held Dina who seemed shocked. *No Boon, I won't hide this from them this is life and death.* He told Boon. *You stupid humanlings, you think everything is life and death.* She intentioned back to him and teleported home. I could feel Ofro felt some humility from that.

Raph went over to Dina and gave her love as she sat in shock. *I did not know he would do that. I could have died. I would never let that happen my love.* I intentioned and knelt by her as she sat on the low cushion. I stroked her hair as we sat quietly.

The next day Dina and I missed practice though Faro went. I understood why he needed to, he still had revenge on his mind for what the World Collective did to his family and it haunted him knowing what was happening now still, and what he was capable of doing.

Dina did not want to miss practice and had gotten past what Ofro did and even tried to defend him, but she felt I was in no mood to discuss it.

Ofro asked to port in that night and I accepted.

"Can I speak to you privately? We can walk." He said in the ancient language. Boon, Dina, and Raph nodded internally that it was alright, and I accepted. As we walked through the flower forest I felt more at ease, as he knew the forest was my place of peace. The gleepers formed a line behind me purring waiting to be pet.

As we walked through the forest my hands grazed the flower trees feeling their liveliness. With the insight I could feel everything now including the earth moving.

"I didn't mean to hurt you. I am sorry. I got carried away as they used to say."

"Carried away to where?" I asked puzzled. It was nice to take a break from intentions though, to converse in this old way, to hear my voice aloud. Though most of the Freedom Founders spoke in old language, they started to intention to us when we arrived. I almost wished that we instead spoke in the old language, sometimes missing it, but I knew they were just trying to be respectful.

"Nothing, nowhere, anyway it's not important. What is important is you know how sorry I am and that it will be difficult moving forward without Dina's participation." At the mention of Dina, she appeared there next to me. She felt my annoyance and I felt her love and sorry.

"I will do what I need to," Dina replied.

"But..." I tried to cut in.

"Atlia, this is my decision and mine alone. I love you, but this is what I need to do to save my people. I may have forgotten that for a time, but I do not feel any less intent on saving them. I agree with Ofro, you need me."

"Fine," I grumbled, it was easy to show anger in the old language, more than the love I felt for her, so I sent that to her too.

"Then it is settled, tomorrow in the great room we meet." He vanished, and we walked home. The whole time I did not talk to Dina. She felt my worry and held my hand sending love. I then intentioned her to go, that I needed some time alone, as one of the gleepers aggressively rubbed against my leg - begging for pets.

I sat for a while with the gleepers in the forest, Dina left me with my thoughts. I wish I could protect her, to practice without her getting hurt. I knew I owed it to the lessers though to release them from the Grand Avo and the World Collective. I pet two gleepers one named Gia and the other Tito. *My head* Tito intentioned, I pet his catlike ears on his fuzzy head. He purred louder, and Gia was silent. Gleepers did not say much, which made them the best people to meditate with.

It will be alright Gia said, surprising me with a high sing song intention. Their intentions felt like little bells in my mind, light and sweet. Tito just turned more, not saying anything, intentioning to pet him more than Gia.

What will be fine? I intentioned back to her and she lay silent happily purring as I pet her belly more.

I let it go, gleepers were smart, as smart as we were but were creatures of few words. I said my goodbyes after the gleepers felt I had pet them enough and ported back to our house. Dina lay beside me, and I watched the breath go in and out of her body. In that moment, I wanted to give her everything. The consciousness she wished for, being the strong warrior she wanted me to be. I wanted to tell her how much I loved seeing her sleep, how peaceful she looked. How all I wanted for her beautiful being was peace. I got close behind her and held her, she snuggled into me sighing. I could see she was dreaming of us on the beach, the one I made when we lost our little one.

It made sense she would go there, we had been through so much, and here Ofro wanted us to go through more. Tears started to fall down my face onto her shoulders. They went down her beautiful brown shoulder, leaving a trail, a clear line down her back. She turned around slowly.

Atlia, my love, what is it?

I can't lose you, not again. I want everything for you. You deserve everything. I cried, and she held me to her perfect shoulders. I felt her love spark inside of me.

You know you are not the tyrant of me and you can't control what happens to me. She intentioned laughing sending me love. *Oh, my sweet Atlia, my sweet fool. I am doing what I want and what I want is to fight with you.* She kissed away my tears and to my lips. I felt her sweet kiss, smelling of the rose she creationed for us in her nut dish tonight.

I laughed with her, feeling her laughter. She was right, I never was in control of her, no one was. I kissed her back. *I will do everything I can to love you.* I intentioned to her my protection and love of her, she matched those intentions.

I know my love. With a sigh and her caressing my back we fell asleep entangled in softness.

The following day we went to the great room and were surprised to see Beleeka there.

I knew it, how could you hide this from us? Beleeka intentioned and Telepa and Nurium showed up. My last siblings I was close to from the World Collective. She was the last person I thought would be angry with me. I felt her anger and my eyes I felt went wide.

What's going on, how can I help with everyone? Curly intentioned and he felt our amusement at his eagerness.

I felt my Dalto, Telepa's sadness towards me first. *Do you not trust us?*

Maybe she felt she had to Nurium chimed in, always the peacemaker.

What did I not tell you? I intentioned in total confusion.

About Ofro! I heard you while forest bathing the other day. Beleeka beamed with sadness and annoyance. *You know that we have… connected. I thought he was Jared but now I find he is someone else?!*

It was the biggest offense to lie to someone you are connected with, to lie to a lover. I sent her my sorry and how I felt for her pain as did Dina, surprisingly.

Boon and Raph ignored us as they often did not get involved in human squabbles. One time, Raph compared us to the ancient animals they called chickens when they talked to each other incessantly.

Faro ported in first and Dina informed him of what happened and then Ofro ported in.

He could feel Beleeka's feelings of betrayal as she ported out.

Confused I turned to Ofro. *I thought you were only ever connected to Remmi, like Dina and I.*

All the writings are not correct though I loved Remmi with all my heart, I am one of those who falls in love with multiple people. Remmi was the one who was solely connected with me. He filled me in those days with such intense love, I needed only him. Now Beleeka I have connected with and I am afraid I may have ruined it. Please give me a few moments and start practice. He intentioned with his usual old world elegance. Ofro ignored my other siblings and left to talk things out with Beleeka.

We let Telepa and Nurium know what we were doing. They seemed afraid and accepted it.

You will need a healer after the battle Telepa said thoughtfully.

And an Intentioneer or two to help if things get rough with them. Nurium intentioned with Beleeka in mind as well.

Faro, Dina, Boon, Raph, and I conversed and agreed we needed them. Curly also wanted to help but Telepa and him fought about it. Telepa loved Curly so much and Curly helped him heal.

I better let Rachel know. He teleported and sooner than later Rachel appeared. I was so consumed with everything I had to do I missed Telepa and Rachel connecting as well. Rachel stormed up to us *Of course I am fighting beside you, I don't care if I have the rage those people took my family.*

We agreed, there was no arguing with Rachel once she had her mind set it was impossible to deter her.

We waited until Ofro came back. More people started to port in, as more knew about Ofro.

What is happening?! I intentioned to everyone confused they put two fingers to their hearts.

It's your army Dina intentioned with pride.

I don't need an army though I intentioned.

Dina laughed at this *Of course you do love, and they need to fight for their homes as well. Who are you to take that right away?*

Ofro welcomed everyone and set me up to teach the basics. Everyone had a little bit of the insight in them, so we taught that. We also found a few more people who had the rage, we found it was more prevalent in the previous lessers. The great room was soon filled with people sitting cross legged ready for telebattle lessons.

Beleeka, Nurium, and Telepa talked battle strategy and how and where we would battle. They created the ideas for what our three battles would be.

I started to do evening practices with Dina, Ofro, and Faro. Each lesson with Dina was extremely difficult and it weighed on us both. Dina had soon caught up to me and so did Faro. Ofro used us all in difficult situations. From poisonings to hangings, to even impossible things like the sun moving closer to scorch us.

It seemed impossible, both of us were so tired, we brought out ilia sleeping mats instead of using the hammock. On our mats, we just touched fingers at night, our bodies tiring out until the next morning.

I could see how everything was weighing on Ofro. Now the whole village knew, and they seemed to change how they felt about him. They were weary and untrusting at times. Our people on the opposite side were completely supportive.

There was a day when Ofro could not instruct us, Beleeka was gone too.

Boon said he needed time to rest and Raph decided to instruct everyone that day.

What is happening I asked Boon. She seemed as if she did not want to say anything, but I nudged her internally.

He is pushing too hard and is getting weaker. He built up a wall after Remmi to make sure the rage never came back. He feels the wall is falling.

Stunned I sat there in my cross-legged position as Boon instructed us that day using a different technique with the insight. Instead of using the rage to break out of a fight, she taught us to use the warmth, love and compassion to connect with the other person to break out of their battle sequence. She said that this tactic was ancient and anyone who could naturally feel their insight could do it.

When I stepped back I saw everyone, all our people glowing in gold wisps of smoky light. It was beautiful, you felt the joy in the room.

I like this so, so much better than the rage I intentioned to Dina.

Dina calmly responded next to me in crisscrossed position *That is because violence is not comfortable for you, for me the insight is harder, it is not my natural state.* That is when I noticed how I could feel her gritting her teeth to keep her concentration. I had no idea she struggled with anger like me. Even if it was not uncontrolled rage, still, having anger was difficult to control in general when the feeling suppressors were turned off.

Boon then instructed us to connect with each other to increase our insight. Our insights grew, we felt everyone, buzzing together with joy, laughter and happiness though we looked still and meditative. We felt the insight grow around us until it boomed out of us spreading.

Shocked we all opened our eyes.

Is that bad? Telepa intentioned.

No, everyone will feel beyond the Earth the next few hours, you have just healed anyone who was injured in any way. Boon intentioned as if it was not a big deal. People were intentioning to one another, cautious of this power too, even if it was just spreading goodness.

Could the insight be used for bad? I intentioned to Boon.

She looked directly at me *There is no bad when goodness is brought into the world. What humanlings do with goodness, how they manipulate it, that is bad.*

We felt the weight of her words. This was a powerful weapon that our people who did not have the rage could use during the battle to heal us, make us stronger in winning against the World Collective.

Dina and I ported to our secret water hole on the mountain. We tried to take rests there now to relax from the most painful days of practice.

I sat next to Dina as she read via Eden the history of the kinderling. Ofro shared so much knowledge in our telegraphics and Dina was in love with the history of the ancients, so much like my Avia Carlo. I wondered how he would feel, us learning this violence tempered with love.

She could feel me watching her. *What* she intentioned with the fire in her voice that typically accompanied it these days. Her intentions were usually sweet, her voice silky and smooth, but that day I could feel she was annoyed more than usual.

It's just, I don't understand how you...

How I put up with you? That is easy, I just ignore you. She said with her breathy thoughts, the fire seething underneath them.

No... I filled her with my laughter and she would not budge. *How you have a hard time with your insight.*

I felt her rage, it was not the first time I felt it, but I felt as if it had built on top of itself.

Do you know how hard it is to feel love after most of your life all you felt was pain? Do you know how hard it is to feel the love for yourself? Her eyes had frustrated tears in them, she was looking at me now and I felt her pain.

I sent her my insight and my love, and she tried not to feel it, her rage shoving me off.

See it is so easy for you. Dina replied in sadness as she felt my love temper her rage.

I laughed at this she felt my laughter. *You think it is easy for me? Dina, I may not have had your upbringing, but I have uncontrolled rage. I feel it all the time.*

She then looked at me sharply feeling for what I felt. For the first time, I released more than I typically do and she felt my rage and was shocked.

How do you... Dina asked quizzically, her silky intentions back.

I don't have a choice. I struggle with it every day. But I think because of all the people I love, even Avia Carlo who is not here, I feel I can temper it. I let her feel my insight and she let it in. The neon pink smoke powder filling her with the love I had for her.

I had to use Boon for the longest time to get some balance. I intentioned to her. She had never thought of working with Raph that way, not that he offered. He usually let Dina come to things on her own with little to no guidance.

Dina thought about it. *I will try with him.*

And with me, I can share my insight with you, I may have not lived what you have but I can share all the love I can with you. I intentioned as I kissed that soft spot on her neck and she let go of her rage, her insight and my insight filling her. She laughed at the feeling, tears coming out of her eyes and mine. I knew she rarely felt this, though she felt intense love for me, it was hard for her to accept the love, her being still recovering from her previous life.

Later, Ofro surprisingly showed up for the meeting we had with Rachel, Telepa, George, Faro, Nurium, and Beleeka. We were going to discuss strategy of what the World Collective battle would look like.

Since Atlia rage fired the last battle, they will want to eliminate her, Beleeka started with her light voice, saying what we were all thinking.

I don't know, they may want to use her as a weapon and capture her

Telepa intentioned, knowing the World Collective was more hypocritical than how they pretended to be. *Do you think they will come past the southern borders?* Nurium intentioned quizzically. *I think they will do anything to take Atlia, as Telepa said, Atlia is a valuable weapon.* Ofro replied in his elegant intention. I could feel my anger rising but tried to quash it gently with insight and before anyone else could say anything I intentioned *I am not something, I am a person, and I am here. If they think I am a weapon, why not just give me up and I can take care of myself?*

I am not sure that is a good idea Beleeka responded in her solemn intention, her usually high voice intention lowered to that of a hum *They know what the rage is and when it is uncontrolled, since Ofro they have created weapons to control the person who has it. They will experiment on you until they can control you.*

We could use her as bait. George intentioned in his old world voice and felt some shock and trepidation and curiosity to it.

It is not a bad idea Ofro intentioned.

There is no way we would let her risk that alone Faro intentioned.

I felt Dina's intention of *Over my dead body* in our private channel.

What if we did something like one of us turned all of us in? We can make them think that one of us betrays everyone. They probably think that we are naive enough to underestimate them and go into battle. I intentioned and I felt Dina's agreement.

Beleeka should do it Dina intentioned and we felt Rachel, George, and Faro who were unsure why Dina would offer up Beleeka.

Beleeka without hesitation intentioned *I would be glad to do anything for this community.*

We sat there in an awkward silence.

Well, it sounds like you all have it figured out, George said and turned to leave.

Hold on. Ofro intentioned and George stopped and looked at Ofro. *I know what you are George. You could help.*

I have no idea what you are referring to George intentioned and left.

What... what is he? I intentioned to Ofro, confused.

If he won't help us, then it does not matter Ofro responded.

We then discussed strategy of where Ofro thought they may enter.

So, we wait for them? Rachel chimed in, sounding annoyed. She was not very patient.

It is better to fight on our ground, and they will come for her. Ofro intentioned internally nodding to me.

Maybe I can do something to speed things up, like send the Grand Avo a message? I intentioned and I felt Dina internally pinching me. She was not happy with this idea.

That would work. Ofro intentioned and I felt the others agreement.

Still sitting cross legged in our circle, I reached out to my Grand Avo, for the first time in a long time. I blocked her in the past, so she could not reach me, but I knew she would have a line open.

When she connected I immediately connected her to all our channels, her face showed up in the middle of the circle.

My spring, my she intentioned right away and felt everyone else. We then all felt her discomfort and anger as her love washed away. It was a very cold anger, slowly seething.

I see this is a battle call. She intentioned.

Avo, I am not hiding from you or the World Collective anymore. I know that the International Unity wants me as well. I am here. Come and get me. Before she could say anything more I cut off our channel.

Then Beleeka nodded and connected with the Grand Avo, secretly displaying her private channel with the Grand Avo to everyone.

Sweetling, did you see how your Dalta spoke to me?! I could feel my Avo's rage, now I did not have to wonder where that came from. I could feel it in her now, not tempered with insight.

Beleeka calmly responded *Avo, I am afraid for her, I believe she has become a lesser, I am sorry I could not connect with you before, they were watching me, I had to keep my image.* I felt Beleeka's fake intentions that even had me questioning if she was really a spy or not.

It is okay, spring, just tell me where you are and give me all the information of the camp.

We felt an internal nod from Ofro and Beleeka shared all the information.

I felt our Avo get excited and thankful and send Beleeka love. *You have always been the best member of the World Collective. Kind and smart in all your learnings sweetling. I am happy to see you did not become a beast like your sister.* I could feel Beleeka almost give into sadness and anger for my Avo saying that, she released it in the group private channel.

Everyone felt for my feelings, but I had put them in a private channel with Dina. It was a great sadness instead of anger. The person who birthed my consciousness, she of all people should love me no matter what. How she could so quickly view me as something less than human was extremely painful.

Beleeka nodded internally and sent love to our Avo as she sent love back and they cut off communication.

That was really convincing, Dina said to everyone, but then noticed my pain and sent me love as I swallowed hard and tried to hide it in our channel. I shook my head and felt Dina's insight with my own.

She does not feel ready, it seems we have some time, but we need to up our dome shield around the village. We need to prepare for battle. Ofro intentioned. *They are crueler outside the World Collective, more physical, they will wipe out the whole village to get to you Atlia, we need to be ready.* He then vanished to warn his people as we did ours. The dome was erected and Beleeka and Nurium were on the lookout to feel for intentions with their self-made algorithms of who would try to surpass the dome walls.

Avia Carlo I remembered saying "There is always a loophole," he said in English out loud, his eyes crinkled with amusement. I wondered what he would think of me now, coming this far with everyone. Nothing was ever as simple as we planned it to be. I sighed and sent insight to whatever realm he was traveling now.

I hoped for his sake I could carry on his legacy, that we would win this battle.

Humanling, I will be with Raph tonight Boon intentioned. Boon often slept in our cottage unless Dina wanted time to ourselves. Boon rarely took time with Raph, and I did not even know they were lovers until Boon told me specifically. She laughed at me and would tell me kinderling love was deeper and did not need touch to keep solidifying it. But tonight, I was guessing she was drained of her insight and needed his love.

As we sat in the cottage drinking our flower root tea, Dina I could feel was not intentioning everything she felt. *What is it?* I asked Dina.

We need our own plan Atlia. We need another plan in case we fail again. I could see Dina was nervous to intention this, she always wanted to support me, but did not feel as positive as I felt all of the time.

I went over and held her gorgeous face in my hands *If we fail I will intention us out far away from where we are. We won't look, we will just jump and hope for the best.*

Your plan sounds like it is more likely to get us killed. I felt her sadness and kissed her and shared with her my love and worry too.

I will try my best not to get us killed.

What will we do if we win? She asked with some hope.

Ofro has a dome prison to put them in, Beleeka helped creation it. I am not sure what to do with them except for collect them, feed them, treat them like people but not let them out. I intentioned and I could feel Dina thinking.

Maybe in time, they will change and come to understanding. Dina intentioned with more hope sharing her insight with me.

Maybe, we can win it all. I shared my insight with her and we had done something we had never tried. Our insights came together in a clash of love, joy and passion, as I kissed her. She lovingly caressed me and brought me towards our sleeping mat. As she caressed me I could see the beautiful insight dance across my skin, this golden powder of light. It was warm and filled with pleasure like I had never felt before. I did the same to her and our love built as we moved with our fingers and mouths over each other's breasts, shoulders, face, lips and down to our pleasure centers. As I licked her and caressed her moving in and out she moaned as I did as she caressed mine with her mouth. Our pleasure, and happiness and shear ecstasy built so fast, and was beyond anything we ever felt before. As if we were one body with more pleasure than anyone in the world. Our release came at such a crescendo the golden, pink light was sent in a circular explosion outwards with a clear beautiful jingle of sound. We stayed in that moment, it was as if we had fifty of the best orgasms we ever had, feeling each other having them, only made it more pleasurable and we came again. Afterwards, I lay on top of her, my heart racing, our breaths ragged together. We could still feel the after-shock waves of pleasure coursing through us. We tingled all over with a feeling of pure bliss.

I love this insight. Dina intentioned and I laughed. There was no better way to prepare for battle than to love the person you loved most in the world, before one of the hardest days of your life.

21

WAITING

I was not sure how long it would take for my Avo to attack, but a week had passed. We still practiced every day, Ofro's tests did not get any easier, though he was not testing us anymore. We were testing each other. Faro made the best and worst possible tests for Dina and I while we also made some almost impossible ones for him.

It was better with using insight, it would temper the memories of the test battles. Waiting was hard though, especially for me. I felt ready and I wanted her to come. Even though this fight was bigger than her or me, I could not feel more tense about getting through it sooner. Dina tried to calm my nerves as I turned at every possible suspicious sound and person.

I was walking through our nourishment center once and heard someone drop something, it made a loud banging noise. I turned and sent my rage on alert and sent fire to their telegraphics. Except, it did not go to their telegraphic, it formed right before my eyes, blue and white flames bursting forth from my outstretched hand and flew towards them and pushed them back. Telepa fell to the ground with a thud screaming. I quickly used my insight to put out the fire and ran towards him. Time moved slowly as I felt like I could not run fast enough, feeling my pants fly in the wind, shuffling as I rushed towards him, as if they were holding me back. I saw his face as he fell in sharp amounts of pain.

I held my hand to his head and saw the gold, orange, and red smoky bits of insight take it away. He then looked up at me afraid for a second. I will never forget his face, eyes wide in fear, a half grimace with his breath taken away. Seeing my tall Dalto become so small in that moment. I felt everyone in the village who saw this, I felt their fear of me. It was there for just a second and he smoothed it over with a nervous smile. *It is okay, Atlia, I am fine.*

No, I... I stammered and teleported to the cottage.

Dina was surprised to see me. *What's wrong, where is everything I need for eve nourishment?*

My hands were shaking wildly. I tried to still them as I started to pack our things in a hammock bag, the one Dina and I took for camping.

What are you doing? She intentioned to me. I could feel the tears coming down my face silently. I tried to push everything in the hammock bag, not everything was fitting as I was trying rapidly to stuff it in. Then I felt Dina's hand on my face. Her warmth and insight touching mine.

Hey she intentioned and turned my face onto her chest, hugging it as I cried.

I have to go I intentioned.

What?! She intentioned quizzically and angrily.

I stood up and looked Dina in the eyes as I tried to pack again. *I am one of those ancient ticking bombs, I can't control myself and this is what she wants. She wants me to go insane waiting for her, she wants me to just go off!* I intentioned to Dina.

I then felt Dina's determination *Fine, if you want to leave, we will leave.* She said and started to add her things as well to my hammock bag. Before I could argue she said *I know you think that we will end like Ofro and Remmi, that is not going to happen.* She then took my face into her hands. *You, Atlia, are the strongest person I know. Your strength comes from the insight, not the rage. You will always be able to temper it. If you need to get away from here, then, let's do it. But you are not going without me.* I could feel her love and stubbornness. I knew I could not talk her out of her decision.

Fine I snapped and felt her satisfaction because she could feel my worry for her, and that maybe I could talk her out of it later.

Boon then showed up along with Raph. I didn't even try to reason with them or ask them how they knew I was leaving. They did not say a word to me but just curled up in a corner together waiting to go with us.

I teleported us all to a camping spot that was Dina and my watering hole. The top of the mountain felt closer to the sun, it showed through our huge old purple and bright yellow flower tree. I unpacked and hung the hammock up. Dina put the ball of blue, white light in the middle which made a dome around us, a Freedom Founders' invention. We did not say one word as we sat down. Dina read an old book she had packed, one of Avia Carlo's, as she sat on her camping cushion. She dug her feet into the dirt as she always did, she loved the feeling of the soft dirt of the outside world.

I felt Ofro try to call in. To Dina's surprise, I answered. Ofro showed up above the bubble ball of light in the circle we were sitting in.

What are you doing? Ofro intentioned confused, worried, and annoyed.

You know what happened with Telepa today, I can't be around anyone. I intentioned to Ofro.

You need to be here to protect these people, you have a whole army here behind you! You are not me Atlia, you have control...

I have control of nothing when she is around! I barked at him the rage seething inside me.

I see I have no choice. He said and left the conversation.

What... I had no idea what he was talking about. I felt Boon sigh as if she knew what would happen next.

I tried to ignore whatever Ofro was trying to say, and I tried to keep my rage at bay. It was so high from worry, and stress of when my Avo was coming, I could not help but hear it try to cajole me with feelings. That I needed to burn everything.

I tried to go to sleep that night in the hammock with Dina. I heard something, it was an intention I felt as well.

Atlia...

I knew that old world voice. In an instant I was falling to the ground with a thud, somewhere totally different than where

I was. Boon was with me I saw, and she did not fall at all she was standing there, and I felt her annoyance.

I knew you would come and try to ruin things, I will protect her from you I heard Boon bellow and I looked in the direction of where she intentioned. There stood George. Of all people he was the last person I thought I would see.

Atlia, this is the final step, the one I have been waiting for kiddo. And creature, it is fine, I will not hurt this one. George said, I saw his eyes gleam for the first time.

What are you? I asked George, remembering Ofro asking him to fight with us.

Remember when Boon said the people of the South had magic? Well that is me. I am one of those ancient people, more ancient than humans. He bowed to me, an old custom I had only read in books, but never in person.

You are insane I intentioned perplexed, nervous, and confused.

I am a mage. He said *I will let it sink in. I was captured not too long ago by the World Collective. I could have left but I felt you and who you were. Atlia, you are going to save all of us, at a very high price for you.*

What? How do you...

I know, and so does she, your kinderling. Have you not wondered why you are different, why you can control uncontrolled rage? He stepped closer to me, I did not want to hear the answer, but knew I had to.

How?

You are one of us. You are descendant from the line of Alison Singer, she was one of us. You think a human could have made that technology? It was what she made to save the Earth, using what we had and making it artificial, so those stupid humans would not end our world.

I sat down on a cushion that George brought over. *That means my Avo.*

Not your Avo, your Avia Carlo.

My Avia Carlo? I saw his face again, eyes crinkled in laughter. How many secrets did he keep from me?

What about Beleeka, she is Avia Carlo's direct littling.

Ahhh, your sister. She shuts off that self of hers, you can ask her about it. She hides it deep inside herself, she always wanted to be human. She uses her telegraphic to dampen the feelings she has still.

I had to think about this. It meant Beleeka had the rage too, and the insight, just as much as I did. I would have to ask her how she did this later. This is what my Avia Carlo meant when he said to take care of her. He knew, the whole time he knew we were not...

Ofro knew, but he wanted to speak to your... humanity. The thing is you are not human, you never were. There were always two species of humanoids, but humans, being primitive as they were, we had to not make them aware of us, look at what they were already doing to each other. We lived in a world above them, they barely noticed as we lived our happy, fulfilling lives. But then, it changed. We could not stop their pollution and stupid weapons. We never thought it would get to this point.

I am not human? This scared me, and I looked at my hands, they looked like human hands.

No, they are our distant cousins. We are the ones that they call magic, we call it insight.

But humans have insight I said confused.

George got down to my level. *Atlia, distant cousins, stay here with me. All creatures have insight, but we have the insight beyond a human's wildest dreams and we have a way to harness it naturally. Telegraphics, we never even need one. You are a half breed, but the mage gene is powerful, it takes over whatever consciousness a mage mates with.*

Speaking of mates, I thought of Dina *I have to tell Dina, she will be so...*

Do you want to blow up half of the mountain? George intentioned.

No I said with a sigh. *What do I need to do, how will I be able to be there?*

I have traps for your Avo, I know exactly when she will come, do not worry about her. Now I know you saw your insight and rage manifest outside of the telegraphic. That is what we can do. That is what makes us different.

I don't want to...

You need to. I know the World Collective taught you that violence was not the answer. This is not violence, we can use it without hurting people. You need to learn to let the energy out. Ofro has kept you cooped up with

all your energy, no wonder why you were exploding at Telepa.
What do I do?
Get some sleep mageling and we will work tomorrow. If that is okay with Boon.

Boon the whole time was silent and huffed *I hate magelings more than humanlings, remember you will always be half humanling though the mage is strong in you.* She huffed a few more times as I imagined a dragon would sound and lay down.

I lay down next to her taking this in. *How many things could I possibly be?*

I wondered, and I felt Boon reply *You are just you Atlia, humanling, just Atlia.*

To the rhythm of her breathing I fell asleep, wondering how angry Dina would be but sending her love. I sent her a message for when she woke.

The next more I woke to a ringing in my ears. Someone seriously wanted to get in touch with me. I connected to Dina.

Where are you? She seethed, and I could feel some of her rage. Her anger hurt, and so did feeling her hurt and worry.

It's not my fault George didn't…

No one did anything you just disappeared. Where are you! I felt her scream in my head with worry and sadness.

Dina I intentioned her love and I felt her try to bat it away, too angry at me, but she could not hold that resolve and felt it.

It's a long story, I have to be away from you for now.

Tell me what happened.

Well I am not human…

What? I felt her anger wain and her curiosity take over. *How?* She asked suspiciously, I could feel she thought I may be losing my mind.

I am something called a mage.

A what?

A mage, it's a distant cousin of humans. Avia Carlo was one. I could feel she thought I had lost my mind.

Hello George chimed in. *Atlia has bigger problems to worry about Dina, what do you want?*

I could feel Dina's rage again *I want Atlia back, what have you done to her?*

Nothing, I told her the truth of who she is. She is not a kook. She is a mage. What she says is true. What Boon said about the Southern people, she was referring to us.

So, you are one too? I heard some shock but also some acceptance in Dina's voice, as if it explained many things.

Yes, how do you think I helped you so well?

I don't…

That's right you don't, now I want Atlia to stay in one piece, don't you?

I felt Dina internally nod, confused.

Great, I will return her to you when we are done. He cut off my connection with her.

Wait, how did you?

You can do it too. George replied, and food appeared in his hand. It was a spiky bright pink fruit, one of the ones from our camp. Food appeared in front of me in a cloth. *Eat, you need it, after all you are half human.*

What does that mean?

Mages don't eat, we feed off Earth's energy. That is why you feel so connected to the Earth. We are her and she is us. But you, you are half human, though as a half mage you could live without food for a while, you would need some human food at some point.

Oh, great I said sarcastically, still not feeling comfortable with all of this.

Unless you let your mage-half take over. George smiled eerily, and I winced. George laughed at me *you become more and more like your Avia every day, it is good to see the World Collective wearing off you and the ancient language becoming more a part of you.*

I had no idea what that meant and brushed off his amusement of me.

When we finished, George walked Boon and I to the center of a field. I realized we were on the other side of the mountain. I never went on the other side since it was not Founder territory, I could see the beach and the ocean. The deep purple sand and the teal waves. I felt this pull to it.

You feel that Atlia, the world is bigger than you could have ever imagined. So many types of humans, creatures, more than you ever dreamed. You can just leave all of this and explore, like our ancestors did in the old days. You can be above it, like we lived a thousand years ago. Though it was tempting, I sent him my feelings that I could never abandon my people, though I felt that pull. *No, I need to be here.*

Suit yourself, okay, we are going to start. Boon I felt was watching us, her intention of annoyance of George reached us both.

Where is Lila? I asked George, suddenly realizing his kinderling's absence.

She doesn't own me like this one owns you, I go where I please and so does she. She loves the beach so that is where she is camping. You don't have to be together all the time.

I felt Boon's annoyance at this reference and her snort of anger as she went close to George. I saw some light fear in George's eyes, though his mouth was in a half smirk to cover it, not something I expected. *I didn't mean to offend you, you have a... unique relationship.* Boon then backed away and sat down.

Now, are you ready Atlia?

Ready for... Before I could say anything, I was put in a dome cage. *What?!*

You need to learn to control your insight and rage. I am not going to let you kill everything. Now you see the grass in front of you?

I looked down at the bright blue grass.

Now I want you to grow a flower plant there. Put all your insight into it.

More training - great I thought I could not get sicker of training. My rage flickering. I felt a tap in my head *Ow* I intentioned.

Not rage, insight, use your insight.

I felt Boon growl at him and I felt him intention her patience.

I then found my insight, as that is what I imagined what he meant by use it. I felt for it and tried to feel for how I would inspire to grow something. I sent love to the blade of grass and it vanished.

George laughed at me, hollered actually. *That, that is so funny.*

He said wiping tears from his eyes.

Already put on edge my rage flared and flames shot out to the blade of grass and turned it to dust.

George stopped laughing and was thoughtful. *You have so much anger mageling, how will we do this?*

You need to describe it to her, she is not a naturally born mageling I felt Boon intention with annoyance.

I know that, I have never taught a halfling before. George snapped back.

I looked at the blackened spot. *Great, I can make dust.* I intentioned and George laughed again.

Now, halfling, feel your insight, I want you to at the same time feel... He looked and saw I had no more grass to work with in the dome he put me in. *Oh, right* He opened a new space for grass.

Now feel the grass, feel the Earth, can you feel it grow?

I did what he asked. At first it sounded unreal, but then I did, I felt the grass, and I felt the roots grow little by little I felt the grass feeling the soil and the soil feeling the grass. I felt every part of the grass as it slowly left the ground, the life in it growing. It was so different than any animal life. It felt a part of the Earth, as if she was putting little bits of herself into each and every plant, no matter how small the amount. Excited I nodded internally.

Now feel, expand your reach and feel for a flower tree.

I felt past the dome and beyond where we were, I felt to where Dina was. It was as if I was moving at the speed of light I saw everything. I went to the tree Dina and I loved and saw her there, reading to pass the time. I felt her, and she could feel me watching her. I felt her gasp and look around with her awareness of me.

Focus I felt George intention and I then headed towards the tree and felt it growing in the soil, feeling all of it.

Now use that feeling and grow it here. I used the feeling of it growing and I intentioned it to grow. It was deeper than a telegraphic intention, it was not just feeling emotionally, I felt it with smell, taste, sound, and actual feelings of my hands. I smelled the wet dirt and tasted it in my mouth, it was sweet and light like how earth smelled when it was covered in morning dew. I felt it physically grow me and I pushed it out with all the strength I could muster, it felt as if I was lifting a heavy stone. I felt it though as I pushed through it.

Faster halfling or we will be here all day. Release it.

I am trying to I said my breath heavy with trying to grow it.

NO, release it I felt his intention and finally, it was like a switch. Everything that was in me, rage, insight it came together and with a roar I released it.

I felt the energy flow out of me with the roar of blue green and gold powder smoke that covered the area. Wisps of light smoke that was golden, red, and green went into the ground. I felt the tree spring up fast with the force of my hands, I felt I was lifting nothing. I released everything, the pain of what I lost and for the people suffering, the love I felt for Dina and everyone, all of it together sprang forth.

I painted my arms out in front of me, my hands contorted. I didn't even notice I was using my body to send everything forward. I heard a whistle and saw Dina and my tree standing before me with purple and yellow that reflected the sun's shade to the ground where I stood.

There that is it! I heard George's excitement.

How did I do that?! I exclaimed in wonder. *It was rage and insight...*

Those words are just labels to help channel your energy. What it really is, it is just your energy. Together it can grow things, destroy things, you can even go where no man can go.

As mysterious as that last statement was, I was not going to follow it now. Now I felt I can battle.

I am done, right? I feel so much better.

No, do it. Now again. I felt a pull and I could not move. I sighed.

I grew an entire forest. It got easier as I went, like this is what I was meant to do. The energy flowing through me as music flows through the fingers of a musician playing their instrument. The beauty of creation in these trees was indescribable, though I will try. I felt as if the Earth and I were one. As if I could help her grow, and as if she let me, with this growing, bursting feeling inside of me that grew, my body buzzed with a warmth and energy. It was the energy I felt when I touched nature or animals, one that was such a small little murmur at first.

I bet Boon told you the Earth healed itself. When we had the ability to help, we gave I heard George say proudly and Boon snort.

It could have grown back without you, the kinderling did just as much as you did She retorted, and he laughed at Boon but did not challenge her.

George taught me everything about being a mage. From how to naturally control others' feelings, telegraphics, intentions, everything no matter what blockers or technology was installed.

As much as he taught me to create he taught me to destroy as well. He took me back to the forest I created.

You must learn that destroying is a part of the Earth as well, it is as important as creation.

Destroying what? I asked *Isn't destroying anything the Earth has evil?*

To mages we do not believe in good and evil when it comes to energy. It just exists. Creating something can be as evil, such as creating any type of weapon or way to harm someone. Look at what the World Collective did without magic. Pitiful creatures the humans they captured. I am happy to help their cause after seeing their conditions. I felt real sincerity here.

So, he continued *You will learn to destroy the forest you created.*

But it's so...

Destroy it. He intentioned firmly his bony white hand in a fist.

I felt Boon who I felt agreed with him.

I then harnessed both energies and imagined them dying, I sent that energy to them. They started to die, I felt their dying energy come into me, ghostly whispers they were white and see-through. I felt George stop me as if I hit an invisible wall.

No, no, no, that is all wrong! He said annoyed and stopped me. *Don't destroy things as you grew them. That is dangerous, that is taking the energy. You need to release the energy when you destroy things, so it*

196

goes back into the world. Unless you want to become a walking nuclear bomb.

I sighed annoyed he would not have told me this beforehand.

I then used my energy both feelings for insight and rage, the rage for once in more of a lead and chose fire since it seemed to be the natural element of choice I had. I felt the fire I created from both insight and rage. Then I spread it amongst my forest, showering the flower trees with it. I felt a sadness as I saw them die, for it was a forest I had grown to love that I was able to make. I felt each one, the energy release, connected to it. Tears flowed down my face, these were my creations. I could not help but feel this is how the Earth felt when we destroyed her creations. I felt their energy leave in peace though.

It won't be peaceful when you do this to humans. I felt his intention and I stopped. I could not imagine doing this to humans.

I can't.

You can, and you will. George intentioned with his old world accent, it sounded haunting. *It is hard to release the energies of any living beings. The plants are easy because they are of the Earth, the Earth is their life force, you are just returning them to grow again. Living beings, their life is their only life force. Once they are gone... who knows what happens to humans. All I am saying is killing is no happy moment. You will feel their lives torn from them. Their energies go to wherever they go to.*

This frightened me and confused me. *Do you know...* I intentioned as the last of my creations fell. I was trying to get through this painful practice as quickly as possible.

Good now constrain it to just your flowers, and make sure none of the debris flies away make the debris dissipate in the air, turn it into oxygen. George intentioned changing the subject, I knew I would get nothing from him now. I focused on what he was asking.

I tried to do as he said, focusing on each element as if it was one of Beleeka's pesky algorithm math problems.

I clumsily felt around and finally contained it and then focused on turning the debris into oxygen. I felt the energy release from the flowers and flow back into the Earth. Their light green energies sinking into the dirt.

Good. Now build the forest again.

This was difficult, as I built and destroyed it over and over again. Every time I felt wrong destroying it regardless what George or Boon said.

I spent days doing that exercise as George taught me about the powers of being a mage. We could create anything, even things that did not exist. He said my imagination was my second-best tool, one that most beings had lost in this new world. It was one I never really flexed in the World Collective, maybe when I read Avia Carlo's stories when I was a littling. Otherwise, I felt as if I really had to reach.

George asked me to create something that never existed before and I struggled to imagine something. It did not help that he entered my mind and would tell me *That exists, that exists, and that exists,* frustrating all of my thoughts. Ofro prepared me well though and I was so thankful to Ofro's many meditation trainings in that moment.

I imagined a flower tree and before he could say it existed I merged it with the idea of a butterfly. A flower fly I thought it was cute and George laughed at me. Purple smoke came out of the ground elegantly floating up and from my hands as small sparks of bright white light formed the wings made from flowers, as if the flower was cut in half and the body that of a butterfly. The flowers were bright blue and purple. The body was pink. I saw the creation in my telegraphic as the light sealed off the last bits of it, a brain and spinal cord. I saw the animal that I created with my eyes as it flew around and landed on my hand. *Hello mother.*

Hi I said fascinated at it, petting its petal wings. It then ported away in a poof of pink smoke.

What?! I said looking for my new creation frantically and George laughed at me with his cackle.

Littling, you created a little one who wants to explore as much as you do. Lesson learned that the Earth will always create what you truly desire.

I felt sad the creation I just made flew away, I felt the cord between us, the line of energy of the consciousness I created out of the Earth. I sighed, not knowing what I had created but wishing it well, hoping it brings love to the world.

I learned next how to take and exchange energy from the Earth, how to harness electricity, fire, wind, water, stone, and any Earth element. Each one had a different feel and smell. Each was so beautiful, the more I practiced with them, the more I was able to see how it was made and create it myself.

It was exciting, but more and more I felt less human. That I was connected to so much more than humans, how could any human understand what it was like to be a part of the Earth? Then I remembered Dina which grounded me. She was as close to the Earth as I was, I smiled at the memory of her digging her feet into the dirt.

As I was settling in with the energy of the Earth and practicing moving objects around me, George burst in.

We have to go now. They are coming. He said with almost glee.

You are crazy I intentioned to him.

This battle will be won before you know it.

He intentioned all of us to Dina, who before she could mutter anything as much as a "hello", he teleported everyone to the camp. The camp sirens were going off in our telegraphics with bright lights and the intention of *be ready.* The army we had built was at all sides of the dome.

I went over to Beleeka, Telepa, Rachel, Nurium, and Ofro who were all standing together in a circle looking towards the dome in a stance ready to fight, hands out in front and going back and forth to their sides.

I felt Dina look me over for a second and she touched my arm. *You have changed,* I felt the worry in her soft intention.

Though I wanted to hold Dina, and kiss her, I instead ignored her. I knew we did not have much time. *Beleeka, I know what you are, join me.* I intentioned with love and new understanding.

I felt her grit her teeth, *I don't know…*

We don't have time Beleeka,

I am human. George wanted me to train with you, but I am not what you are, I won't let myself be. You do what you have to, I will always love you. But you can't make me into you.

That's not...

Telepa pulled me aside. I figured I would finish that argument later. *So, George filled us in on your vacation, welcome back, we have been holding them off for three days.* He said with some annoyance Curly on his shoulder intentioned at the same time *Atlia where were you? We missed you! What were you doing?* I felt their concern.

I went to face Curly and put my finger up to his nose, so he could sniff I was healthy. *See Curls, nothing to worry about.* He sniffed, licked, and preened me. I could feel Telepa's amusement to this and his love for Curly.

We have to move now Ofro intentioned in a rushed manner, not his typical elegant intention to me and Dina. We took our places in the battle circle.

Then I saw the dome break down with a crack as if lightning had struck it and the army moved in slowly surrounding us. Before they could teleport in I stepped forward and heard my name intentioned by Dina *No Atlia...*

I ported out of the dome to my Avo. I was what she wanted after all, might as well make it real. I tried to send the rage to my Avo when I entered. I saw her at her camp with her telegraphic map of our village in front of her, the one Beleeka sent. This just filled with more rage until I felt numb.

Hold her. I felt my Avo say and looked around me realizing I ported into a circle of smoky, orange light. I could not do anything, though I tried. My Avo came towards me, smiling. *Atlia, I am sad that you are... well not who you were, my little spring.* I felt resentment and anger in her intentions as well as love that was still there. *We were expecting you and we know what you are. Your friends, they are all going to die. All of them are not humans, they chose beings lesser than humans versus their own species.* She came over and held my chin. At that moment I bit her.

Ow she intentioned and pulled her hand away I smiled at her as I tried to figure out this new cage, feeling from the Earth the energy she provided me. Examining every crevice of my cage.

You are not a human Atlia, which makes you even worse than the lessers. You have to know that they have to die. And you my love, you are going to be our greatest weapon that kills them all.

No I said smirking, *You can't make me.*

Really? Then I saw her bring in Latla, Liat and their family, Dove and Leaf. The littlings had grown so much in the past few months, but they still clung to their mothers. Their eyes were wide in fear.

Don't you dare… I felt my rage ignite and tried to send my insight to the family, to create a bridge out of my cage.

My Avo laughed at me, the leaders I noticed were around her laughed as well. All of them believed this, there were still fifty leaders who supported the rights. I could not believe it, that these people were my family.

You are mine again Atlia, just like your Avia Carlo, I practiced on him. He loved you girls so much I felt her intention Beleeka and me. I also felt her love for him too, despite everything, and her dissonance made me feel nauseous.

But you loved him I stalled her, hoping to speak to her humanity. She was fully human with the rage herself, maybe I could reach her, I hoped. *You can stop all of this now Avo, stop it and feel the love I still feel for you. I forgive you Avo. You can move past what you are doing.* I sent her my love and then was surprised to feel her love back but then her disgust.

I don't forgive you, spring. You broke my heart. You are too much like your Avia. I loved him, and I love you, but it does not matter for the greater good. This is not a person. She grabbed Liat by the hair and Latla cried out for her as my Avo rang a shock through Latla's telegraphic. *This is what she is.* And I felt her rage go through her as Leaf and Dove cried for their mother and Latla stretched out to hold Liat's hand.

We could feel everything Liat felt. Her heart racing and being squashed at the same time. The pain excruciating in her head. I could feel my Avo drawing it out with pleasure. The look on Liat's face, I will never forget. That look of fear of dying, tears streaming down her face into her agape mouth that was mouthing out quiet screams of pain. Feeling her greatest fear, of not being able to watch her littlings grow older, or to hold them one last time.

Her littlings watched her, crying harder, reaching out for their mother. Latla looked torn she could feel Liat's pain, it was excruciating.

Liat's eyes started to roll to the back of her head, her breaths got shorter.

Let me go, I love you. Liat's last words rang through everyone as my Avo committed telecide and Liat's body convulsed and fell to the floor, the light leaving her eyes.

NOOOO! my rage and insight unleashed the love and sadness I felt for the families of the World Collective over what my Avo did. I saw my gold, blue energy fly around me like flames trying to climb through the cage my Avo put me in. They raged against it. The energy I exerted bounced off the cage and into nothingness.

There is nothing… My Avo intentioned with a smirk, I felt her happiness at what she did, her glee at the littlings cries and Latla's sadness for her wife perishing.

Then I felt a crack in the cage.

No my Avo intentioned her eyes wide in fear. I pushed through the crack with all my might and the invisible wall shattered with my blue, gold, white light. I immediately grabbed my Avo by the neck with my energy, the blue powder of the light surrounding her ominously, waiting to break her.

No, spring, stop, I'm sorry. She cried I felt the apology was not sincere, just her fear of dying. I laughed at this and moved forward, but Latla came up to me and put her hand on me, tears still in her eyes.

Stop, there is enough death for the littlings today. Latla said, strongly, I felt her sadness, anger, and fear… fear of me.

I let go of my Avo and with a roar of flames went to the middle of the field where my people were battling the World Collective.

I knew I could risk no one else. I knew what I was, and I knew this was not our plan but this is what I had to do. With both of my hands I lifted them up and my rage and insight already at its highest point and let it out towards the people trying to port in with force. I screamed at them, with all the rage and sadness and love I had for my Avo, and for what I had just witnessed. The invisible force pushed everyone trying to port in fifteen feet in the air and backward landing on their backs. I felt the fear of my community but tried to radiate calmness, that I was not uncontrolled.

Atlia I felt Dina intention.

Yes, you feel me, my love, I am fine. This is what George taught me.

Yes, I am just going to watch you from the sidelines George said, laughed, and disappeared.

I did not care where George went I was focused on releasing the energy of every greeder I found. I felt for a group of them and I used my fire and released their energies as they screamed to death. I saw my light and blue, white fire consumer their outer bodies, and I felt glad. I felt satisfied, to feel their pain. I wanted to feel all their pain, for what they did to Liat, for what they did to all of the lessers, to Dina, to everyone.

I then ported back to the leaders. I saw the fear in their eyes. They felt me watching them. I then ported them back to the camp and put a dome around them. Their eyes were wide in fear.

I saw my Avo looking at me as if I was some creature.

I went up to her and I felt my energy radiating from me, showing them my might.

No Avo, I am not some creature, I am not some beast like you I intentioned, and I sent her into a sleep. She curled down and slumped over.

I stood there looking at what I did. Thousands were laying on the ground in a great circle around me. I was somewhere above it, feeling as if I had done what I had to. I saw it through Dina's eyes. Blue light was shining from my eyes, so bright everyone else was squinting. The blue, gold powder light was all around me, so fine but thick, as if the northern lights were one with me. The fine powder was flowing in and out of the Earth. I could feel Dina in awe, and with less fear since she could feel my feelings, that I let out the violence I could. That no matter how awful the leaders were, I did not want to harm them. I wanted to be done with their threat and now I was. I did feel her fear though at what I did to the rest of the World Collective army, they were decimated around me. When I showed her what had happened to Liat, she intentioned understanding, but still… fear.

She came over to me and kissed me, I kissed her back. *Come back to me Atlia, you are my person. You are love and light, not violence.* I felt her and suddenly I felt a pull deep within me, the person I wanted to be, the one who was love and light. I came out of my trance, of feeling above everything. Though I still felt justified in what I did, the pang of guilt crept forwards, the words *could there have been another way?* rang through my head.

I took in some of my light, feeling the fine powders come back to me as I felt them with my hands. My team looked at me with fear and awe, as I took the light back in and let some go into the Earth. I then nodded letting my team know they could move and bring the other leaders to the dome cage. I felt their fear of me and I smiled at it, though there was guilt inside. *What was I now?* I thought to myself.

I will not see you like this humanling, Boon said and vanished. I felt her sadness but chose to think about my next move. I knew we did not have much time.

I went into my Avos mind. She was there, sad, frustrated, and angry.

What are you? You are not my spring! She cried at me. *You are worse than your Avia, you are a murderer.*

I suggest you stop talking and sit down. She did just that, as I controlled her, though you could see she wanted to do otherwise.

You stole my child from me, you raped Dina, yes, I knew you helped her owner with that I saw all her faults and made her feel them. She winced. *You lied to me, you killed Avia Carlo, you murdered Liat, you killed so many of your own people. What kind of beast are you Avo?*

I felt her sadness and her knowing of something else. It was locked in her brain. Like my Kamma taught. She laughed at me. *You see I knew you were one of them, when I saw your uncontrolled rage. I knew it, and you will never know why Carlo died. You will never know about me. You still have not figured out why Avia Carlo gave you that memory? As long as I am breathing you will never know.*

I could not talk to her anymore and I pulled out of her mind and left her there. Her words pained me, more than anyone else's - still. This was a woman who said she loved me. Even though we had won, her words made me feel like we had lost.

You need to see if there are more soldiers and protect our people like you just did. Ofro intentioned and I nodded, I felt Dina's worry at my recent conversation with my Avo and how I was feeling in that moment. I looked past her worry and searched. I found no other army. I had no idea how many people I had fallen. So many lay on the ground, at least twenty thousand. Seeing the size of the army though, it meant the International Unity meant destruction. There were people from all chapters of the unity.

I could not believe these people supported the eating of the lessers.

They are gone. We must bring the fight to them I intentioned to Ofro. I then ported to Dina and my cottage. I calmly unpacked as she exploded in.

How dare you be so calm she intentioned and I felt her rage, and worry, and fear. *Have I lost you?! I read all about mages, most of them were insane.*

Avia Carlo was a mage, I am a mage. Beleeka is even a mage. That's it. It is nothing to get...

She grabbed my arms and looked at me in the eyes. I saw her sincerity as she brushed a ginger curl out of my face. *You are blind if you don't see something is wrong. Atlia, a couple of months ago you could not kill anyone. Today you killed thousands.*

Thousands of beasts like my Avo. They were attacking us. She murdered Liat right in front of me. Besides I released their energies.

What does that even mean? If they are not breathing, that means they are dead. And you will become like her if you think any differently. I felt love, fear, and annoyance.

She has good reason humanling Boon ported in. I thought about it for a second and felt my calmness. It felt like numbness, like a nice numbness though.

You are right, and I can think about it later. I said after some thought.

No, you will think about it now, she said sternly.

Fine. What do you want me to do about it?

I want you to use your humanity and feel for the people who lost their lives. Maybe we can try something different next time.

I realized she was right. Here I was so calm, but I was filled with guilt, my human side felt it. But it is true. They were my family, all of them. I felt the pang of sadness, but I did not let it take hold.

There, I felt it. I intentioned and then intentioned all of us to the great room. Rachel, Telepa, Nurium, Ofro, and Beleeka were there in a circle talking and sitting on cushions.

Everyone looked at me. I felt their fear as I sat down and smiled at them and sent love and insight to help calm them.

Everyone I am fine. I am sad about what I have done, and in the future I will just capture them. I felt my first intention lie seep from me. They felt calmed by this.

We can now enter Kalea. Nurium, what is the best point of entry? Ofro intentioned.

Through the back of the dome. Nurium responded showing us in her mind where it was, where Latla and I ventured first.

Let's teleport there. Then we teleport to the leader center and, Atlia, that is where we need you. I need you to safely teleport the Intentioneers out and detain them.

I can also detain the Peacers at the same time as well as the Intentioneers. I said calmly and felt the worry from my team.

Okay said Ofro.

We are coming with you, I felt Boon intention and Raph in agreement. I felt Boon wanted to watch me, to make sure I did not decimate everyone again. I sent an internal shrug, I could feel Dina's relief at this.

We intentioned to where Nurium said to, keeping our momentum. We knew if we caught them we had only a short amount of time to take Kalea from the World Collective. At the spot of the dome I felt through the dome and lifted it before Nurium could unlock it with her telegraphic. I went to the leader center and I detained them all as they were working one by one. I then detained the Peacers, I felt all of their shock and terror as I put dome bubbles around them and floated them from the center. My bubbles popped, and they joined the others in the Smooth Square.

Everyone else ported into the empty leader room. Everyone was not shocked anymore at what I was capable of, but I felt their fear. I steadied myself against it, trying not to feel my sadness at the people I was closest to, fearing me.

Now we need to get to the center of the telegraphics. I guided them to the center. One man did not get out of the center. He was tall and very skinny. His eyes were a steel colored blue, his face was tan, his eyes were thin, and his hair was blue.

Boon I felt was surprised *No* he ported her and Raph out.

Why would you do that and Who are you? I asked annoyed and was flung back as he smiled and thrust his hand toward me.

You are not the only mage in the world.

Without their consent I ported everyone back and blocked this section from them. I could feel Dina's annoyance and fear.

So, you are for the collective.

The International Unity. He smiled and again tried to fling me, this time I brought up energy from the Earth quickly and blocked him.

I see you are well taught. Impressive. You could join us you know, there is a state of us in the south across the ocean.

Really, I said intrigued for a second *I did not know mages were owned by anyone.* I said with a smirk and blocked another attack.

We are not owned, we just like to play nice with humans.

He then did something unexpected and pulled me into a battle of wills. I could not hold up against his will, it was too strong. I ended up in the first battle sequence.

22

VANQUISHED

hy fight the human way? I asked as I felt what his next
move would be.

Isn't it more fun? I bet George did not teach you that.
I saw Dina. *No, it can't.* But it was her. *No, she can't be here,
take her away. This is between you and me!*

I shouted at him, I felt his name. *Darius, you are like me. We
can talk. We don't need to involve others.*

*Why do you care for this human so? Yes, you are half human, but
these people don't even believe she is full human.* I felt her pain as he
created it in her chest and blood started spilling out of her
mouth.

Dina, stop, stop Darius! I intentioned with both the rage and
insight. I stopped the whole sequence.

Well that is no fun. Darius appeared in the black space of
nothingness we were in. Dina was breathing heavily, and I sent
her my insight as I felt her annoyance at Darius trying to hurt
him with her rage.

Awe, isn't she cute. Darius said as I was about to attack him
he froze me.

*I am stronger mageling. Don't try it. I will let you have Kalea, if you
beat me in battle.*

Why? I asked exasperated and angry as I rubbed Dina's
back.

*Because I feel like I want to see what you will do. You see I don't care
about any of this, I joined in for the fun. If you take Kalea, we will just
make you a part of the International Unity anyway. That is my offer.
Win against me and Kalea will be yours. I will even give you the rest of*

the World Collective as well. With the mages behind you they will just hand it over. All you have to do is win against me.

And if I lose?

Trust me, you just don't want to lose.

Hold on.

Go ahead, talk it over. He said as if he was giving us some sort of mercy.

Atlia, you don't have to do this. We have the Grand Avo, we can go back right now. I felt Dina's love and worry, and I looked deeply into her brown green eyes.

I sent her my love and how much I looked forward to our future, us with a family.

We can't have that if I don't end this, they will always come back for me. I said as I held the side of her face and felt a tear running down, feeling her knowing it was true.

Fine, but I stay with you this time. This time I would not argue. I knew she would have never forgiven me had I tried to tell her to go.

I kissed her and intentioned togetherness. She felt this, and I felt her deepen our kiss, holding on for dear life.

Precious, now time to play.

One condition.

Yes?

You do not use Dina to get to me. What fun is that for you when it is so easy? I said, trying to appeal to his competitive nature.

Fair point. Done. He said, and we went into the first battle sequence.

We were in one of those ancient houses I saw during Ofro's story of our ancestors. I was holding two ropes one above me and another to the side of me.

Dina was in front of me stepping on a button.

Don't move Dina intentioned. I nodded internally and felt with her what he was playing at. If I let go of the ropes the house would explode from one of those ancient devices, so would Dina if she took her foot off.

I felt him deeper and pushed down the barriers he built. I felt his laughter as I pushed against them trying to figure out pieces of the puzzle.

We only had four minutes to figure it out. I noticed then that we had old cloth on. She had a sweater, pants and sandals, and I had boots, a skirt and tank. I started kicking off the boots towards her.

What...

It's the cloth, I will give you my feet wrappers and then you can give me your top. I intentioned, at the time I did not know all the names of the cloth we wore.

She took the boots, reaching for them, keeping her foot on the button. The last boot was too far away but she reached and reached and used the rage and almost took her foot off the button but at the last second she got the boots and put them on the button.

She then quickly tried to take off her sweater, though she was not used to clothes.

C'mon love I intentioned

I am trying. She intentioned back and got it off and before the last few seconds of our timer, I quickly transferred one string to Dina and she and I tied both strings I was holding with the sweater. I stepped away and we went back to the black.

Darius clapped. *Good job, so entertaining to watch. I thought I would start out with an easy one.* And then I lost the battle of wills again and we were transported to a dome filled with fire. We felt it eat at us and it stopped. We were chained to the dome ceiling. A person came in, a woman with long nails and sharp teeth.

Welcome, I am here to torture you. She said, and she touched my heart. I felt a searing pain and smelled my flesh burning, it smelled of nourishment. That kept me going. Dina cried out and I could feel her fear so well, like never before.

I can't touch her, but that is what is fun, you will also feel her pain of losing you.

I felt her hand touch me again and I felt all the deaths I caused. Every single person, I felt their energy leave. I felt their fear, sadness, and pain. I felt Dina's pain as well at this creating excruciating screams from me. I tried using my rage and insight and felt it helping with the pain.

No cheating We felt Darius say. And I stopped, so tired.

We are so close, love Dina intentioned and I felt her love. Her love filled, as much as my insight would and as the woman touched me again I was able to resist the torture. I smiled at her and let Dina fill me up more and joined my love for her. It poured out of us and all of the sudden we were back in the black nothingness.

Yes. Darius intentioned and I felt his happiness. *You see mageling, you don't just need insight, or rage, your love with Dina is more powerful.*

I am confused, why are you happy, you lost? I asked waiting for another fight of some sort.

He laughed *Oh mageling, I am not here on behalf of the National Unity. I am here on behalf of the mages to see what you are made of. I have to say I am impressed. Tell George I say hello. And yes, us mages have a great hold, that part is true. We will support you in your new leadership of the World Collective.*

Darius left. I intentioned out of my telegraphic and saw that Dina was ported into the intelligence center by Darius. Dina and I looked at each other in front of the intelligence center. We hugged each other, and I kissed her forehead as we breath hard from coming out of battle not believing we won.

I kissed her, and she kissed me, I felt her love fill me with such joy and I sent her the same, breathing together. Our kiss literally slowed down time as I noticed her eyes, lips and her smile shining through, her pride, and love, and happiness at our ability to survive. When we had come apart we noticed the rest of our team there.

What happened? Rachel asked, and we laughed. *What are you crazy now?*

No, maybe a little. Dina said laughing. Everyone laughed feeling her laughter, a laugh of relief. We showed them what happened with Darius and they were as confused as we were.

Beleeka secured the intelligence area as we headed to the Smooth Square. All the people who were left from Kalea ported in. We stood at the top of the slant of the Smooth

Square.

I connected to their channels.

People of Kalea, you will now be governed by the Freers. All lesser beings are now free. I severed all the connection between owners and lessers. The lessers and some members cheered.

If you don't agree with this we will happily move you to another colony, however, there is no other colony that eats lessers. I suggest you get used to progress.

I felt all the people and they could feel me. Some did not want to change, but saw they had no choice, while others were relieved.

The mages stood by their promise and we were able to take back the whole of the World Collective. We had all the members who were not supporters of the new government have a choice of being moved outside of the World Collective or to go to rehabilitation. Some chose to go outside the dome while many others sought out rehabilitation.

Though we had Kalea back, we did not want to live there. Dina and I had grown quite fond of our cottage with the Freedom Founders, that we decided to stay there. The Grand Avo was there too and, though I never saw her, I wanted to be there in case she ever tried to get out. A rehabilitation specialist was working with her, but of course, nothing was working.

Dina and I turned back to our lives, she got more creative with her plant creationing, and even took to gardening like Liat, and in her honor, used many of her methods that she learned from her. She loved to make nut cheeses from the nut trees that we found in the garden the Freedom Founders had, as well as an ancient food called bread that she learned how to make from a plant called quinoa. Since the battle, we were able to grow our knowledge of plants, now that we had time to learn. Our telegraphics knew all of the old plants that had existed before, but we also had to update our telegraphic with the new plants that Liat had found and created.

I took up building as the task I liked to do, using the Earth and my insight to create new building types out of the Earth, the flower trees, and the grass. I thought creationing would be a way to heal from the battle, though the guilt was still there. The worry was there as well, as how I can keep my humanity and be a mage. I hid this from Dina, though I felt she knew, and I tried to act normal. I would come home smelling of dirt and Dina would smell so sweet that I would kiss her even if she pretended she did not like the way I smelled.

As soon as things quieted down, I went over to Ofro and Beleeka's to have a tough conversation. Beleeka knew right away and sat down at the stone table she had in her stone cottage. I sat down on the hammock chair across from her.

I know what you are going to say. She said as she drank her tea from her bubble tea cup, a creation she made that popped after you used it, creating no waste. *I am not interested in being a mage.*

But that is what you are...

No, what I am is half human. Atlia, I have settled. Here with Ofro. I can't and don't need to explore anything. I loved our Avia, but he was a dreamer of adventures. I have had enough adventures for a lifetime.

It is not about adventures, it is about being who you are. You are a creationist and you could do so much more as a mage.

Maybe I like doing it as a human she said with kindness and love to me. *I don't want to feel insight or rage. I am happy with my controlled world. I don't want to be a... a...*

A weapon I finished her sentence. It was what I was called by my Avo. To Beleeka, to everyone, I was still a beast. I might have saved them, but I felt their fear of me. I intentioned her what George showed me, the ocean and the idea of the world I did not know, the world that the World Collective kept us from.

I felt Beleeka smile at this, seeing this. *You have always wanted to explore. I know Dina is ready to start a family though. What will you do?*

I felt her thoughts as she felt mine. I knew Dina liked our settled life while I longed to know more. I wanted to learn about who I was, what I was meant to do.

Then I felt something, something in Beleeka that shocked me.

I was going to tell you Beleeka intentioned, embarrassed, *we have a new consciousness coming.*

I got up and hugged Beleeka, she giggled and hugged me back. Now I understood why she did not want to try anything new, especially with her body.

Ofro then came in and I hugged him as well, he felt our conversation had ended and that Beleeka told me.

I left her house smiling, though our conversation left me more perplexed.

I went to see Boon. Boon enjoyed the new quiet life and so did Raph. I could feel she was still worried about me and she would check in occasionally, she said to make sure I was still a humanling. Our connection had grown too with my findings of the insight. We could even grow more together and would often go to empty places of the Earth and grow more.

She was sleeping in a garden next to Raph. I put my forehead to hers, she brought up her head. *What is troubling you humanling?*

I am not sure what to do. I said, expressing my bewilderment. Here was Beleeka easily moving on. It was hard to imagine everyone moving on when my first little one...

You are not ready to. Boon responded simply, nudging my head.

What about Dina, I owe it to her.

Dina will understand. She might be rushing things to forget as well.

Boon was always so wise. I sighed and gave her a kiss.

Why not try for a while, see what happens, who knows, life might surprise you. Some tears fell down my face and I brushed them off, trying to not think of the littling my Avo took from us. *Coralina* even saying her name brought such pain to my heart, I pushed it down inside me. If I thought of her, who knows what uncontrolled power I would need to release?

Everything was back to normal, well as normal as could be. All of the twelve freers who were leaders of the camp outside the dome we incorporated into the new leadership. That meant Dina and I had to teleport back and forth from Kalea, commuting to deal with daily batch of new problems. Building new infrastructure, teaching how to make plant nourishment, and more.

The gleepers were commonly at our cottage now, Boon and Raph tolerated them, though they would come over and gently move them out of the way if they wanted to get pets instead. The gleepers would glare at them, and then Tito typically would come around them anyway and plop down, expecting to be pet at the same time.

The gleepers and the kinderling were the only comfort Dina and I had in our lives. It was hard, we tried to retain control of the World Collective as we lived in the Free Colony, the new name of Ofro's village. Some people from the World Collective, mostly lessers, chose to move to the Free Colony, wanting to move far away from their past and the oppression.

The only person who disappeared was George. I did not see him until months later.

I had still the feeling that I had something bigger to do and that there was something wrong. I did not tell Dina though she could feel it and did not push me on wanting a family. We were in our hammock one night, both of us reading via our telegraphics when I felt a huge push in my head. "Ouch" I cried out and I felt who it was.

I had heard an urgent intention of George to let him in. I saw him stumble into the room, his leg was all bloodied and so was his head.

George what happened I intentioned.

Your Avia Carlo, he is alive. George intentioned and then he collapsed, out cold.

The words "he is alive" crossed my mind, and little did I know, that this was just the beginning.

ANA LEVLEY

AFTERWORD

This book was written with the scenes inspired from real events. The slaughter, dairy, and all other difficult scenes of what happens to the lessers, with the exception of the egg scene, is what happens to animals in this day and age. The only thing I changed was their ability to have telegraphics. Please, choose kindness and go vegan. I hope this inspires you to connect more with animals, and to see we are not so different being animals ourselves.

To go vegan, here are some resources that helped me on my journey:
    nutritionfacts.org
    cowspiracy.com
    dominionmovement.com
    onegreenplanet.org/channel/vegan-recipe/
    heart2heartmeals.org/vegan-recipes/

I verified with Amazon that these books are printed without the use of any animals products.